T0357769

THE
MEADOWBROOK
MURDERS

ALSO BY JESSICA GOODMAN

They Wish They Were Us

They'll Never Catch Us

The Counselors

The Legacies

THE MEADOWBROOK MURDERS

JESSICA GOODMAN

G. P. PUTNAM'S SONS

G. P. PUTNAM'S SONS

An imprint of Penguin Random House LLC

1745 Broadway, New York, New York 10019

First published in the United States of America by G. P. Putnam's Sons,
an imprint of Penguin Random House LLC, 2025

G. P. Putnam's Sons is a registered trademark of Penguin Random House LLC.
The Penguin colophon is a registered trademark of Penguin Books Limited.

Visit us online at PenguinRandomHouse.com.

Library of Congress Cataloging-in-Publication Data is available.

ISBN 9780593698716

1st Printing

Printed in the United States of America

LSCH

Design by Rebecca Aidlin
Text set in Aldus LT Std

This book is a work of fiction. Any references to historical events, real people,
or real places are used fictitiously. Other names, characters, places, and events are
products of the author's imagination, and any resemblance to actual events
or places or persons, living or dead, is entirely coincidental.

The publisher does not have any control over and does not assume any
responsibility for author or third-party websites or their content.

To Mom,

thank you for just about everything

THE DAY
SHE FOUND THEM

Amy

Sarah wakes up before I do. She always has, since we started rooming together as freshmen. Her voice carries. A giggle or an ABBA song. A muffled whisper on the phone with Ryan. Goddamn Ryan.

I expect to hear her rasp this morning. The last day of senior welcome week.

But our suite is silent when I roll over, crust packed into the corners of my eyes. I pause and listen for her through the wall that separates our bedrooms, each so tiny they only fit a twin bed and a tall dresser. The school's obvious attempt at creating intimacy, roommates pushed into shared common spaces to avoid our cramped rooms. It worked for Sarah and me, finding comfort on our ratty couch, bonding first over soccer and then all at once over everything, slipping easily into the kind of friendship I wasn't quite sure existed, the kind that was defined by knowing how the other's breathing changes when they fall asleep, what might make them snort by accident from laughing too hard, how it sounds when they scream into a pillow.

I reach over to the space where Joseph was last night, but it's cold now. I press my nose into the sheets, smelling his shampoo.

Excitement churns in my stomach, but it's short-lived when I remember what preceded Joseph's visit, why I called him in the first place.

Sarah must still be mad about our fight. That's why she hasn't bounded into my room to wake me up and stand over my bed with a blueberry corn muffin, holding it hostage until I say I'm sorry for the things I said last night. But I'm not sorry. *I* should be the one who's furious. She should be breaking down my door to apologize to *me*.

But Sarah won't do that. It's not her style.

I should take a cue from her playbook. Demand my own *sorry*, withhold a cherry chocolate chunk scone. But as soon as I think it, I know there's no way. I've never demanded anything of Sarah, and I'm not about to start now.

There's a deep ache in my chest telling me I've got to make things right. Every moment that passes is another moment of senior year that we're at odds, another moment we don't get to spend together, on the same side.

Maybe if we talk now, sober, away from Ryan, Kayla, and the others, the warm cans of beer, the rank smell of the boathouse, she'll understand.

My bare feet hit the floor and I rub my eyes as I swing open the door into the common room, my vision blurry from sleep. I bump into my desk before finding my way to the baby-blue mini fridge. Sarah had surprised me with it last week when we moved in. She had already filled it with our favorites—cans of Diet Coke, little glass pots of French yogurts, single servings of hummus and guacamole. Students aren't supposed to have their own appliances in the dorms, but Sarah shrugged when I brought up the rule.

"No one stopped me." She smiled and began explaining the color-coded labels she made to keep the groceries organized.

I swing the door open and reach inside for a plastic cup of iced coffee, saved from yesterday's outing into town.

It's watery and too sweet. But it'll do until I get to the dining hall.

I knock on Sarah's door. "Sar? You up?"

No one answers.

"Cool silent treatment, but can we talk about last night?"

I take a sip from the straw, then another, everything around me a little fuzzy. The curtains are drawn, and the room is dark, but sun peeks through the corners. The digital clock below our TV flashes 8:00. *Shit.* I overslept. Senior Sanction is in an hour. A full day of welcome rituals reserved for our class, while we're still the only ones on campus. Maybe Sarah left for breakfast already, didn't wake me up as part of her *I'm-pissed-at-you* campaign.

I pad back into my room and fumble as I call Sarah. The line goes straight to voicemail. Her recorded message rings in my ear and my shoulders tense. She ran a six-foot extension cord from the outlet near her door to make sure she could charge her phone right next to her bed while she slept, said she'd rather die than wake up with less than 20 percent battery.

"Sarah?" I call again, stepping into the common space.

That's when I notice it.

The stench.

The rotten smell of iron. Pungent and everywhere, lodged in my throat. My nostrils. My stomach.

My heart pounds as I dial Sarah again, wait for a ring that doesn't come.

"I can't come to the phone right now . . ." her voice bleats in my ear.

Suddenly I'm lightheaded, like I can barely breathe. Because once the rest of the room comes into focus, I realize it's not only the odor that's odd. There's an overturned lamp. A thick red smudge caked onto the hardwood floor near the window. Another one on the chair next to Sarah's desk.

I shake my head, trying to remember if the room was like this when I got home. I was drunk. Of course I was drunk. But Joseph wasn't. We didn't even turn on the lights.

I close my eyes, can picture us bumping into one another, laughing as our limbs tangled in the dark. We paused once, when Joseph noticed his paring knife, the one he takes with him to work. He had let me borrow it the day before when we were slicing peaches at soccer practice, and I had left it out as a reminder to return it to him. The mirrored blade caught a sliver of light from the moon, shining in the darkness. His initials carved into the solid wood handle. But when I look at the coffee table now, the only thing on top is one of Sarah's photo books on Cape Cod, unopened, the edges thick and sharp.

I should call campus security. The Meadowbrook help line. I should call Kayla or Coach or even Dad. Maybe Joseph would remember. I should call him, too.

I don't.

Instead, I take one step closer to Sarah's room. I wrap my hand around her doorknob and twist. I don't think twice about opening it.

I hear myself scream. Feel the coffee slip from my hand. My vision narrows to a pinprick as I stand there, staring. I can't speak. Can't do anything.

My toes are sticky and cold, covered in milk, day-old coffee. My legs are like lead when I am finally able to move, stumbling into the hall. I see Mrs. Talbert, her wispy white hair in rollers. I say her name. *Sarah.* And then I fall to the floor as the others stream past me, finding what I found, seeing what I saw.

Their screams echo, sharp and piercing. I vomit on a stray slipper.

Someone shakes my shoulders, grabs my hand. But I don't see them or hear them or remember who they are. Because all I can see—all I will ever see—is Sarah lying in her bed like she had been doused in crimson paint. Her dark hair matted, wet, and sticky, and her red toenails poking out from the bottom of the blankets.

People say that images get seared into your brain like a brand, but this one doesn't. Brands are raised and bumpy. They scab, then scar. This scene isn't a scar. What I've seen has altered what I knew to be true and good. This image is now as much a part of me as my own pinky or my left earlobe.

It's surprising, then, that it takes me so long to realize there were two sets of feet. Twenty toes, four ankles.

Sarah's, of course, and, undeniably, Ryan's.

Mrs. Talbert appears in the hall, her face a shock of white but her rollers still perky, perched on her head.

"They're dead," I choke out.

She nods, her mouth agape, and my world splits like a cleaved-open melon. Forever, my life will be divided into two halves, a before and an after, one with Sarah and one, horrifically, without.

Liz

"Where the hell is the nut graf? I told you last night it had to be right below the lede." Kevin groans, but it's not my fault this Hunter S. Thompson wannabe thought he could get away with passing off a literary essay as a breaking news story in his first article of the year. Not that I'm now editor in chief.

I thought I made it very clear at the end of last year that my version of *The Meadowbrook Gazette* will *not* tolerate purple language, certainly not in a story that's supposed to be about the controversial new freshman curriculum, which forces all incoming students to take an ethics seminar.

Kevin chews the inside of his cheek and crosses his arms. "I'll give it another shot," he says.

But it's almost 8:10 in the morning and all of these stories have to go online as soon as possible or else no one will see them before Senior Sanction. "No time," I say, resting my hands on the keyboard in front of me. "I'll fix it for you."

Kevin sighs, but his jaw relaxes and his shoulders drop from their hunched position as he leaves the room. I should have known better than to recruit the floppy-haired Jack Kerouac devotee from Mrs. Herschel's English seminar to be a reporter—even if I *was* desperate to find more bodies to join the staff of our fledgling high school newspaper. He spent all of this past week writing poetry in a leatherbound notebook. I bet he didn't even read the Susan Orlean reporting packet I handed out at our first staff meeting.

I tie my hair back in a ponytail and crack my knuckles. I'm not going to let Kevin bum me out. Not today.

It only takes a few minutes for me to rewrite the first fifty words of Kevin's piece, and after another read-through of the dozen articles we spent the past week working on, I finally feel ready to post them all to the *Gazette*'s website.

I close my eyes for a brief moment and remind myself that I've been waiting for this day since I stepped onto Meadowbrook's campus as a freshman three years ago. I was the only kid from Milwaukee—the entire state of Wisconsin, actually—to attend Meadowbrook, an impossible-to-get-into boarding school no one from my hometown could even find on a map, and I'd come here with one goal: to run the school paper.

After I got accepted to Meadowbrook on full scholarship, Mrs. Gilbert, my middle school English teacher, told me that once I got here, I'd find my people. I took that to mean that the students here might also read Joan Didion's nonfiction for fun, devour true crime tomes like *I'll Be Gone in the Dark* in one sitting, and obsess over the latest drama between cable news networks' election coverage.

Unfortunately, neither Mrs. Gilbert nor I could have anticipated that none of my peers had any interest in journalism or debating the merits of objectivity in media. She didn't even realize that the school news outlet had given up on a print newspaper five years earlier and that the *Meadowbrook Gazette* only consisted of a website that, when I was a freshman, was updated with new articles a few times a month.

But that didn't matter. Sure, no one else wanted to nerd out over the latest issues of *New York Magazine*, but that also meant I had no competition when it came to running for editor in chief. I could be in control. I could dictate what was considered news and *how* we'd go about finding out the truth behind Meadowbrook's dark underbelly. Though, after three years, I'm not even sure there *is* a dark underbelly.

Besides, if I'm being honest, I like calling the shots more than I like following someone else's orders. Grandma calls me her take-no-shit lovebug for a reason.

I inhale deeply as my mouse hovers over the publish button. Within seconds, all of our articles load on the *Gazette*'s home page, blaring the headlines we've spent the past week work-shopping: "New Ethics Course Raises Eyebrows," "Take a Tour of the Renovated Science Wing," "Soccer Stars Aim for Gold at Regionals."

We could have done better. I know that. But as I scroll down the site, a swell of pride grows in my chest. There, at the bottom, is the masthead, with my name at the top: Elizabeth Charles, editor in chief. I suck in a breath of air, nearly dizzy with excitement.

My focus shifts to the other open tab, the one with all the information for the Page One college scholarship. The text has practically imprinted on my computer screen at this point since it's been open for so many years. I zero in on the words at the top of the page:

The Page One scholarship is awarded to one high school journalist who has demonstrated a tremendous amount of promise in the field of media and intends to study journalism upon entering college. The scholarship recipient will receive a full tuition grant to the higher education institution of their choosing. Applications due October 15.

I keep reading, even though I know what I'm going to find, a list of past recipients I've almost fully memorized:

2023: Tyler Hill, "Plagiarism Scandal at Gilcomb Academy Leads to Mass Resignations and One Arrest," attends Northwestern University

2022: Paul Steinberg, "Superintendent's Beach House Bought with Illegal Funds," attends Yale University

2021: Rio Suarez, "Cold Case Finally Solved at Famed Los Angeles Public High School," attends Stanford University

There's a common thread among them all: illegal activity uncovered by a dogged high school reporter.

I flip back to the *Gazette* homepage. None of our articles come close to being of that level of importance. No criminal activity in sight. No unlikely villain. Just write-ups of who said what at the six-hour-long student government plenary.

Grandma always said it was bad luck to wish for horrible things to happen, but I can't help but hope for something a bit more dramatic to take place here at Meadowbrook. Just a little financial fraud. A cheating incident from a top donor's kid. Something that could launch this sleepy Connecticut town into the national discourse. Allow me to show my reporting chops, how I handle difficult situations with care and professionalism. But there's still a few months before the application is due. There's still time for something *exciting* to happen.

Outside my door, I can hear the other senior staffers assemble. Backpacks hitting the floor. Coffee pouring into mugs from the communal pot in the hallway. I asked everyone to gather before

Senior Sanction so we could toast to our first stories with orange juice and donuts from Rex Taylor's, and my stomach settles, grateful they all came.

"Holy shit," someone calls from the hallway. A few more gasps ring out.

I smooth out my skirt, straighten my button-down blouse, and roll up my sleeves to my elbows. I stick a pencil through my ponytail and grab the box of donuts as I make my way into the main room.

"Are you serious?"

"That's what I heard . . ."

"In a *dorm*."

I straighten my spine. Perhaps I introduced a mistake in Kevin's nut graf, missed a typo in a headline. Maybe if I fix it fast enough, no one will notice.

I set the pastries down on the counter, expecting to see the *Gazette* staff semicircled around the desks, mugs in hand. But everyone is glued to their phones, eyes wide. Kevin's hands shake so hard he drops his water bottle.

"What's going on?" I ask.

Rachel, the sports editor, looks up, her cheeks red, bottom lip trembling. "Sarah Oliver," she whispers.

"The soccer captain?" I cross my arms as I picture Sarah's pretty freckled face. We've had a few classes together, though she was obviously annoyed when we were paired as lab partners in physics and begged Doc Kolner to let her be with Peter Radcliffe, our class president. They'd been best friends since they were born, a fact they loved to share with any and everyone who would listen. "What about her? Did she get recruited somewhere? That girl is nowhere good enough to play D1."

Rachel shakes her head and for the first time I notice her skin has paled so much, she looks gray.

"What?" I ask, tapping my fingers against the steel filing cabinets.

"She's dead," Rachel says. "Ryan Pelham, too."

I run back into my office and grab my phone from my bag. But I don't have any new messages or push notifications. Nothing.

"Where are you seeing this?" I tear back through the hallway.

"On the app Melody created."

"App? What app?" It takes every ounce of self-control not to yank Rachel's phone out of her grasp.

Rachel's eyes flick up to mine. "Are you not on it? She created it as part of a hackathon. Some encrypted thing so we don't get caught messaging about parties or whatever."

I clear my throat and tilt my chin up. "No, I don't . . . I'm not on it."

Rachel's cheeks flush, and she turns her phone over to me. "Here. Take a look."

"I think it's invite-only." Kevin's voice is a whisper behind her, and I pretend not to hear him as I read the messages on Rachel's phone.

Sarah and Ryan were killed in Getty House . . . Amy found them this morning.

They've blocked off the entire wing of the dorm. I'm so scared.

WHO DID THIS?

This has to be a joke.

Not a joke. Police are coming now.

I heard Mrs. Talbert say the M word.

WTF is the m word???

MURDER, DUH!

I blink, reading the words again. I look up, out at my staff still in shock, hands over their mouths, tears beginning to form.

My heart thumps hard in my chest, adrenaline and fear coursing through me. A killer, here at Meadowbrook Academy. The idea is impossible.

But as I look out the window and hear sirens, see cop cars lining up at the gates, my stomach lurches into my throat. This is real.

Rachel hears them, too, and looks up, frightened. She turns to me. "What do we do?"

"I—" I start, but there's a wobble in my voice, a lump in my throat. I roll my shoulders back, projecting as much confidence as I can muster. "Well," I say, speaking slowly to mask the terror. "We're journalists. So, we'll do what we're trained to do. We'll report on the story."

Amy

I sit up on the bed in Nurse Gwen's office, realizing, with horror, that I'm not wearing a bra.

I clear my throat, scratchy, and Nurse Gwen turns around from her desk. Her eyes are red and her cheeks are wet. "Um," I say. "Can I have a sweatshirt?"

"Oh," she says, looking at me with pity before leaning toward the hallway and calling out, "she's talking!"

My cheeks burn. "A sweatshirt? Something to . . ." I motion to my chest, flopping around under my threadbare Meadowbrook Soccer T-shirt.

"Right, right." Nurse Gwen fumbles through her cabinets until she finds a maroon school crewneck and places it next to me, patting the cotton. I tug it on, though it's too warm in this room, and as I'm searching for something to say, a reason for why I'm here, she grabs my hand.

"Amy," she says. "I'm so terribly sorry."

I pull my hand back. I've never been one for physical touch, especially from near-strangers. Sarah likes to attack me with hugs when I least expect it, so I don't ward her off. Joseph's is the only touch that makes me want to lean in. But mostly in private. When we're in town or walking through practice, I barely let him hold my hand. At least I don't jump away like I used to last spring.

I look to the exit, and outside the doorway I see Head Teacher Egan and Coach Jensen rushing toward the room. Coach is dressed in her signature tracksuit, a low ponytail tied at the nape of her neck with a ribbon. Her normally cheerful face is splotchy and red, and she's biting her lip. I never really saw a resemblance between her and Joseph, not until now.

Egan's wearing a tweed skirt suit and a flouncy silk top, her Meadowbrook Academy brooch pinned to her lapel. She looks older than she did at the end of last year, but composed and stoic like usual, her pale blond hair tied up in a French twist. She pushes through the door first and enters the small room, taking up all the space.

Nurse Gwen dabs something cold and wet on my temple, and I recoil, my whole head stinging. I reach up and touch where she pressed. When I bring my fingers down, I see blood. Smell it.

I'm back in our dorm, swinging open Sarah's room, spotting a tuft of curly blond hair—Ryan's. Sarah's limp arm, dangling by her bed.

Their feet sticking straight out of the white sheets still wrapped around their ankles.

I saw them there. Dead.

In our room, our home. Our favorite place in the whole world.

It must have been a prank. Sarah likes to pull gags. Like last Halloween, when she left plastic spiders in my bed. Or Spring Fling, when she convinced me to set off a glitter bomb in the bouncy castle on main quad.

It was a joke. Obviously. To make me pay for last night.

But the blood on my finger is so real. Just like it was on Sarah. I try to speak, but no words come out. Only a rush of green—

sticky, sour bile dribbling out my mouth and onto the floor, masking the smell of blood.

Egan and Coach reel back, while one of Nurse Gwen's aides rushes in to mop up my mess.

I close my eyes and picture Sarah, with her nail-bitten fingers, her loud, deep laugh. Her dark brown eyes and her big bear hugs. Sweet Sarah who let me come to her house for Thanksgiving when my dad's work trip went long, who offered me my first sip of gin behind the crew boathouse, who always passed me the ball, even if she knew I wouldn't score. Sarah, who bought us matching mugs and sandals and scrunchies and throw pillows. Two of everything, two of us.

Sarah. The closest thing I had to a sister.

Sarah, who, just last night, called me selfish. Who I screamed at, the word *traitor* sitting easy on my tongue.

Sarah.

I blink open my eyes and try to focus on Head Teacher Egan standing next to my bed. Her brow is furrowed, and her hands are clasped in front of her, knuckles taut. Coach has backed up into the corner of the room, leaning against the wall. Her eyes are red and puffy.

"What happened to them?" I ask, my voice hoarse.

Egan shakes her head. "The police are doing their best to find out."

Coach approaches and wraps my hand in both of hers. "I'm so sorry, Amy. I know how close you were to Sarah. Ryan, too."

I bite my bottom lip. Don't think about Ryan. *Don't.* But I can't help it. *This is all his fault.*

"The police want to talk to you," Egan says. "But before they do, we wanted to check in. You've just experienced incredible trauma. You're in shock. We're concerned about you."

The only other times I've had one-on-one conversations with our head teacher have been in the presence of my dad, an alum whose recent donation helped build the new science wing on upper campus. I know how she sees me—an extension of Derek Alterman, class of 1991. An average student, by no means the best, but someone to keep happy. Someone to placate to keep those funds rolling in.

Coach, though. She's been honest with me since day one, when she told me I'd have to push myself harder to make the varsity team. She was right. When I got my period sophomore year, too embarrassed to tell the other girls that I had only just begun to menstruate, she's the one who taught me how to use a tampon, instructions given with a kind lilt from the other side of the bathroom door in the locker room. And when Joseph and I told her we were together last spring, she hugged me fiercely, telling me Joseph was the lucky one, even though he was her son.

"Can you tell us what happened last night, Amy?" Egan asks, softening her voice. She lowers her head as if she's about to whisper a secret. "Where you were? When you last saw Sarah? Anything that might be useful? The police will ask all of these questions and it's best you tell us first."

Coach looks down to the floor, avoiding my gaze, and suddenly I understand what this meeting is about. Egan wants to vet my story before the cops hear it. She wants to know where we were last night—what we were doing and how it might look when the news breaks.

I should tell the truth. Sarah and Ryan are dead. *Murdered* in our dorm. Everyone will want to know how I slept through it.

Why I didn't hear a thing, why I didn't call for help. Why I'm still alive while they're gone.

But I can't answer any of those questions because I don't know myself.

"Why don't you start with the party?" Egan says. "The one at the boathouse? After your senior soccer dinner?"

I snap my head up. "You know about that?"

She smiles. "We know more than you think."

Egan is testing me. I can feel it. But the party . . . everyone's going to find out about that anyway. I lean back against the pillow and close my eyes, picturing the racks of crew boats, dozens of empty beer cans, my friends laughing in their Meadowbrook hoodies.

"Okay," I say. "We can start with the party."

Liz

My inbox pings with an email from Head Teacher Egan, canceling Senior Sanction and all of the other team and trust-building activities we have scheduled for the day. She cites the reason as "unforeseen tragedies," which is a hell of a euphemism for "double homicide." She even notes that the underclassmen who are supposed to arrive tomorrow won't show up until further notice.

She urges everyone to return to their rooms and stay there, but I got permission from my dorm advisor, Doc Kolner, to camp out in the newsroom. "Okay, Liz," she said, sounding defeated over the phone. "Just make sure someone's with you."

She doesn't need to know that no one else wanted to stick around.

I pace the length of my small office, bring my thumb to my teeth to tear a cuticle. Out my window, I can see the whole campus. Usually, it's bustling, with uniformed students tossing balls back and forth, lying on blankets with books, speakers, and oversized water bottles. But right now, my peers are rushing to their rooms, fear and frenzy palpable as everyone peeks over their shoulders, wondering what might happen next.

It occurs to me then that I should lock the door to my office, and I spring up, latching the dead bolt into place. I ease into the seat behind my desk, feel a buzzing in my head, and my fingers seem to vibrate with nerves as I place them on my keyboard. I lean forward and start scrolling through socials, looking to see if there are any updates on what's going on, but no one's said anything just yet.

If only I could get into that dumb app Melody set up. Kevin said it was invite-only, but I can't imagine someone would let me in *now*, especially once they realize I'm there to do some reporting.

I look down at my notebook, a blank page in front of me. Usually, we have no problem getting students to talk for stories. Everyone wants their opinion heard on matters of new offerings in the cafeteria or renovations to the dorms. But this . . . who would want to talk about *this*?

I shoot off a text to Carly Kleary, who was my hallmate last year and, more importantly, social chair for our class. That meant she was always seeking me out, asking me to publish glowing pieces about how fun the spring formal was sure to be or what new rides students could expect at the homecoming fair. Perhaps someone like Carly, someone who prided herself on knowing everything that went on at Meadowbrook, might have some information to share.

Trying to figure out what the hell is going on. Have you heard anything? I ask.

It only takes a moment for Carly to reply.

Mariah lives in Getty House and says that whole section of the dorm is cordoned off. Apparently, Mrs. Talbert called it a "bloodbath."

My stomach turns queasy, but I fight the nausea to respond. That's terrifying. Everyone else okay?

As far as I know, Carly writes. But Kayla and Hillary were seen moving all their stuff to a new room since they were the closest to Amy and Sarah. Mariah said there's yellow caution tape and everything. I heard they took the bodies out through the tunnels underground so no one would see them.

I have no idea what to say as I read over her texts, blinking.

This is all off the record, by the way. Please don't use my name ANYWHERE.

Of course, I write back. I would never.

I lean back in my chair and tap my foot against the ground. The idea of something like this happening *here*, at Meadowbrook Academy, a place that has always felt secluded from reality, like the gate that kept us from the rest of town was impenetrable, is impossible.

But at the same time, I know that disaster can find you anywhere. That truths you thought were fact, set in stone and undeniable, can be proven false in an instant.

I learned that when Mom finally came back into my life when I was ten, after having been "away on business" for a decade of my childhood. When Grandma finally told me the truth, that Mom had really spent the early years of my childhood living in a van, growing weed with some dude named Harold, and that she was finally ready to come home and be a parent, I was so furious.

Of course, at Mom for leaving me, but at that time, I didn't even know her. She was a myth. A mannequin in photos. It was my grandmother who had raised me, who received most of my ire. I screamed at her, demanded to know why she couldn't have explained that Mom wasn't ready to be a caregiver, that my surprise arrival freaked her out so much that she ditched her responsibilities completely.

It pained me that Grandma didn't think I could handle the truth, that "being away on business" might soften the blow. It only made things worse when I learned that Mom wasn't off brokering important deals that were so consequential they overshadowed the needs of her daughter at home. Instead, she was spending her time doing something so insignificant, so inessential—and yet, so much more meaningful to her than raising a child.

I reread Carly's texts and even though I'm tempted to use her eyewitness account to get a story up right away, I'd rather go back to Milwaukee than publish an article with one betrayed anonymous source. That's a surefire way to get folks *not* to trust you.

Maybe I should make a list of potential sources, folks who might talk to me to give me a nugget of information.

At the top of my notebook page, I write *Amy Alterman*, though I have a feeling Sarah's roommate is probably out of commission right now.

Coach Jensen. Everyone always said she got along great with Sarah. Maybe she'd share some details or theories.

Peter Radcliffe. He's Ryan's best friend, co-captain of the crew team, and class president. If anyone on our student body were to know something it would be him. But based on the fact that we've barely spoken outside of *Gazette* dealings, I'm not sure how forthcoming he might be in a cold call.

Head Teacher Egan. I tap my fingers against the keys. I know the obvious answer is the Meadowbrook administration, but I can't imagine that Egan would talk to the press yet. She barely gave us a quote about the new ethics curriculum.

The police. There's never been a reason to drag them into Meadowbrook Academy reporting. Now, though. Now's the time to start.

I force myself to pick up the phone and look up their number to make the call. I tap my foot against the floor, losing my nerve with every passing second. But as I'm about to hang up, someone answers. "Meadowbrook PD, Brenda speaking. How can I help you?"

I straighten up and put on my best *adult* voice. "This is Liz Charles, calling from the *Meadowbrook Gazette*." She doesn't say anything, so I continue. "I'm hearing reports that there was a double homicide at Meadowbrook Academy. Care to comment?"

Brenda sighs and I hear her type something.

"Hello?" I ask, trying not to sound timid.

"We're not talking to the press."

I pause, plotting my next move. If this woman works at the police department, chances are she lives in town, and if she's like any of the Meadowbrook folks I've met, she must think this school is full of a bunch of stuck-up assholes. All I have to do is keep her talking.

"That makes sense," I say. "Especially since you know how all those hoity-toity parents would react if word got out."

Brenda lets out a grunt. "That's for sure. One time at High Meadow Farm . . ."

I let her go on for a while about prep school parents as I gaze out at the window, facing the quad, a grassy enclosure gated in by the four Meadowbrook dormitories, and two academic buildings, all made of bright red brick. The first time I saw photos of campus with its shiny windows and manicured lawns, I thought it was a college, expansive and full of possibilities. Now, though, it's empty. All those rushing, scared students tucked safely inside their rooms. But our rooms aren't safe. Not anymore.

Except . . . there, just outside Getty House, I see a small door opening below ground level. It's an entrance to the tunnels, a system that was set up in the fifties after Meadowbrook got walloped by snowstorm after snowstorm, and the administration didn't want kids missing classes due to weather. Thanks to some old engineering, there are underground walkways everywhere, with a clandestine exit right where I'm looking.

One member of the Meadowbrook Police emerges first, looking around to make sure no one is there. He then motions down into the stairwell and soon, the stretchers are lifted, two black body bags coming into view.

I nearly drop the phone as I watch them roll the stretchers onto the walkway until they reach an ambulance waiting on the street. The bodies disappear inside, and I swallow the lump in my throat. They drive away, quiet. No sirens. Which can only mean there's no one to save.

". . . And then I said, 'No, Sally, that's *not* how you bake a proper pie!'" Brenda pauses. "You still there?" she asks.

"Yes." My throat is like sandpaper and my mind spins with headline ideas and a potential lede. I need her to confirm the news—I need her to confirm that the police are investigating a double homicide.

"Brenda," I start. "I just saw with my own eyes two body bags being rolled into an ambulance, escorted by Meadowbrook Police. You sure you can't confirm to me that the department's investigating the deaths of two students? Murder?"

She pauses. "What paper you say you're with?"

"*Meadowbrook Gazette.*"

"Hm," she says, and it dawns on me she has no idea I'm with the school. Then she lowers her voice. "Well, you didn't hear this from me, but yes. Yes, I can confirm."

My fingers fly to my keyboard, and I pull up the local news, the one that reports on town hall meetings and lost cats. There's nothing there, nothing about our school at all. When I google "Meadowbrook Academy + murders" I get nothing. That's when I realize this story hasn't broken. *I* can break it. *I* can own it.

"Can I say this information came from a source at the Meadowbrook Police Department?" I ask, breathless. If I get this qualifier, I can run with the story. I can publish.

She pauses. "Okay. But again, you can't use my name. Nor my job. Just . . . a source. Got it?" And before I can say yes, she's gone, only static left in my ear.

I wiggle my fingers above my keyboard as I look at the blank document in front of me, cursor blinking, ready.

That's when I start typing.

Amy

"So I'm clear, you're telling me the party started at nine at the boathouse," Egan says. "And you left near midnight?"

"That's right." At least I'm not lying *now*.

"And how did Sarah seem to you at the party?"

"She was kind of mad." I scratch the inside of my wrist, an itch I can't relieve.

"At who?" Egan asks.

"Me."

Coach looks up.

"It was silly," I say. "Boy stuff." The words pop out, but as soon as I say them, they feel wrong. We did fight about Ryan and Joseph, but it wasn't silly, and it was deeper than the words *boy stuff* can convey. It was about the eroded foundation of our friendship.

I had wanted to mend it—and she did, too. But neither one of us knew how, not in that moment. It was like I didn't have the language to say, "You hurt me," and neither did she.

"I left the party after that and figured we'd make up in the morning."

Egan looks back to Jensen, who nods, confirming what she knows about Sarah and me, that we *do* make up. We always do. Except we had never fought like that before. We had never fought about Ryan and Joseph. We had never let them come between us. Though in reality, the fight wasn't about them. It was about us.

"And you went straight back to your dorm?" she asks. If this had happened any other night at Meadowbrook, Egan would have been able to check the smart lock system to see when I entered, to confirm that I had indeed used my key card, that I was accompanied by someone else, someone who did *not* go to Meadowbrook Academy and was barred from entering any dormitories. But since it was technically before school was in session, the security system wasn't recording our movements.

It's why seniors always party during this special week. Usually, the administration looks the other way. Coach told me it's a good way for us to get our ya-yas out before the underclassmen arrive.

I blink, looking between Coach and Egan. I knew this question would come up. If I tell them the truth, then today could be Coach's last day at Meadowbrook. There might be a trespassing charge for Joseph. Egan's done it before, when a sophomore let her cousin sleep in the dorms without permission. She almost had them arrested until she found out their grandmother was on the board at Cornell, where Egan hoped to send a few students every year.

But Joseph. He doesn't have a golden parachute, not like that.

All he's got is a crooked smile and a tiny gap between his front teeth, a sweet swoop of dark hair that falls away from his head when he's bent down over a plate, adding a final sprinkle of salt or one last grate of Parmesan to a bowl of pasta. When I saw him last night, he had smelled of garlic and olive oil, of the trays of focaccia he had spent hours prepping at Rex Taylor's. The little café was his happy place, a launching pad to Michelin star restaurants in New York, a future of scalding oil and "yes, chef!" A future so different from mine but still, a future.

Telling them about where we were would jeopardize all of that. The lie sits on the tip of my tongue, salty and forbidden. Sarah always says—*said*—that I don't trust myself enough, that I need validation of my decisions and I never go with my gut. But right now, my gut is telling me to lie—the smallest of fibs, one that might not even matter. I'd have to repeat it back to the police, of course, but saying I went to bed alone won't make a difference, because Sarah and Ryan are still dead and there's nothing I can do to bring them back. The only thing I can do is protect Joseph.

I look right at Egan, trying to keep my face still. "I went right back to my dorm," I say. "And didn't wake up until morning."

Coach walks beside me across the quad, strange and quiet without students who are hunkered down inside their dorms. I look up and see faces in the windows, staring back at me, pressed against the glass. Yesterday, while Sarah and I were getting ready for practice, we talked at length about how cool it felt to be here on campus with only our class, how *special* we felt. Seniors wait three whole years for this one week where we get to run around with so few responsibilities. The past few days were filled with soccer practice and dorm bonding, but also the kinds of boathouse parties you can't get away with when the normal school year is in session. Peter had even found a way to get a keg for last night's festivities.

We had been free to roam the school like we ran it, like we were just that: free. Only days ago, we walked this very route after midnight to visit our teammate Olivia, who got stuck in Holbrook instead of Getty, clearly a clerical error the school rectified as soon as they could. Sarah had cartwheeled across the grass, laughing as her T-shirt fell down to her chin while she flew through the air, revealing a strong stomach, toned and tan from a summer at the beach.

"Come on, Amy!" she called to me, but I demurred, wondering who was watching from the turrets. Likely no one, I now realize. But today, I can feel eyes peering down at me.

I duck my head as we walk past Getty House. I can't even look at the building with its redbrick facade and arched entryways. It's always felt so safe to me, more like home than my dad's modern cube in Palo Alto, gated and secured like a fortress.

I don't know if I'll ever set foot inside Getty again.

"Where are they putting me?" I ask Coach. She's carrying a small tote bag full of Meadowbrook Academy warm-up gear she grabbed from the locker room and a few pamphlets from the student mental health center. One peeks out of the bag, and I see the words "Managing Grief."

"Holbrook," she says, nodding toward the dorm on the opposite side of the grassy lawn, the farthest one from Getty. "Apparently someone there got a single, so it's the only senior bed left on campus."

"Do you know who?" I ask.

Coach shakes her head. "Mrs. Talbert said she'll arrange for a few of your things to be brought over once . . ." She stops herself and we both know what she's going to say. *Once they're done treating your room like a crime scene.*

We're quiet for another few minutes, the air heavy and warm, a reminder that summer doesn't end just because the calendar flips to September. It smells like soccer season, like new beginnings, like arriving on campus and cracking open a fresh notebook for the very first time. It smells like meeting Sarah freshman year, our dorm windows wide open to let the old building cool down, like hugging her and realizing she was about to change my life.

Coach Jensen must feel it, too, because she grows stiff beside me and when I look up, I see tears wet against her cheeks. I hate lying to her, especially now. Joseph always says she loves us all—her players—that she would take a bullet for any one of her girls. I have to remind myself that my silence will keep her safe. Joseph, too. Admitting that he was with me won't bring Sarah or Ryan back.

"I'm sorry," I say, because I don't know what other words might suffice.

"Me too." She gives me an awkward side hug, and I choke back a gurgling sound in my throat.

Coach's phone chimes and she releases me, looking at the screen. "Oh no."

"What?"

"The news is out," she says. "Egan was hoping to keep it contained for a while, but . . ."

I look over her shoulder and see she's looking at the school newspaper's website, where a huge headline blares the words "Double Murder in the Dorms." I scan the screen and see it's written by Liz Charles.

Everyone knows Liz since she's often carrying around a reporter's notebook and recorder as if she's about to break some Watergate-level story even though we're in the middle of nowhere. I never thought much of her, not when she tried to recruit more reporters at the club fair last fall or when she stood in the middle of campus on winter mornings, asking passersby for quotes about midterm exams. She seemed a little too chipper about conducting interviews in subzero temperatures.

Besides, I'd never engage with a member of the press, even if the *Gazette* is a student paper. "They're vultures," Dad warned me in the weeks after he filed the divorce papers. The paparazzi's light bulbs flashing through the tinted windows of our SUV proved him right, put an exclamation point on the truth. "Whatever you do, never trust a reporter."

His words ping in my brain as I peer over Coach's shoulder and catch a glimpse of the article.

Meadowbrook Academy students were shocked to learn that two seniors were found dead during the penultimate night of senior welcome week. Sources describe it as a grisly and violent scene . . .

I stop, my feet suddenly heavy. "She's writing about them like they're not real." A lump forms in my throat and I can't swallow it, no matter how hard I try.

Jensen shakes her head and puts her phone away. "Come on, let's get you inside."

I move with her, but I can't shake the icky feeling in my stomach, the one that's telling me that Liz's article is only the beginning. It's the same feeling I got when I was twelve, when all the tech blogs picked apart the divorce filing, making listicles about assets and publishing claims of infidelity alongside photos of my mom on a white-sand beach in a sarong.

"TechBoom CEO's Wife Ditches Him for a Trainer in St. Tropez" made for a hell of a headline, though I doubt those reporters thought for a second about the kid in the middle of the split or how it felt for me to go to school knowing that everyone in my class had read the posts about my parents. Reporters camped out at our house for a week, trying to get photos of my mom packing up her stuff. Some trash site ran them and didn't bother to blur out the little kid—me—crying in the window.

I follow Coach through Holbrook's entrance and up the mahogany staircase to the second floor, where Doc Kolner, head of the physics department, is waiting with her hands clasped in front of her stomach.

"Oh, Amy," she says, her voice dropping. "Come this way." She leads me down a hall, where I can see girls' heads poking out of their doorways, eyes wide and bulging. For the first time I realize I'm no longer Amy Alterman, a seventeen-year-old from Northern California, halfback on the soccer team, average student, lover of spicy salmon rolls and sad girl pop. I'm now Amy Alterman, the dead girl's roommate.

Doc Kolner stops at the last room and pauses, knocking on the door.

We're all standing there awkwardly, and it dawns on me that I'm going to have to room with someone who's *not* Sarah, someone I'll have to make small talk with about the weather, who won't understand the whole situation with my dad, someone whose rhythms are out of sync with mine. And I won't even be able to complain about it to Sarah. I won't be able to do *anything* with Sarah ever again. I wipe my eyes with the back of my palm.

Jensen squeezes my shoulder as the door opens and when I see who's there, I can't help but step back.

Doc Kolner looks at me, confused, but I can't take my eyes off the girl standing before me, with her head cocked, her lips pursed.

"Hi, Amy," says Liz Charles. "I guess we're going to be room-mates."

Liz

Amy stumbles backward into her coach, arms flailing. "I can't room with her." Her voice shakes as she looks up to Doc Kolner, her eyes pleading.

My cheeks burn. I should have seen this coming, known that Amy would be furious to learn she had a new roommate.

Amy turns her head to Coach Jensen. "I'm not living here." She shakes her head, backing away from me. "She's going to be spying on me."

Oh. So, I guess it is about me personally.

"I'm so sorry, Amy . . ." I start to say, but as soon as the words come out of my mouth, it's obvious they're the wrong ones. Amy's eyes flash fire and her mouth thins into a straight line. Behind her, other people on my hall poke their heads out of their doors, trying to see what's going on.

I lean in and lower my voice. "Do you want to at least come inside?" I motion back toward my room. Coach Jensen offers a quick nod and gently pushes Amy through the threshold.

The common room is small but tidy, void of houseplants in pastel ceramic pots or neon signs displaying catchphrases that are so popular in the other rooms. It never seemed important for me to keep things like that since I spend so much time at the newspaper office. "Your room's over there," I point to the open door on the left. "And the other closet's empty."

Amy stares at me, narrowing her eyes. "That's *not* my room and I'm not living here." She turns to Coach. "They have to put me somewhere else. A freshman dorm. Fielding House. I don't care." Her teeth are gritted and she keeps her arms crossed over her chest, her fingernails digging into the cotton of her sweatshirt.

Coach sighs and pats Amy on the shoulder. "I'm sorry, but Egan wants you with the other seniors. She said it's for the best for you to keep some semblance of normalcy."

"Normalcy?" Amy echoes. "That's a joke, right? I just found Sarah and Ryan dead and Egan wants me to feel *normal?*" She clenches her hands into fists by her side. "This is unbelievable."

Coach rests a hand on Amy's shoulder. "I can try to talk to Egan, but her mind was made up."

Amy lets out a strangled sound and a lump rises in my throat. All of the books I've read about journalism, all the interviews I've watched with reporters, all the tips I've studied on how to interact with sources . . . none of them could have prepared me for being face-to-face with someone who woke up to find her friends murdered in the room next door.

Coach turns to me. "It's not like Liz is going to write about *you* or violate your privacy, isn't that right?"

"I won't even be here, really," I say. "I've got a lot to do at the *Gazette* office."

Amy glowers like she's trying to wound me with her gaze and I look away, clenching my toes deep inside my loafers.

"Your things will be brought over soon and, in the meantime, here." Coach hands Amy a tote bag full of stuff and turns back to me. "Maybe Liz can loan you anything else you might need?"

I nod, even though my wardrobe consists of our school uniform, one pair of jeans, a few moth-eaten sweaters I found at the vintage store in town, and a dozen white T-shirts I got on sale at a big box retailer five minutes from Grandma's house. Amy's probably the type of girl who has seasonal changes of clothes—vacuum-sealed bags of cashmere sweaters and sundresses for every day of the week. "Of course."

Amy stares at me, and I begin to fidget with the hair tie around my wrist.

"We'll come get you when the police are ready, okay?" Coach says to Amy, who finally turns away from me. "It should be sometime this afternoon."

"Can I see Joseph?" Her voice is small now, like a child's, and there's a noticeable break when she says his name.

I turn around and try to pretend like I'm not listening, reorganize a few books on my desk. I've met Joseph before at Rex Taylor's, where he works as a chef, whipping up egg sandwiches on homemade brioche or assembling berry-topped bowls of overnight oats. He's always come across as sweet and gentle, laughing politely at customers' bad jokes and sliding free cookie samples to kids across the counter. When I found out he was dating Amy Alterman last spring I was admittedly surprised, since she seemed so stuck-up. She was the only person in the entire class to bring someone from outside school to the junior formal last spring.

Coach responds in a low voice. "I don't think you can leave campus now."

"He can't come here?"

"I'm sorry, Amy. Soon, though, okay?" Coach's phone buzzes and I sneak a peek over my shoulder to see her shoulders sag as she looks at the screen. "Egan," she says. "The detectives will come for you in about an hour." She reaches for the door, Doc Kolner by her side, and gives Amy and I both one last look. "Take care of each other, girls. This is an awful, awful day."

They both leave and for a moment there's an awkward pause, the kind I know reporters are supposed to leave empty, let the source fill. But this isn't an interview. I'm not on the job. I may be a student reporter, but right now I'm just a student. I open my mouth and try to find something comforting to say, but before I can speak, Amy turns around and heads toward the open bedroom, slamming the door behind her.

This is not how I thought things would go when Doc Kolner told me that Amy Alterman would be moving into the spare room an hour ago. I had been thrilled to receive the one single last week, thanks to the fact that they had originally paired me with Tara Simon, whose family moved to London over the summer after room assignments were already doled out.

But in a moment of naivete, I thought rooming with Amy might mean that I could convince her to talk about Sarah and Ryan, about what happened.

I slump down in my desk chair and squeeze my eyes shut. How foolish.

My phone screen lights up and I reach for it, seeing a text come in from my mom. Even though she moved back a few years ago, most of our communication still goes through Grandma, who prefers handwritten letters and care packages full of sour candy over digital communication. I received her first letter yesterday and smiled when I saw she included a clipping from the local paper talking about the new addition to the library.

You would have written a much better lede, Grandma had scrawled on a sticky note. I hung it up on my corkboard last night and her handwriting stares back at me now.

I hesitate to open Mom's message, but I do it anyway, unease settling in my stomach. I never trusted her after she came back. My therapist said it was because I couldn't believe she would stay put, or that she was telling me the truth after so many years of lying. Rebuilding all of that trust would take time, I was told. But Mom doesn't seem to want to wait for that to happen.

I just heard the news—the school emailed all the parents. ARE YOU OKAY??????? CALL ME.

The last thing I want to do is call my mom in order to calm her down, but I shoot off a text. I'm fine. We're on lockdown. You don't have to worry about me.

She responds fast. Of course I have to. I'm your mother.

I curl my fist around my phone as if I might break it with my grasp.

Only when you want to be, I type out. But I don't hit send. I delete the text, letter by letter, and turn my phone over on my desk.

I swivel around in my chair and stare at Amy's closed door, searching for a way to make things right. My eyes travel to my bookshelf, where I had unpacked all of my novels and nonfiction books yesterday. Right in the middle is *Beyond the Woods*, a true crime investigation by my favorite reporter, Yalitza Luna, who broke the story about the serial killer in the Catskills in the early 2010s. I devoured it in one sitting over the summer.

I reach for the book and flip open the pages to a section in the middle, a chapter called "Sourcing Up."

At first, the townspeople in Mount Cherry didn't want to talk to an outsider. They didn't want some smarmy reporter from the big city coming in and picking apart their way of life or finding the ways they were at fault for the killer's actions. Getting them to talk to me took months, sometimes years. But after speaking with more than two hundred people in the community, one thing became clear: they didn't want someone to be their mouthpiece. They wanted someone to listen.

I reread the passage, my heart thumping hard in my chest. Maybe that's true for Amy—for everyone who knew Sarah and Ryan better than I did. Maybe that's the way to break through.

I grab a sticky note from my desk and etch out a few words, my pen flying fast.

I'm sure I'm the last person you want to talk to, but please know that if you do need someone, I'm here.

My phone pings with a notification and when I check the screen, a sense of urgency fills my stomach. An email from my advisor, Mrs. Herschel:

Subj: Your article

Liz—meet me in the newspaper office ASAP.

I grab my phone, a backup recorder, and a small reporter's notebook and stuff them all in my bag. As my hand reaches for the knob, I hear a rustling behind me. When I turn around, I see my note sliding all the way under Amy's door.

Amy

The door to the suite shuts with a bang and I throw Liz's note into the small plastic trash can in the corner of the room and flop on the bed. It's made up with thin cotton sheets—not mine, that's for sure. I stare up at the ceiling, flat and smooth after getting a fresh coat of paint this summer. Whoever slapped it on probably thought this year would be like all the others—boring and uneventful. They were so wrong.

How could Liz possibly think that I would want to confide in *her*, of all people?

For the first time since this morning, I realize that I'm alone, like *really*, horribly alone. This room looks exactly like mine across campus, except it's bare, void of the decorations that Sarah and I spent hours hanging on our walls a week ago when we arrived. Ryan had been sprawled out on the common room floor, twisting his hands around a Rubik's cube and shouting out "higher" or "lower" while we strung fairy lights from one corner to another. I hadn't complained that he was there, hadn't pulled Sarah aside and said this was *our* special time, our *last* time decorating a room together, even though I thought it. I kept watch for her when they disappeared into her room for an hour, making sure Mrs. Talbert didn't come back to find Ryan inside our dorm.

I should call my dad. That's what anyone else would do—get

in touch with their parents. I'm sure half my peers have already placed frantic, worried calls home, letting their guardians know they're wholly traumatized and desperate for comfort. Maybe a care package containing their favorite baked goods from the café near their house might help. A new pair of jeans or designer sunglasses. Emergency therapy sessions and perhaps a re-up of Xanax. Some probably begged for a first-class ticket home, or to be picked up immediately.

But Meadowbrook is my home and the last thing I want to do is call Dad. I know how the conversation will go: He'll be concerned, of course, but his first thoughts will go to his own schedule, his next flight. The guilt will get to me and I'll have to reassure him that no, he doesn't need to fly back from wherever he's doing business, and yes, I'm fine. Yes, *really*. The lie will slide out through my teeth, the same kind of fib I'd tell when he would ask me how I was dealing with the divorce and the media coverage. *Fine* was the best course of action, the only answer that would indicate *No, you don't have to worry about me, too. Not on top of everything else.*

He'll ask me to forward Sarah's and Ryan's parents' information to his assistant, Drew, so he can send them sympathy packages, though Drew will undoubtedly call me as soon as he receives the email, asking for a few personal specifics he can write on the card to make it seem like my dad actually knew who they were. Neither one of them will realize the added burden this nicety places on me. The whole interaction will make me want to smash my phone into a million pieces.

So, for now, I'll put off contacting Dad. He'll call eventually, when he gets an email from the school or when he sees something on the news.

My heart rate quickens and suddenly I'm sweating, so hot my

sweatshirt sticks to my skin. I reach into the stomach pouch for my phone and pull up Sarah's messages inside the app Melody made over the summer so we could all text under an encrypted signal. I enter the password and my thumb moves with muscle memory, her name the most typed, the most loved.

When I see our last exchange, tears spring into my eyes.

Sarah: where are you?? did you leave???

Amy: why would I stay? Seriously?

Sarah: BULLSHIT

I wipe my face with the back of my hand. We never spoke to each other that way, not in the three years of friendship. Even as I slipped away, leaving the party without telling anyone where I was going, I assumed that we'd have a chance to make things right. She was drunk and furious and would certainly calm down in the sober light of day. So would I.

But she never made it to morning.

There's a knock on the door to the suite, loud enough that I can hear it from my bed. I freeze, my heart rate picking up. I don't want to talk to the police. Not yet.

"Amy," someone calls, their voice muffled. "Are you in there? It's me, Kayla."

I press my head deeper into the pillow, wishing I could disappear into the extra-long twin-size bed. The last time I saw Kayla Liu, she was smirking at me from across the boathouse right before Sarah and I fought, like she knew Sarah was about to unleash on me.

Maybe Sarah had confided in her yesterday. The thought jolts me and I sit up straight. Kayla had grown up with Sarah in New Canaan, Connecticut, along with Peter Radcliffe. They all went to the same country club and elementary school, taking tennis lessons together in the Oliver family backyard.

Kayla never warmed to me, an obvious threat to her friendship with Sarah, and I'd be lying if I said I didn't relish the fact that when faced with a choice of who to sit with on the soccer bus or in the library, or who to bunk with once we were able to pick our own suitemates, Sarah chose me. She always chose me.

But still, Kayla's pounding on my door, while Sarah lies in a morgue.

"Amy," Kayla calls again. "I know you're in there."

I push myself up to stand and walk barefoot through the common space. When I swing the door open, Kayla's there in an oversized T-shirt and shorts, her face red and swollen. She throws her arms around me, nearly knocking me to the floor.

"Oh my god," she says. "I can't believe it."

She smells of lemon and soap, like she just took a shower, and I wonder if she had to walk to the far bathroom in Getty, if the one that separated our suites was cordoned off with yellow caution tape.

My arms hang limp by my side and finally Kayla lets go. Her long dark hair is tied in a high bun and she looks younger than usual, her face free from the dark eyeliner she favors, the peach blush she's never seen without.

She shakes her head. "I don't even know what to say."

I look down and shrug. "Me neither," I finally mumble. "How did you get here? Aren't the dorms on lockdown?"

"I begged Talbert," Kayla says. "Figured you'd need a friend right about now." She looks around at the bare walls, the lack of decor. "Who did they put you with?"

"Liz Charles."

Kayla scrunches her face up. "The newspaper editor? Don't they know that the media basically ruined your life in middle school?"

I nod, remembering I had told her that after one too many shots of Jameson in the boathouse sophomore year. At the time, I was embarrassed that I had revealed so much of myself. But now I'm grateful that she gets why it would be so disturbing to room with someone like Liz, even for a night. "Hoping they'll find room for me somewhere else."

"Can't you just ask your dad to yell at Egan? Work some donor magic?"

"Maybe," I say, though I would never have Dad fight my battles. Even this one.

Kayla sniffles and plops down on the small couch in the common space. Back in my and Sarah's room, it was the first area we decorated with fuzzy throw pillows and thick potted candles on the coffee table. Sarah had placed a photography book about Cape Cod beaches beside it. I hadn't even had a chance to thumb through it.

The air between us is heavy, laden with resentment as thick as the humidity. Kayla breaks the silence first. "Have you . . . did you hear anything? Do you know who . . . ?"

I shake my head. At least I don't have to lie to her, not right now. "I have no idea. I didn't hear a thing."

Kayla starts to cry, her sobs quick and angry. My cheeks flush, embarrassed for her, and I watch as she leans back against the couch and closes her eyes, trying to catch her breath through the tears.

"It's just so awful," she ekes out. "I can't believe it."

A sickly feeling rises in my throat and I swallow hard, desperate not to puke in front of Kayla. But another feeling arises, too—rage. Kayla wasn't there. Kayla didn't see what I saw. Kayla wasn't furious with Sarah when she ran from the boathouse, hoping they'd resolve their fight in the morning. Kayla gets to live with the fact that her last interactions with Sarah were likely pleasant and kind.

But then Kayla looks at me and I catch a hint of suspicion, as if she's wondering where my sorrow has gone.

"Did you two make up?"

And for a second, it's like I've been punched in the gut. Kayla glances down at her phone and doesn't let me answer. "Shit. The Olivers just got here. They're with Egan."

I sit up straight and try not to seem like I'm peering at her phone, but when I get a glance, I see there's a long text from Sarah's mom in what looks like an ongoing conversation.

I don't think I've ever had a real talk with either of the Olivers, aside from them asking me where I wanted to go to college and what I wanted to study. Sarah gave me her mother's number in case she broke her phone or dropped it in the pond. But I'd never think to text with Mrs. Oliver like she was a friend.

Sarah never did either, preferring to keep her uptight matching-sweater-set mom out of her daily life. Her father, too, though at least he looked the other way when we swiped vodka from their library bar in New Canaan. Early on, she and I bonded over being only children in a sea of families that had enough siblings to start a basketball team. Kayla is the oldest of five girls, two of which are twins, already at Meadowbrook as sophomores. It always surprised me that she was so desperate for Sarah's friendship when she had a built-in network of her own, four girls who idolized Kayla as their leader, their hero. Sarah and I only had each other.

Last October, she burst into our suite after mail call one night grasping a small cardboard box, her eyes shining with excitement. "I got us DNA kits," Sarah said, tearing the package apart.

"What?" I had put down my chem textbook and watched as Sarah opened each pouch, reading the directions as fast as she could.

"Think about it this way," she said, swabbing the inside of her cheek with a long Q-tip. "Neither one of us have siblings, but what if we're related? What if one of our parents boned the other and never told us? A total *Parent Trap* situation."

"They've never even met."

"That we know of."

"You're ridiculous."

"Oh, come on. Let me dream a little."

I rolled my eyes but obliged her by going through the motions of swabbing myself, too, secretly hoping that when the results came back, they might reveal we *were* long-lost sisters, paired together by fate.

They only revealed the obvious: I was 99 percent Ashkenazi, and she was a mixture of English, German, and Irish.

Sarah shrugged at the results and tossed them into our trash can. "Who needs blood to be sisters anyway?" she had said, quickly kissing the top of my forehead.

"Mrs. Oliver says she's in Egan's office and that I can go see her. Do you want to come?" Kayla's looking at me with wide eyes as she stands, her hands wrapped around her phone.

A lump sits in my throat. I know I should try to comfort them and remind them how important Sarah was to all of us. But their emotions might not be limited to sorrow and pain; they might also be full of ire. Because how else can a parent react to the news of their dead daughter than wonder why the girl sleeping next door was spared when their precious angel was taken from them?

Kayla looks at me expectantly. The skin around her eyes is red and puffy and she bites her bottom lip as if she didn't lob an arrow at me, asking me about the fight only moments before.

I shake my head, grateful to have an excuse. "I can't. I'm waiting for the police. Interview and all that."

"Right. Sure." Kayla turns for the door fast, and I know I should take back my words, go with her to the Olivers and let them hold me and cry and scream at me for living. I should tell the cops to wait, that I have a duty. But I don't. I let Kayla go and stumble back to the unfamiliar room that is somehow now mine. I pull the thin sheets up over my head and draw the blinds, and finally I cry.

Liz

Mrs. Herschel is late so I post up behind my editor's desk and start searching to see who else has picked up the news. All the local papers have developing articles, and there's even a national wire making the rounds. None of them have very many details, but they all contain the same thing, a link to my story, quoting it as the definitive confirmation that two students were found dead at the esteemed Meadowbrook Academy this morning. I'm deep in to reading through my news feed when a slamming noise causes me to jump.

"Elizabeth Charles, have you lost your mind?" Mrs. Herschel is standing in the doorway, wearing wide-legged trousers and a short-sleeve cotton top. Her usually neat hair is frizzy and out of place, and she's not wearing any makeup, which makes her look about fifty even though I know from my sleuthing that she's thirty-five. It's as if she learned about the news while she was getting ready for the day and stopped halfway through. I wince as she starts walking toward my desk in the back corner.

"I understand why you're mad, but you always say to take action when news breaks. This is a once-in-a-lifetime story and—"

Mrs. Herschel holds up her hand to stop me. She sucks in a puff of air and presses her lips together. "I cannot believe you published that piece without giving me a heads-up. Do you know that the administration is furious with you? And me, by extension? Do you know what you've done?"

"But—" I start.

"No *buts*."

"Aren't they a little too busy to be worried about me? Shouldn't they be more concerned that two students *died* on campus? In *dorms*? In what seems like an incredibly violent double murder?"

Mrs. Herschel's eyes flash fury as she sits down in the seat across from me. "Egan is doing everything she can to cooperate with the police, Liz. Everyone wants to find out what happened, and if anyone else is still at risk. Whoever did this is still out there. People are terrified."

My hands drop from my keyboard into my lap, my fingers clasping together. Of course it occurred to me that other students might be in danger—that *I* could be in danger. But the thought hadn't deterred me from trying to figure out what happened.

I remember reading an interview Yalitza Luna had done with a student reporter at her alma mater. When they asked her what makes a good journalist, she said something I'll never forget: "When danger strikes, most people with good sense run to safety. But journalists, we're compelled to rush toward it. That's what makes us different. Foolish sometimes, but different."

That's how I feel in this moment, an undeniable pull, tugging me toward danger.

I tilt my head up. "What's my punishment?"

Mrs. Herschel rubs her temple with her thumb and forefinger. "You can't cover the story, Liz. Not like this."

"But—" I start. My mind spins, trying to put together an argument: our classmates deserve to know the truth about what happened to their friends. No one can tell this story better than we can. What if Sarah and Ryan weren't the only targets? What if other students are in danger? And finally, though I'm not proud to admit it, I know that reporting out these murders is a surefire way to win that Page One scholarship.

"There are more important things than that scholarship," she says, as if she knows what I'm thinking. She blinks fast and for a second, I think she might cry. "Two of your peers are *dead*. On the campus of the school *you* attend." She shakes her head. "This is different than writing about a new debate coach or an inter-school mixer or even the crimes of notable alumni. This is . . ." She trails off and throws up her hands. "This is unimaginable. It's murder."

We're both quiet, letting her words hang in the air. *Murder.*

"This is about more than some prize money," I say, and as soon as the words come out of my mouth, I know they're true. "It's about the finding out what happened, *who* did this. How the school allowed it to happen. Don't we need to know?"

"That's why we have police, Liz. This is their job. Not yours."

"But you know the media plays a huge part in these kinds of stories." According to Yalitza's book, the police weren't even close to finding the Catskills Killer's identity until she started reporting, until her articles led them to that cabin in Greene County. They never would have solved the case without her even though they tried to dissuade her from investigating.

"What am I supposed to do?" I ask. "Let the local news write a bunch of garbage stories? Wait for reporters from all around the country to descend? You know they will and they'll say whatever they want about Meadowbrook Academy."

Mrs. Herschel turns her head so she's looking out the window toward the quad, right through the same pane of glass where I saw the stretchers carry Ryan and Sarah away.

"Sarah was supposed to be in my homeroom this year." Mrs. Herschel lets out a little smile. "I was excited to get to know her. All of her previous advisors loved her. Said she had an infectious laugh. Worked harder than an ox. Fought like hell for her perfect GPA."

I press my teeth into my bottom lip. It's always so weird to me when people die and everyone pretends they were perfect, that they never did anything wrong or bad or mean. Sarah may have been funny and smart, but she was just like the others—the spoon-fed Meadowbrook students who assumed life would work out for them. They never had to think about who would pay for their college applications, let alone their tuition. They never had to worry that their parents wouldn't show up to family weekend, that they'd be the only kid in class left alone.

Sarah was never mean or malicious, but she was coddled and self-absorbed, only seeing what was right in front of her at that exact moment. Even after we were paired together for a physics lab that took two weeks to complete, she ignored me in the halls, pretended we had never worked together, that I had been forgotten as soon as I left her line of sight. The ambivalence—the disinterest—was almost worse than if she had been cruel.

It was fitting that she got together with Ryan, another athlete who seemed to only see certain people from certain places, the rest of us objects moving around him. Freshman year, their adoration for one another flooded the halls like noxious gas. You couldn't walk three feet through our class lounge without watching them paw at one another, his arm draped around her slight frame. That year, the *Gazette* ran a special Valentine's Day issue, highlighting couples on campus who seemed so in love. It was *not* my idea, obviously, but George, the editor at the time, asked me to interview Sarah and Ryan. He handed me a list of questions that started with "Can you define love?" Barf.

It seemed ridiculous, asking two fifteen-year-olds to define something no one could, and Sarah laughed off the question, curling into Ryan's underarm. "I don't know."

But Ryan turned to me and leaned in, his gaze unwavering. "All I know is that I don't want to be anywhere without her."

I blushed, surprised by his honesty, and the quote ended up being our headline, blasted on the *Gazette* website for a week. He never spoke to me again, barely looked at me. But I'll always remember that brief moment where he shocked me, made me think that perhaps he wasn't plagued by indifference.

Neither Sarah nor Ryan was perfect. They were human. And perhaps one of the greatest tragedies of their deaths is that they'll never be able to grow and mature into people who understood the power they wielded and how their actions affected those around them.

"Sarah seemed very genuine," I say.

Mrs. Herschel looks at me. "This is a time for you to respect your peers and your teachers. You have no idea what everyone else might be going through, how people are grieving. You are a reporter, yes, but you are also a member of the Meadowbrook Academy community."

"I know that," I say, my voice small. "But what happens if I continue to cover this?"

Herschel purses her lips before speaking. "You really want to test your luck?" She pauses. "Egan could strip you of your editor title or, worse, suspend you. Maybe even expel you. Forget about college recommendations or support for the Page One."

My mouth drops open and I want to challenge her yet again, but before I can, my phone chimes with an email from Head Teacher Egan sent to the entire senior class.

I skim the message and find she's calling an assembly.

"We should go." Mrs. Herschel begins to gather her things and stand.

I follow her lead and reach for my bag. "Do you think it's off the record?"

She looks at me with narrowed eyes.

"I'm *joking*." I try to offer her a smile, but it comes out halfhearted.

Herschel shakes her head. "Come on."

I follow her out of the office, but before we head into the hall, I reach for her elbow. "I'm sorry you won't have Sarah this year."

"Me too," she says, patting my hand. "Me too."

We walk together in silence through the quad, the rest of the senior class streaming out from the dorms in silence. All around me, I see tear-stained faces and wrinkled shirts. Dead-eyed gazes as if everyone is under a spell. There's a commonality among them, a collective shock and grief, though I can't feel it myself. I should. I'm a student here, a part of this.

But perhaps I'm not. Not really. Not when I've spent the past three years on the perimeter, reporting on my peers like they're lab specimens best viewed through a lens. That's the truth, a reminder like a bruise, pressed only for pain.

Amy

Someone knocks on the dorm room door. "Amy Alterman?" A deep male voice calls out. "Detective Fitzgerald with the Meadowbrook PD. Here to escort you to Head Teacher Egan's office."

My fingers tingle as I open the door to see two men in uniform standing in the frame. One's tall and thin with a scruffy goatee and a small gap between his front teeth, and the other one is short and round, with a baby face that makes me think he became a cop last week. Nothing about them gives me hope that they'll find who did this.

None of us talk much as they walk ahead of me outside Holbrook, but as soon as we get into the quad, they pause, looking around, and I realize neither of them know where we're going.

"This way." I step in front of them and walk toward Egan's office in the main classroom building on the north side of campus. But as we reach the walkway, doors all around us open and students start streaming through them, heading in the opposite direction toward the auditorium.

I duck my head, but it's no use. Everyone stares, and as we walk by a group of debaters, someone whispers, "I heard she found them dead, covered in blood."

My eyes sting and I swallow a lump in my throat. I expect

the police officers to huddle close to me, to protect me, but they seem oblivious so I pick up my pace, my heart pounding, until we finally reach the building. I dart to Egan's office, tucked in the corner of the first floor.

As soon as we're shut inside, I let out a breath. The room is light and airy, with floor-to-ceiling windows that are opened wide, letting the September sunshine right on through.

Egan's not there, her big mahogany desk empty, but Coach Jensen is pacing back and forth across the deep burgundy rug, looking even more exhausted than she did this morning. I wonder if she's been home to see Joseph.

"You're here," she says.

"Where's Egan?"

Coach shakes her head. "She had to call an all-class assembly. I'm going to supervise."

The cops clear their throats and move around the room, seeming more nervous than I do. I can see the younger one's hands shake as he pulls out a recorder, setting it on the coffee table between us.

It blinks red and menacing. Before they can ask a question, my phone buzzes and I look down to see the word *Dad* blinking back at me.

I spoke to Janet, he texted, referring to Egan. She filled me in on what's going on. I'm in the air for the next few hours but call Lisa Brock if you need anything. Love you, kid.

The name Lisa Brock sets off an alarm bell in my brain. She's the family lawyer based in New York, the person who cleaned up messes and found my dad a shark of a divorce attorney. Not that Mom wanted to fight for custody anyway. I haven't seen Lisa since Dad's fiftieth birthday party two summers ago at our home in Palo Alto.

Thanks, I write, and stuff my phone into my pocket.

Even during tragedy, he's all business, as if keeping emotions at an arm's length might save him grief in the long run. Sitting here, in Egan's office, I'm reminded that I, too, can shut off emotions if I try hard enough. Mom always joked that Dad learned to keep things surface level and businesslike after spending most of his free time in board rooms, trying to prove his prowess to investors. I wonder if he passed that down to me.

My phone buzzes and I pull it out again to see a text from Lisa Brock. Heard the news. So sorry, Amy. But I'd be a shit lawyer if I didn't tell you NOT to talk to the cops. Let me know when they want to interview you and I'll come up, okay?

I ignore her. I have nothing to hide.

Well, almost nothing.

The older detective cracks his knuckles and looks at me, though his eyes roam, barely making contact with mine. His name tag says Detective Diaz. "So, Miss Alterman. Your head teacher told us you were Sarah's roommate? That you found her and Ryan this morning?"

I swallow, my throat sandy and raw. "Yes." It comes out a whisper.

I wonder if we have now seen the same number of dead bodies—if these were his first, too. Everyone knows the biggest crimes in Meadowbrook consist of parking violations.

The other cop, Detective Fitzgerald, clears his throat. "Can you walk us through the events leading up to this morning? What happened last night?"

I close my eyes and start to recount the same story I told Egan this morning, the lies coming out slick and easy, too fast for me to take them back. My face flushes, and for a moment, I believe my words. *I went home after the party. I slept through the night. I didn't hear anything.*

When I finish, I glance up at Coach to see she is nodding along, arms crossed, as if I have done the right thing.

The cops look at one another and Fitzgerald clears his throat. "I guess I'm confused how you didn't hear anything. That crime scene was . . ." He shakes his head.

I fumble with my hands and shrug, my cheeks burning. "It must have happened before I got home."

Fitzgerald frowns and exchanges a look with Diaz.

"The medical team is still working out the details but . . ." He pauses, glancing at Jensen. "It seems a little odd that even if you did come home after the incidents occurred, you didn't notice anything."

I think back to what I witnessed this morning—the smudges of blood, the broken lamp, the stench—and for the first time since I sat down, I wonder if I *should* let Lisa Brock come up and do all the talking, stand between me and these two feeble men.

The questioning seemed so simple and necessary. The witness, the best friend, explaining what had happened. But the older guy is looking at me through downcast eyes, narrowed in suspicion. If something goes wrong, Egan won't cover for me, no matter how much money my dad gives to this school. There are plenty of alumni donors with deep pockets. My dad's fortune doesn't compare to the kind of generational wealth that someone like Ryan's mother, Dottie Pelham, has been cultivating since the Gilded Age.

"I was drinking," I say, trying to keep my voice even. "We all were at the boathouse. I didn't even turn the lights on when I got home."

"And you were alone, you said? Just you?"

I swallow and whisper a response. "Yes."

Fitzgerald looks down at his notebook, tapping the page with his pen. "Do you remember seeing her cell phone anywhere in the room this morning or last night?"

"Her cell phone?"

Fitzgerald nods, looking up at me.

I shake my head. "I tried calling her this morning, when I thought she was already at breakfast. I wanted her to get me a muffin. But she didn't pick up. I tried twice."

The cops exchange a look, one that tells me something is amiss.

"I assumed it was somewhere in her room. You didn't find it?"

"No, not yet," Fitzgerald says. "It looks like it was turned off so we can't track its location. We can still see all her texts, photos . . . everything in the cloud. But you never know what's on someone's phone these days with all those secret apps. CSI is still collecting evidence, but if it turns up in your things, we expect you to let us know."

I nod my chin up and down, wondering where it could be. But then I remember the words we exchanged, the vitriol we traded. Maybe it's best that no one finds those. Thank god for Melody's coding skills.

"And what was your relationship like with Mr. Pelham?" Fitzgerald asks, his pen hovering over a notebook.

I hesitate, unsure how to sum up what I thought about Ryan, how our lives intersected and collided. He was only ever one thing to me, a barrier between Sarah and me.

"He was my best friend's boyfriend," I say slowly. "We hung out a lot as a group. Not much one-on-one."

Fitzgerald seems to consider this. "We hear they were very serious, those two."

I focus on the bookshelves across the wall, hundreds of old spines staring back at me. "They were together three years. A lifetime."

The detectives exchange glances but don't say anything else.

Diaz riffles through the papers in a folder on his lap, but he's clumsy and a bunch of them spill onto the floor, spread out on the plaid wool rug. I bend down to pick up what I can and when I pull the papers up, a gasp emerges from my throat. I'm holding a photo of Sarah, mid-laugh, in her grass-stained soccer uniform on the field. It was taken only a few days ago during preseason practice. I can tell by her hair length, shorter than it was last year, freshly cut at a salon in New Canaan, sun-kissed and lighter than it had been in the spring. In the photo, her arms are above her head and her face is turned toward the sun, eyes crinkled, freckles strewn across her nose.

I'm in the background, gazing at her with smiling eyes and my hands clasped together, forever her fan.

The grief expands in my heart, thick and molten, like I can't breathe or move or scream. This is how I want to remember my friend, my Sarah. Not what I saw this morning.

One detective takes the papers from my hands, gingerly tucking them back into his folder. "Looks like a good kid," he says. "Both of them. A real shame."

Coach clears her throat and approaches, placing a hand on my shoulder. "I think that's enough for now."

"But we just have a few . . ."

Coach steps between them and me. "You've got all you came here to get," she says. "We're done."

The cops don't protest, not anymore, and Coach starts to usher them out the door. But before they leave, I find the words lodged in my throat.

"You're going to find out who did this," I say, a statement not a question.

The cops glance at one another, but then Diaz turns around and looks me in the eye. "That's certainly our intention."

I nod, not sure what words could convince me that were true. Finally, they leave and I'm alone with Coach. I sit back down on the couch and drop my head in my hands.

Coach clears her throat and I look up to see her standing in the doorway, peering out of the glass pane like she's watching the detectives walk down the hall.

After a beat, she motions for me to stand. "Come on," she says. "Quick."

Her tone is urgent, and I stand, following her out through the door and away from the way I came in. She turns down another hallway, one I've never been down before, and pulls open a narrow door. I peer around her side to see a dark staircase descending into the tunnels that connect all the buildings, the ones I brought Joseph through last night.

"Where are we going?"

Coach doesn't answer. She just heads down the steps and I follow. The tunnels are only lit by a few bulbs attached to the ceiling every five feet, and I never took the time to memorize the maze, like some of my peers. It didn't seem like a worthy effort since I didn't get in trouble for sneaking around the usual way. None of us athletes ever did.

I can't see anything ahead of Coach. All I can do is follow and trust her as she leads me through the maze. I pretend like we're at practice, jogging around the field, Sarah up ahead leading us in cheers to make our lungs stronger.

Suddenly Coach turns left and presses her shoulder up against another door, sending a spray of daylight into the tunnel. I squint but follow her up the cement stairs and out into a grassy knoll I quickly recognize as the staff parking lot, where we often help Coach load her minivan full of gear.

Her car is nowhere to be found in the nearly empty lot but there's one I do recognize. A cream-colored sedan with a ding right below the right front headlight, a friendship bracelet I beaded hanging from the rearview mirror.

"Joseph." His name is a prayer, a hope, and within moments he sees me and flings open the door, rushing to me, wrapping me in his arms.

I can't exactly pinpoint the moment where it began to feel like this—like seeing him set off an electric current inside my body, like he was a magnet pulling me toward him. It was something I had never experienced before, something that jolted me alive and clouded my brain. It didn't happen right away, not in the beginning when we were getting to know each other last winter, or when we first had sex last spring. Maybe over the summer, when we were separated by time and space, and the only thing that kept us tethered to one another were video calls and constant texts. His descriptions of summer produce—tiny fairy-tale eggplant and sweet yellow corn—and what he was making at Rex's, how he couldn't wait to bake me a tomato galette when I returned to Connecticut.

That need, that desperation to be near him, it's what nearly broke Sarah and me. She felt that way, too, with Ryan. But neither of us wanted to admit what that meant for our friendship. That while we were busy indulging in our hunger and our desires, exploring what it meant to not only give yourself over to someone but to receive them as well, we had abandoned one another. It was when one of us turned to the other, looking for comfort or solace, that we realized a barrier had been erected between us without either one of us ever noticing. When we finally did, it was almost too late.

"You're okay," he whispers into my ear, clutching the nape of my neck with one hand. I lean into his chest, wetting his thin cotton T-shirt with my tears. He smells of melted butter and fresh chives, as if he had spent the morning making French omelets.

I pull away and look at him, his eyes sunken in like he hasn't slept since I saw him last night. His dark curly hair is matted in some places, sticking up in front, and I run my hand through it to remind myself he's real.

"How are you here?" I ask. "Coach said no one could come in."

He looks to his mom behind me and then his gaze refocuses on me. "We figured now was the only time since everyone's in assembly. I can't stay. Mom . . ." His voice breaks. "She knew I needed to see you."

"Thank you," I say, not knowing if it's to him or her. All that matters is that Joseph is here now with me, and I'm finally, finally safe.

Liz

By the time I get to the auditorium for the assembly, most of my peers are already in place. The only sounds are those of seat hinges squeaking open, hushed apologies as students slide past one another. Unlike other all-class events, where people huddle together in little groups, spreading through the entire space, all 104 seniors are crowded together in the first few rows, as if being closer, being *together* will keep us unharmed.

I take a seat next to a bunch of theater girls from my dorm. They nod in my direction, like we're all coming to the same battlefield, preparing for what's to come. I crane my neck and see Peter Radcliffe in the first row, sitting next to Kayla Liu and Hillary Steinberg, two other soccer players who were close with Sarah. The girls keep their hands clasped together between them and Peter has his arm around Kayla's shoulders, sniffling every few moments. She hands him a tissue and squeezes his knee, an act so intimate I feel the urge to look away.

I scan their row for Amy but she's not there. She's not any-where. Maybe she's still with the detectives. Maybe they're keep-ing her sequestered.

Head Teacher Egan walks onto the stage, and whatever noise was in the air ceases. The whole room quiets and she looks up and out at all of us, the students she called "brave and bold" at last year's stepping-up ceremony, as if we were different from the classes to come before us. But we're not, at least in terms of numbers. I studied the data for a story on admissions last year. We have the same average makeup of scholarship kids, legacy admissions, foreigners, and scions of billionaires who had been taught Russian math at age three. We are not special. We are just like all the others. But it's Egan's job to make us feel superior—and to keep us cocooned from the rest of the world. I wonder if she realizes she failed.

Egan looks out at us, a deep frown on her face. "We have gathered you all here today because there are many rumors swirling about what has happened this morning and while there are still a number of unknowns, we feel it is important to be together as a class in this time of great uncertainty and grief." She pauses and purses her lips before continuing.

"This morning, two members of your class, Ryan Pelham and Sarah Oliver, passed away. We are working with the Meadowbrook Police Department to find out what exactly happened as quickly as possible."

I press my hands to my thighs to feel my phone in my pocket. Slowly, trying not to attract attention, I retrieve it and hold it to my side, pressing record to capture the audio. Who knows when I might need it.

"All programming has been canceled for the week and we are making all of the counselors in our mental health services office available to you at any time, day or night. For now, we are asking for your patience while we try to understand what has happened."

Down in the front, an arm shoots up in the air. I crane to see Melody Sidhu, class vice president and the person who made that messaging app, leaning forward in her seat. She glances at Peter, who nods, as if giving her the go-ahead.

Egan's eyes dart toward her and it's clear she doesn't want to hear what Melody has to say. But still, she nods curtly. "Yes, Melody?"

"How are we supposed to feel safe here?" she asks, urgency rising in her voice. "Can we go home for a few days, at least until classes start?"

I lean in, eager to hear her answer. Egan licks her lips and pauses like she's been waiting for this question. "The police are asking that all students who were on campus for the past twenty-four hours stay put," she says. "They still need to question students, and we want to make sure that they can do so with ease. We must cooperate with their investigation."

"So, you're saying we're all being held here because we could be *suspects*?" Melody's voice goes up an octave. "When really, we're all potential targets? My parents are demanding to see me and I can't imagine that mine are the only ones who are terrified." She's practically shouting now, something you would only do if you were certain that your place here was never questioned. The Sidhu Visual Arts Studio had its grand opening last year on lower campus.

All around Melody, students start to voice their concerns, talking over one another until the room reaches a fever pitch.

Egan pumps her arms like she's trying to get us to settle down after a misunderstanding. It takes a moment, but everyone quiets.

"You are quite right, Melody. You are not the only student whose parents are concerned after these . . . events. For that reason, we have invited any parent who wishes to see their child to come to campus for any amount of time. We are offering up guest housing on Kensington Avenue and at Fielding House for anyone who would like to stay over. Your parents, along with everyone else's, are being notified this very moment."

Melody slumps down farther in her seat and Peter raises his hand but doesn't wait to be called on. "Are the underclassmen still coming tomorrow?" he asks. "As senior class president, I am concerned about how to welcome students to campus under these circumstances."

Egan shifts her weight from foot to foot. "That is currently up for debate."

Peter leans forward. "What do you mean by that?"

Egan sighs as if she did not want to answer this question. "We have been advised by the authorities to delay the arrival of all underclassmen until further notice."

All around me people start to speak, murmuring to one another until Peter's voice rises above the rest. "Will classes start on time?" Taking a look at Egan's frustrated face, he adds, "I know this is painful to discuss, but we all have questions and need clarity. You always say that as seniors, we get treated differently. Like adults. If you can't do that now, then when can you?"

"Thank you, Mr. Radcliffe," she says, though her voice tightens. "You are quite right. We do view you as adults, which is why I've been so forthcoming." She grips the podium in front of her. "It may surprise you to know that we in the administration are still finding out new information every moment. We are in the midst of an unbearably horrific moment in Meadowbrook history. Two of our very own are gone and I cannot underscore just how devastated we all are. But for now, we must band together and support one another *and* this school. Please be patient with us as we work with the authorities to find out what exactly happened and how best to proceed."

She pauses and then stands up a little straighter. "Above all, I want you to know that your safety and well-being are our top priorities." Her eyes roam the rows, pausing to make eye contact with as many of my peers as she can. "Everything we do from here on out is to ensure you are taken care of, mentally and physically." She pauses as her focus lands on me. Her gaze is hard and knowing and I have to fight my instincts not to look away. A chill runs through me.

Finally, she breaks eye contact and continues down the row. "We are asking that everyone stay on campus and keep your movements to a minimum. Employ a buddy system when possible, and please do everything you can to help one another during this trying time. Your advisors will be available to you as well as mental health professionals led by Nurse Gwen." She pauses, picking up her papers. "Be kind to one another. Now more than ever."

She disappears offstage as people stand up and start to walk to the back exits of the auditorium, filing out one by one. I slip my phone back into my pocket and let the recorder roll, but I stay in place, allowing the theater girls to head out in front of me. Finally, the last of our class begins to ascend the steps and when Peter gets to my row, I reach for his arm. He flinches as I make contact.

"Sorry," I say. "I didn't mean . . ."

"It's okay," he says when he registers me. "I'm a little jumpy."

When I get a good look at Peter's face, I realize I should have anticipated that. His cheekbones are hollowed out and he's got dark circles under his eyes. His glasses are smudged and he's wearing a Meadowbrook Rowing shirt that has a small toothpaste stain near the collar. I've never seen him looking anything other than polished, and the effect is jarring.

"I was hoping—" I start, but he cuts me off.

"Let me guess, you want an interview for the *Gazette*?" He folds his arms over his chest, but he doesn't look mad. But then he turns around and I see Kayla rest a hand on his shoulder.

"You okay, babe?" she asks, and I take note of that last word. *Babe.* I heard they broke up last year, but maybe that was bad intel. As much news as I can gather, I can never quite grasp the fast-moving social machinations.

He gives her a half smile. "I'll meet you out there for dinner."

She doesn't move for a moment, as if she's scared to leave him in my presence. But after a beat, she takes her hand away and gives a quick nod. "Be careful," she says to him, though her eyes travel to me. My face flushes and I try to keep my fingers from flexing.

"This isn't on the record," I say, making a mental note to not use anything from the recording I just made. It was for backup. That's all.

Kayla bites the inside of her cheek and motions for Hillary Steinberg to follow her up the stairs, so Peter and I are left alone in the auditorium.

"You're right," I say, when they leave. "I do want an interview. I know this is a horrible time, but you said it yourself, you're the president of the class. Ryan's best friend. You've known Sarah since she was a kid."

He swallows and I watch his Adam's apple jump up his neck, his eyes turn downward. I search his face, wondering if I'm about to watch Peter burst into tears.

"People want to hear from you," I say. "Comforting words or otherwise. Maybe you want to share them with me? We could do a piece about how the student government is handling all of this? How you're making sure students feel safe and supported?"

"You do realize two of my best friends were just found dead." His eyes meet mine. They're red-rimmed and glassy, and his bottom lip trembles. I take a step back like he needs space, but maybe I'm the one who does.

Before today I never saw grief like this up close, the desperation and frustration boiling so close to the surface. On Amy it looked like rage, with clenched fists and pursed lips, but on Peter, it's despair, his mouth an open wound, his eyes pleading for answers.

"I'm so sorry."

Peter pushes his sandy hair out of his eyes and wrinkles his nose so his glasses move up on his face. He blinks a few times, his complexion regaining its rosy hue. "I heard you weren't supposed to write about the murders."

I jerk my head back with the realization: he was warned by Egan—by *someone*—not to talk to me.

"This isn't a story about the murders. It's about the school." As I say the words, I start to believe them. Maybe there *is* a way to write about all of this without touching the case, the specifics. "We need your voice to help give some comfort."

"Okay," Peter says slowly. "Tomorrow after lunch? Meet me in my office?"

"Definitely."

Peter starts up the stairs, but then he turns back around. "I know what you're trying to do," he says.

"Excuse me?"

"My dad is the chairman of New York News Network. I know

how this works. You're trying to make a name for yourself with this story. Prove you can handle something like this."

I want to protest, but something about the way Peter is looking at me, like he's unafraid and unbothered, makes me want to tell the truth.

"I am," I say.

He nods, an understanding passing between us. "Just do it right, then."

Amy

"We only have a few minutes," Joseph says, glancing at his mom, who's waiting in the car on the other side of the lot, giving us a few moments of privacy. "How did the interview go?"

We're sitting on the curb under one of the big oak trees and I inch closer to him, our knees pressed together, his arm around my back. "I said I went straight home after the party, and that I fell asleep and didn't hear anything. I didn't say we were together."

Joseph's eyes go wide.

"What?" I ask. "We said we wouldn't tell."

He runs a hand through his hair, his cheeks growing pink. "That was before . . . I didn't expect you to lie to the police."

"I'd get kicked out if I snuck someone in. Your mom could lose her job."

"But don't you think . . . I mean, Ryan and Sarah *died*, Amy. If there ever was a time to cut you some slack for breaking the rules . . ."

My heart rate speeds up, doubt pricking at my chest. "Should I go back? Should I tell them?"

He drops his head, quiet for a second. When he looks up, he shakes his head. "No, no. You're right." His dark curls fall down over his eyes and I reach up to push them away. "If they knew I was there, they might try to pin it on me."

I lean back, lower my hand away from his face. That thought didn't even occur to me.

"You never know," he says, sensing my discomfort. "It'd be too easy for them. 'Townie Kills Prep School Students.'"

"Don't say that." I rest my palm on his bare knee.

Joseph shakes his head. "I can't believe you saw all that."

I blink, my eyes stinging.

"Do you want to talk about it?" he asks, toeing the ground with his beat-up white sneaker.

"Not really."

He grinds his foot into the ground harder, specks of dirt ballooning into the air. "It must have happened before we got there," he says. There's a hint of eagerness in his tone, curiosity.

"I guess."

"I'm just glad you're safe. What if it had happened after I left?"

A strangled sound escapes my throat. It never even occurred to me to think what could have been if I had been in our suite, too.

Joseph clears his throat. "Do they have any leads?"

I look up at him and see him lick his lips, his eyes wide.

"I don't know." I shift away from him, shrug his arm off my shoulder. "You're asking a lot of questions."

Joseph leans back. "Sorry," he says. "I've been so worried about you. The news makes it sound like a serial killer is on the loose and any Meadowbrook student might be next. It freaks me out that you have to stay here."

"They moved me into a new room," I say. "I'm bunking with the school newspaper editor."

"Liz Charles? She comes by Rex's a lot. Olly thinks she's cool. She seems harmless."

I let go of his hand, frustrated that his first thought is *harmless* instead of *that sucks*.

I thought he understood when, over the summer, on one of our hours-long video calls, I told him about everything that happened with my parents—the paparazzi, the tabloids, the incessant noise surrounding our lives. He sat in the hammock outside his mom's house, quiet and engaged, until I was done speaking and then he looked right at me through the camera. "Fuck them," he said softly. "Fuck them all."

I laughed, remembering the girls in my middle school, the ones who I thought were my friends but ditched me when their parents told them not to hang out with me for fear of winding up on the *Daily Mail*. None of them had been on my side so obviously, so unconditionally. I thought Joseph was.

Coach flashes the lights on the car, and we both know what that means. Joseph rests one hand on my thigh, the other on my cheek. He leans forward and kisses me softly, his thumb grazing my chin. I give in, pressing my mouth to his, harder, as if that might change anything, as if either one of us has the power to rewrite the past twenty-four hours.

Kissing Joseph won't bring Sarah and Ryan back. It won't make me forget. But at least his warmth, his breath, reminds me that I'm still alive.

When we finally break, I see tears in Joseph's eyes. He doesn't bother to wipe them away. "Text me later?"

"Of course." I nod, a promise. "Of course."

Liz

The cafeteria is buzzing as students take their seats for dinner, looking over their shoulders while setting cloth napkins on their laps, pouring themselves water or iced tea from the glass pitchers.

I grab the last spot at a table with Kevin and Rachel and a few kids from the yearbook staff. No one from our group stands, so I pop up. "I'll get the food."

Carly mumbles a thank-you and I get in line with the rest of the fetchers, waiting to take platters back to the table. It's a Meadowbrook tradition to have most dinners like this, as if we assemble makeshift families every evening to discuss the day's happenings. But tonight, few people have any words at all.

The line is silent as we move forward, inching toward RJ, the head chef who's been at Meadowbrook for decades. I crane my neck to see him silently hand trays over to the students, his wrinkles deeper than I remember them being last year.

"It had to have been someone on campus, right?" Iris Lopez says to Jonas Kreizman, the first chair saxophonist, in front of me. "How else could they have gotten into the dorms?"

I can't help myself. "You think so?"

They both turn around, startled, but then Jonas ducks his head toward me. "I wouldn't be surprised if it was someone who everyone *knew* was a creep." His eyes move over to RJ, only a few steps ahead of us now. His hands shake as he moves behind the counter, mumbling to himself.

"Oh, come on," I say.

Iris shrugs and they both turn away. I keep my eyes trained on RJ as I get closer.

The *Gazette* did a profile on him a few years back, revealing he started here as a maintenance assistant, mowing the sports fields, but when he expressed an interest in cooking to his supervisor, they moved him to the kitchen. He's as much a part of this school as the formal crest, the academic honor code. But that doesn't mean everyone loves him.

I've never had an issue with RJ, but I've also heard the rumors just like everyone else. How he stopped smiling at school after his wife died of cancer ten years ago, how he stalked the halls after hours because he had nowhere else to go, how he gave some girls the ick, his gaze lingering too long.

It's my turn to retrieve dinner and I pause as I face him, searching for a sign of something sinister hidden below his frown lines.

"Miss Charles," RJ says, turning around to retrieve a metal tray piled high with Parker House rolls and leg of lamb, broccolini with garlic, and a mound of mashed potatoes.

"Thank you," I say, trying to move forward, but he nods at the reporter's notebook tucked into my armpit.

"I read your article."

"Oh?"

He shakes his head. "Too many monsters in this place. All the goodness. It's gone."

I swallow the lump in my throat, goose bumps appearing on my arms. "It's a real tragedy." My grip on the tray tightens and I turn away before he can say anything else.

My scalp tingles as I make my way back to the table, trying not to drop dinner while I turn over RJ's words in my mind. They mean nothing, I'm sure of it. But I can't shake the disturbing sensation filling up my stomach. I make a mental note to look into RJ's past a little deeper tomorrow.

The dining room is vast, with wide, expansive windows overlooking the nature preserve, the pond visible in the distance. The sun is starting to set so there's a golden glow in the room as everyone hunches over their plates, huddled close to their own.

Finally, I get to my table in the back corner and unload the tray, passing around the heavy ceramic plates and serving spoons. I plunk down in my seat and look up to find Rachel staring at me.

"What?"

"I wish you would have talked to us before publishing that story." Her voice shakes.

"I didn't—" I start, but Kevin cuts me off.

"Ryan was my freshman-year roommate." His voice breaks.

"I'm so sorry," I say quietly. "I felt like I had a duty—"

"My cousin lives in New Canaan and she said that *your* article is how all of Sarah's friends back home found out. They didn't even get a phone call." Rachel's mouth stiffens and the rest of the table falls silent, staring at me.

"I didn't name them," I say. "I just said two—"

"Yeah, well, someone in the comments did," she says, looking down at her plate. "Imagine that, learning from a news article that one of your friends was murdered." Rachel's shoulders heave and Kevin reaches to pat her arm.

I shake my head and blink back tears. "I'm sorry."

Rachel stops me, catching her breath. "Not all of us are on the *Gazette* to win awards or whatever. I don't even want to be a journalist." Her cheeks are blotchy, pink stains spreading on her skin. "Some of us just like to write and think it's fun. But this . . . this isn't what we signed up for. I'm not trying to *cover* the murder of my friends."

My stomach sinks and a feeling of guilt settles into my core even though I disagree. Just because they don't see the journalistic value in what I did doesn't mean it's not there. "I'm sorry," I say again. "Mrs. Herschel says we can't keep writing about the case anyway."

Rachel nods. "Good."

Kevin moves a piece of broccolini around on his plate with a fork. "Just remember," he says, "they were people. Not stories."

THE DAY AFTER

Amy

The locker room is silent save for the sound of metal doors closing and cleats treading over the concrete floor. Everyone's strapped on their shin guards, pulled their socks up high below their knees, and tied their hair up tight.

Coach appears in the doorway between the locker room and her office wearing a rumpled tracksuit, her whistle around her neck. She doesn't have her usual clipboard and she takes a seat on a wooden bench, motioning for us all to gather round.

Joseph said she didn't sleep at all last night; he could hear her puttering around the house, making tea, watching old *Seinfeld* reruns. He didn't either, but it was mostly because we were video chatting until I finally drifted off to sleep around two. I woke up with my phone dead in my hand, in the unfamiliar, unadorned dorm room, with Liz on the other side of the wall.

"I wanted to gather you all here before we go out onto the field." Coach's voice is shaky and she sits on her hands, rocking her body back and forth. "We cannot change what has happened. We cannot go back in time. All we can do is stick together. At least for now. No matter what you're feeling, how deep your sorrow is, remember that you are still here. You are still together. And that's what we have to focus on."

My eyes sting with tears and I wipe them with my wrist.

"Sarah was our captain," Coach says. "Number fifteen will be hers forever. And she will not be forgotten." Her eyes roam the room, landing on each of us before they stop at Iris. "In the interest of maintaining leadership and strength, I've decided to name an interim captain, someone who I know will help keep our spirits as high as they can be in these difficult times." Coach stands and motions for us to do the same. "As varsity goalie for the past four years, Iris Lopez has always been our backstop. Until the rest of the team gets here and has a chance to vote, Iris will lead the team. I know she'll make us proud."

I shift my gaze to Iris, who's standing across the room with a stunned look on her face, her eyebrows halfway up her forehead. "Um, thanks, Coach," she says. Her voice is low and soft, steady as she bounces on the balls of her feet. I offer her a smile, the biggest I can manage, and she nods in my direction. "No one can replace Sarah," she says. "But I'll work hard to ensure we don't forget her, that all our wins this season are for her."

Coach claps her hands once and the group disbands, heading toward the door. I fall in line, but when I glance back over my shoulder, I see Kayla still standing in the locker room, her hands clenched in fists by her sides. She paces for a second before stopping and bending her leg back in the air, launching it forward to kick the locker in front of her with a bang. "Bullshit," she mumbles before retying her ponytail.

I turn around fast and put my head down as I follow the others out the door and onto the field. The sun is bright and high even though it's barely eight in the morning. I can sense Kayla pulling up behind me, can feel the fire in her footsteps, but the last thing I want to do is engage with her wrath, be consumed by it when I'm still figuring out all of the complicated emotions pinging around in my head. Instead, I throw myself into practice.

The next two hours go by in a blur of dirt and sweat and burning lungs. I slide for balls and dribble as fast as my feet can go. I fall hard into patches of mud and don't bother to wipe it off as Iris calls for us to hurry up, to fight harder, to give this team our *everything*.

I let myself forget, for even a fleeting moment, that Sarah should be here. That her voice, not Iris's, should be rising above the rest, calling for us to push ourselves, to run faster and kick harder. It helps, moving like this, acting like my body is not my own, and by the end of practice, my heart is racing and my lungs are on fire. I lean against the fence post and chug from my water bottle.

"Great job, Liv." I fist-bump Olivia as she heads into the locker room with the others. But I'm not ready to leave. Not yet. I lift the bottom of my shirt and wipe sweat from my forehead. When I look at my jersey, there's a swipe of dirt mixed with blood, and for a second the world grows blurry. I cling to the wood fence to keep myself steady.

"Whoa, whoa."

My vision is fuzzy, but I can still make out Joseph running to me, wearing jeans and a faded gray Meadowbrook High School shirt.

"You okay?" He reaches for my elbow and steadies me.

I hug him tight, pressing my whole body to his until I remember I must smell like garbage. "Shit, sorry. Sweaty."

He smiles. "I like you when you're smelly." He kisses my cheek, letting his lips linger for a moment.

But then I remember he can't be here. He's not allowed. I open my mouth to protest, but he cuts me off. "Don't worry. Mom got it okayed for me to stop by and pick her up."

"Oh, good." I force a smile onto my face.

Joseph's eyes move over my shoulder to the locker room, where the rest of the team is changing. "So, are there any updates? Any suspects?"

I shake my head. "Not that I've heard."

He crosses his arms over his chest. "They should have some leads by now. Didn't they swab everything? Run a whole bunch of tests?"

I look up at him, his brow furrowed like he's trying to solve a math problem. "I don't know. Since when did you become a true crime fiend?" He's the kind of guy who shakes his head when I suggest we watch a horror movie, who closes his eyes when I bandage up his paper cuts. Back in May, he sliced off the end of his pointer finger while using a mandolin to cut cucumbers and fainted right on the floor of Rex Taylor's.

Joseph shrugs. "Olly and Trent are freaking out. Trent's mom is trying to get Meadowbrook High to hire a security guard, but you know there's no chance of that." He shakes his head. "Did I tell you Olly's supposed to start as a groundskeeper here next week? Was so excited about the job before all of this. Apparently, it pays like crazy, enough to cover a semester at UConn. Now he's terrified."

"Right." I've only met Olly a few times even though he's Rex Taylor's nephew and works at the coffee shop with Joseph. The first time was an accident when I showed up at Rex's without giving Joseph warning. He had put together a special menu featuring ramps, those rare, hard-to-find alliums that only pop up out of the ground a few weeks a year, and I decided to take a bike into town to surprise him. As I rode, I dreamed of biting into one of the ramp-and-cheddar biscuits he wouldn't stop talking about.

But when I came through the door and saw him talking to a guy in mud-stained jeans and another wearing an apron around his middle, his face fell and I knew I had made a wrong move.

"Hey," I said tentatively. "Surprise."

Joseph slapped on a smile and motioned to the first guy. "This is Trent," he said. "In my calc class." Then he knocked shoulders with the guy in the apron. "Olly." He nodded and smiled at me, full enough to put me at ease. "Guys, this is Amy," he said. "My girlfriend."

I searched for recognition on their faces, a sign that Joseph had mentioned me. Trent nodded and then quickly turned to his phone, and Olly, who Joseph told me was one year older and a wee bit more mature, stuck out his hand. "Great to meet you, Amy."

I paid for my biscuit and rushed out of there, embarrassed, and when I asked him about it the following week as we sat in his car, parked near the back entrance of school, he tried to explain.

"I just wanted to keep my lives separate," he'd said, not looking at me. "It's a big deal to meet friends, you know?"

I leaned my head against the window of the car, realizing that he hadn't really met any of mine, in passing at practice. He'd only talked to Sarah once. Barely. An awkward conversation about the weather.

"Are you mad you haven't hung out with my friends? Is that why you don't want me to meet yours?"

Joseph shrugged. "*Mad* isn't the right word."

I turned to face him. "Come to the spring formal with me."

Joseph glanced in my direction. "Really?"

"Yes." I wasn't as sure as I sounded, but I couldn't take it back. Would have rather thrown myself in front of his car. "Really, yes."

Joseph reached for my hand sitting on the console between us. "Okay," he said. "Only if you promise I don't have to wear a tux."

I held up two fingers, a scout's honor. "No tux." Though I held back the last bit, that no one wore tuxedos to spring formal, that most of the boys just threw on jackets and button-downs, not even a tie.

"Can't wait." He kissed me then and everything else dissolved, the tension, the confusion, even my anxiety about his aversion to me hanging out with his friends. Being with him was like blocking out the whole world.

"Joseph," Coach calls from her car. "Free set of hands?"

He holds up both palms and nods his head. "Tonight?" he asks. "Think there's any chance we can find each other? Maybe we could test the rules a little bit?"

"We can try."

He gives my hand a squeeze before taking off. Everything in my body wants to cling to him, to tell him to stay here, with me. But then he's gone, jogging to his mom, struggling with a basket full of target cones. I watch him help her load them into the car, observing the ease that passes between them. Joseph once told me his mom was his best friend, which he thought was embarrassing. But it's not to me, not when my mom and I barely talk, not even on my birthday. She hasn't even reached out about Sarah and Ryan, though no doubt the news has reached St. Tropez by now.

Joseph looks toward me and shields his eyes from the sun. He waves and presses his hand to his heart, and I do the same, watching as he gets in the passenger seat.

"They let him on campus?"

I turn around and see Kayla and Hillary standing behind me, their gaze fixed on Coach's car, Joseph's face visible through the window. Kayla's got her lip curled and Hillary juts one hip out to the side.

"He got permission," I say, suddenly self-conscious.

"Huh." Kayla gives Hillary a pointed look, raising one eyebrow.

"What?" Neither one of them had been that inviting to Joseph when he and I first started dating last year. I overheard Kayla calling him a "townie"—and not in a nice way—behind my back, and Hillary asked him at the spring formal if it was weird to know that our parents paid his mom's salary. I nearly smacked her across the face for that one, but Joseph just laughed as if it were no big deal.

Later that night when we were fooling around in his car, I asked him why he didn't get upset and tell Hillary to go eat shit. He shrugged and looked out the window, not at me. "It would only make her think even less of me." I reached for his hand and he let me hold it. "Besides, I don't have to prove anything to anyone. They're the assholes for thinking this is 1985."

Kayla scrunches her shoulders up by her ears. "I'd be wary of outsiders right now. The killer could be anyone in Meadowbrook." Hillary nods next to her.

Fury sparks inside my chest. "Are you suggesting *Joseph* had something to do with this?"

"I mean, I'm just saying . . ."

"It sounds like you're accusing him of something." I ball my hands tightly by my side. "Besides, you do realize they were killed on campus. In a dorm. Filled with students and administrators and people associated with *our* school."

Kayla turns to me, her mouth open, and once again I'm struck by the fact that whoever did this to Sarah and Ryan was most likely part of our community, a member of the Meadowbrook family.

Hillary sucks in a breath of air and shivers even though it's nearing eighty degrees outside.

"Joseph didn't do it." My voice sounds harsher than I mean it to, but I can't help it.

"She's not saying he did," Hillary protests.

Kayla heaves her duffel bag over her shoulder. "Until the killer is caught, everyone is a suspect."

"You sound like a bad movie trailer." I clench my jaw.

Kayla doesn't break my gaze. "Our friends are dead," she says, her voice breaking. "I don't feel the need to pretend to be anything but terrified right now. How well do you even know him?"

"Well enough to know he'd never murder my best friend and her boyfriend."

Kayla steps back like I've slapped her and her eyes go wide, her bottom lip wobbly. Immediately I feel guilty, though I'm not sure for what—calling Sarah my best friend when I know Kayla wanted Sarah as hers or the fact that I used the word *murdered*, so blunt, so brutal.

"I'm sorry," I say. But Kayla's already turned on her heel, dragging Hillary with her.

With them gone and only the sounds of the birds chirping in the trees, blissfully unaware of the tragedy unfolding below, I let out a shaky breath, my fingers tingling, my joints aching. Because I can't ignore one thing Kayla said. She's right. Until someone is caught, everyone is a suspect.

Liz

The school government office is just down the hall from the newspaper one, but when I get there, I'm reminded how much nicer and more spacious it is, with bay windows and potted plants lining the walls. Each group of class representatives has their own glass conference room, and Peter, as senior class president, has a personal corner office, which he's occupying right now, earbuds in as he talks to someone on the phone.

I take a deep breath and turn on my recorder, anxious not to miss a moment, and stride toward him, rapping my knuckles against the doorframe. He looks up and motions for me to come in, but doesn't hang up just yet.

"Of course, Mr. Pelham," he says. "I'm so sorry. Later today. Right. See you then." Peter takes out his headphones and drops them on the wooden desk in front of him. He pushes his glasses up onto his forehead and rubs his eyes with his palms, looking so much older than seventeen. "Sorry," he mumbles, his voice more juvenile, less rehearsed than it had been moments before. "That was Ryan's dad."

"Oh." A sharp pang hits my chest. *The parents.* Hearing Peter talk to them makes the fact that two families will have to bury their children soon all the more real. "Is he on campus yet?"

Peter shakes his head. "Arriving later today."

I suck on the inside of my cheek to keep from filling the silence, an old journalistic trick that's supposed to force the person you're interviewing to keep talking. But Peter stays quiet, his gaze fixed on a spot on his desk.

"Thanks for speaking with me," I say, shifting my weight around in my seat. "I was hoping we could talk about class morale and how the student government is responding to things."

Peter looks at me blankly. "Class morale? I'm pretty sure there is none right now."

My cheeks burn. "Right. Of course."

"My only focus is making sure the police have everything they need to figure out who did this as fast as possible." He rests his hands on the desk, flexing his fingers wide. "We need justice for them. Every moment that goes by is another moment wasted."

"So, you've spoken to the police?" I ask.

"Of course. They've interviewed everyone who was at the boathouse party. That was the last time anyone saw them alive."

I scrawl the words *boathouse party* on my pad. "There was a party? The night they died?"

"Basically every night of senior week." He cocks his head and squints his eyes. "I guess I didn't see you there."

"Nope," I say. "I don't really go to those kinds of things." Not that I'm invited. "Was there something different about that one?"

He pauses. "Did you make it to any of the parties this week?"

Heat rises in my cheeks, but I ignore it. "Not really friends with athletes."

"It's not always athletes." But then he shakes his head. "No, you're right. It is." He offers me a weak smile. "Next time," he says, "I'll invite you."

I bow my head so he doesn't see my face flush. "What happened at this one?"

"I don't know . . ." He trails off and when I look up, I see his gaze back down at the table, his hands occupied as they twirl a pen around and around. "Everyone was on edge, I guess."

"How come?"

Peter lets out a breath, shaky and slow. "I don't want to say. I mean . . . she's dead."

"Something happened with Sarah?"

Peter turns away from me, his face pointed to the window. "Look, you didn't hear this from me, but Amy and Sarah had some huge fight."

My pen hovers over my notebook and I look up. "Really?"

Peter nods quickly. "It probably didn't mean anything. Your story isn't even about this."

"No," I say. "It's not. But any information might be useful."

Peter wraps his arms around his waist. "Ryan and I were going at it like we usually do, trying to see who was better at flip cup, one-upping each other. The usual." The corners of his mouth droop down and the space between his eyebrows creases. "But once those two started fighting about Joseph, the whole party got tense."

"Joseph, like Amy's boyfriend?"

"Yeah. Sarah once told me she got weird vibes from him, didn't trust him. That sort of thing. He wasn't at the party, but it was clear they were fighting about him."

"What happened?"

"Amy ran out of there really fast. Then I went back to Getty with Kayla. Didn't see Sarah or Ryan after that. I ended up hanging out in Kayla's dorm. Told the cops everything. No use pretending like we didn't violate the honor code when they're dead." His face drops and he shifts his attention to the bookshelf on the other side of the wall. Right next to a copy of *Robert's Rules* is a framed photo of him and Sarah, taken when they were kids, wearing uniforms that don't look like Meadowbrook's.

"That from middle school?" I ask.

"St. John's. We carpooled every day."

A deep well expands in my chest as I watch Peter tuck his bottom lip into his mouth. "I'm so sorry, Peter."

"I just can't believe it, you know? Like two days ago, Ryan and I were talking about applying to Yale together, rooming in New York after college." He shakes his head. "We had it all planned out."

"Do you have any idea who did it?" I ask.

Peter's jaw quivers and he exhales slowly. "Someone who hated them," he says. "It's the only thing that makes sense."

"Who, though?" I ask. "They were like royalty here."

"That's for the cops to figure out, I guess."

We're both quiet, the uncertainty hanging between us. I scan my list of questions, but all of them seem trite now. Everything he's said so far is gossip, not much I can use in an article, but having someone like Peter be this vulnerable is an opportunity I shouldn't squander.

"People are going to be looking for leadership in the coming weeks. What would you say to them to help them move forward or feel safe here?"

Peter turns back to me. "Well, we can't feel safe. Not yet. Not until someone is caught. But what I can say is that we will never forget Ryan and Sarah. We will honor their legacies."

"How?" I ask.

Below the desk, I see Peter's foot bob up and down, tapping against the carpet. "You know," he says, "you're just like the reporters at Dad's network. Asking the tough questions." He smiles. "Maybe if you write something nice about me, I'll tell him to put a good word in for you at the internship program."

I roll my eyes at Peter. "Ha ha, you know you can't bribe me." Though I have to admit, getting on Peter's good side for an internship at NYNN *does* sound pretty ideal.

He lets out a low laugh. "Right answer. Just like the pros." He stands and wipes his palms on his khakis, a signal for me to leave.

"Thanks," I say. "For agreeing to talk to me. Not everyone wants to. Having you on the record will help other people know they can trust me."

"Of course."

"You're not giving other interviews, right? Talking to a million other reporters?"

Peter snorts. "Yeah, right. You can consider this exclusive." His gaze moves behind me and I turn around to see the rest of the senior class government streaming through the doors, moving to the conference room. Melody gives me a funny look, her brow furrowed, and I head toward the door.

But once I get in the hall, my stomach drops. Mrs. Herschel is standing there with a clenched jaw and a tousled ponytail. "Elizabeth Charles, were you just conducting an *interview* after I specifically told you *not* to write about . . . this?"

"I was talking to Peter about how the student government is handling things. It's a 'ra-ra, let's all band together' piece."

She shakes her head. "I have to tell Egan."

"Doesn't she have way more important things to do than try to reprimand me?" It's too late, though. Herschel is already pulling out her phone, dialing, and pressing it to her ear.

She disappears down the hall so I can't hear, and I lean back against the wall, closing my eyes, my stomach sinking. If I just risked my entire education to have this conversation with Peter, I don't know what I'm going to do.

It only takes a minute before she returns, her mouth a straight line. "Well, you're in luck."

I stand upright. "Oh?"

"Egan seems to think your new angle is a good one. You have permission," she says. "But I have to read it first. You cannot go rogue and publish on your own anymore."

I have to stop myself from clapping my hands together. "Thank you, thank you," I say. "You won't regret it. I promise."

"There's one more thing. As a consequence for your actions, Egan wants you to go staff the check-in desk at Fielding House, where all the parents are arriving."

"But I have to write—"

"Not yet," she says. "First, you help. You be a part of this community. And remember, it's all off the record, so don't even think about interviewing one of those terrified parents."

Amy

Dear Amy, we are on campus and would like to see you. Please stop by Fielding House this afternoon. Mrs. Oliver.

The text is bright and menacing on my phone screen, a call to action rather than a greeting. I swallow the lump in my throat and rest my hand on the railing at the entrance of Fielding House, which is more than just a house. Built in the 1800s and refurbished ten years ago, it's actually a luxury hotel with forty-five guest rooms, a lounge that holds a billiards room and a wet bar, a full gym, and a library that rivals the ones students frequent.

The school says it attracts visiting faculty or scholars who like to use the library and roam the historic grounds, but it was built by donor money, meaning the folks who reap the benefits are often parents and alumni who book rooms for homecoming and graduation a year in advance. Giving parents complimentary stays for an extended period of time is way above and beyond what Meadowbrook usually does, but I guess they don't have a choice. Not now.

I run my palms over my oxford shirt, making sure it's tucked into my skirt, and walk through the entrance, but when I see who's standing next to reception, I pause.

"What are you doing here?" I ask Liz, who's holding a clipboard and maroon Meadowbrook Academy pen.

"Concierge-ing," she says. "My punishment for reporting on Sarah and Ryan without permission." She looks at her clipboard. "I don't see an Alterman on here. Are your parents coming?"

"No."

Liz nods slowly. "Right."

"My mom lives abroad. Dad's traveling. They'd never show up." *Shit.* I don't know why I just said that to her. The less she knows about me the better.

"Same," Liz says. "My mom's barely ever been on a plane."

The silence extends between us, but then the door behind me bursts open and I turn around to see two familiar faces, sunken-in and pale to the point that I'm not sure it's them.

But as soon as they see me, Mrs. Oliver gasps and rushes toward me, throwing her arms around my shoulders, enveloping me in a hug so tight, my chest constricts. "Amy," she says, her voice deflating like a balloon.

Mrs. Oliver has always been formal, so different from the parents I grew up around in the Bay Area who insisted I call them by their first names and suggested we participate in morning yoga and meditation after sleepovers. The first time I visited Sarah's home during freshman-year spring break, I made the faux pas of grabbing a seltzer from the fridge without asking, an act that caused Mrs. Oliver to raise her eyebrows and pucker her lips in a way I'll never forget. But now, with her arms around me, I realize that sort of distance may have been preferable.

Mr. Oliver pries his wife off of me and then extends his hand for me to shake. "I wish we were here under different circumstances."

I can't find anything else to say, until finally Liz clears her throat. "Mr. and Mrs. Oliver?" she asks. I give her a dirty look, a knowing one that I hope conveys what I'm thinking: *Don't you dare ask these grieving parents anything about their daughter right now.* She doesn't look at me, but her face turns to one of pity. "I'm so very sorry for your loss. Should we get you to your suite so you can get settled?"

"Yes," says Mr. Oliver, who seems grateful for the distraction. "We were in Head Teacher Egan's home last night." Sarah's mom keeps her gaze on me, steely yet watery, and her fingers clenched tightly around my arm.

Liz slips them a skeleton key and a little map of Fielding House, though they've stayed here dozens of times before for alumni weekends, board meetings, and soccer games. Sarah always said their favorite room was on the top floor because it overlooked the entire grounds and could see all the way to the boathouse.

"Would you like some help with your bags?" Liz asks.

Mr. Oliver starts to reply, but Mrs. Oliver interrupts. "Amy can help us," she says, turning to me. "We wanted to talk to you anyway. There's so much to discuss."

I throw Liz a desperate look, but she's not about to save me and waves her arm toward the staircase, where I grab Mrs. Oliver's bag by the handle and start hauling it up to their suite, where surely, nothing pleasant awaits me.

Liz

I've checked in a dozen sets of parents, mostly people who seem to be friends with Ryan's and Sarah's families, folks who were driven here by personal chauffeurs or flown here on their private jets. They wore thick, shiny watches and carried soft quilted handbags. Their luggage matched and all of them had been here before, to Fielding House. None of them knew who I was. None of them asked.

I look at the clipboard and see that all of the families scheduled to arrive today have indeed come and check the time to find that there is still an hour left in my shift. I slump against the desk, wishing I could head over to the *Gazette* office, but at least here I can scroll the news to see if there are any recent developments.

Just as I pull out my phone, I hear the sounds of shoes against the hardwood floor, making their way toward me, and I shove my phone back in my pocket, stand up straight, and prepare to greet whichever parent is stopping by to ask for a fresh set of sheets or perhaps a golf cart ride to main campus.

But when I look up, I see Head Teacher Egan and Mrs. Herschel making their way toward me, and I swallow the lump in my throat.

"Glad to see this worked out well," Mrs. Herschel says, nodding in my direction. "Everyone settled in okay?"

"Yes." I tap my papers in front of me. "We're all set."

Head Teacher Egan crosses her arms over her chest. "Good." She looks around, as if to make sure no one is wandering into the foyer, and then she takes a step closer to me, so close I can smell the coffee on her breath. I've never had much one-on-one interaction with her, only when she sat for the annual end-of-year interview with the *Gazette* staff, in which she gave elaborate, detailed answers about the school's achievements and what might be in store for the next academic calendar. She had laughed at last year's senior class prank and brought us cookies to celebrate the end of the semester. But now, she's looking at me with a cool gaze like I'm the enemy, not a student.

"I know Mrs. Herschel relayed my message, and asked you not to write about anything regarding the incidents that took place."

"That's right," I say, glancing to my advisor. "Unless it's approved, like the story about how our student government is responding."

Egan nods. "That's correct. I just want to remind you that the school is in a very precarious position. People from all around the country, the world, are watching us in ways they haven't before. Your news outlet has more power than it ever has."

Pride swells inside me, but I'm not sure she means it in a positive way.

"I implore you to use that power for good. You are a member of this community. You are *not* an outsider. Whatever happens here reflects on you as well as your peers."

"I understand," I say, knowing full well what she means. *Make us look good.*

"Very well." Head Teacher Egan turns on her heel and I'm left alone with Mrs. Herschel.

"Was that a threat or am I paranoid?" I ask.

Mrs. Herschel looks out the window at a set of parents walking down the hill arm in arm. Egan stops to talk, placing a hand over her heart. "All of the other journalists descending on Meadowbrook will be angling for the same thing. They'll want to know who did this and how, why this school that was supposed to be safe . . . was not."

"That's what I want to know, too."

Mrs. Herschel rubs her temple. "Let someone else dig into those questions," she says. I start to protest, but then she holds up her hand. "View this as a time to be creative. Challenge yourself. This student government idea, that's where you'll have success. Reporters like Yalitza Luna will move the investigation forward, go the whole true crime route. Think, what will no other reporter ever come up with? What story could *only* a student write?"

"Wait, you think Yalitza Luna is going to cover this?"

She waves her hand in front of her face. "I don't know. I'm just saying."

My stomach flips at the idea of my idol coming here, to campus. Perhaps there's a chance I could meet her, talk to her about story ideas. But I'm getting ahead of myself. "So, all my pitches should be from a student perspective?"

"What other perspective do you have?" Mrs. Herschel sighs and looks outside to where Egan is now driving off in a golf cart emblazoned with the Meadowbrook logo on the side. "I want you to win the Page One scholarship as much as you do. This is a solid way to make sure you can still do your work. Trust me."

"It's not just about the scholarship."

Mrs. Herschel raises an eyebrow. "It's not?"

I haven't told her much about my family, the way my mom left us for so long, how one lie made me rethink everything I thought was true. When Mom walked through that door with a beat-up rucksack and worn leather sandals on her feet, causing Grandma to drop a tray of macaroni and cheese right onto the tiled floor, I knew my world had changed, that my entire brain chemistry would have to be rewired to understand how the people closest to me could lie about something so important.

It's why I began obsessing over nonfiction, the need to report and explain what had happened. The facts. No editorializing. Nothing else. It's the only thing that matters.

"We have a duty to everyone at this school to show how and why this happened. Reporters expose the truth."

Mrs. Herschel wrinkles her nose. "I wish you wouldn't use the word *expose*." She shudders but then begins thumbing through a folder, pulling out a slip of paper and a small object. "Why don't you go cool off at Rex Taylor's?" She hands me the sheet, and I see it's an off-campus slip with her signature on it, a key fob that unlocks the Meadowbrook bikes we're allowed to ride into town dangling from her finger. "Consider this my permission as long as you're back by dinner."

I grab the fob and she pats me on the shoulder before turning around and following Egan's path on foot. Frustrated, I weigh my options. I could head back to the *Gazette* office to sulk, but a trip into town might be refreshing. Plus, it would be nice to see Rex after everything that's happened, or at least get a lemon poppy loaf and a cappuccino.

I pocket the key fob and glance at Herschel's note, which I realize is undated, meaning I can reuse it in a pinch. Outside, I grab a bike from the rack, and soon my legs are pumping, the wind whipping through my hair.

The trip to Meadowbrook's small Main Street only takes ten minutes by bike and by the time I reach Rex Taylor's I've already begun to calm down. I lock the bike up out front and scan the strip. It's the same as it was last spring, with only a handful of storefronts, most of which have been here for decades catering to weekenders and Meadowbrook Academy–affiliated folks like us. There's barely any cell service in town, so most people rely on the storefronts' Wi-Fi, but sometimes I like to turn my phone on airplane mode and bask in the disconnectedness of it all, the quaint small town feeling that makes it seem like you're in a different era completely.

There's the Meadowbrook Diner, known for serving fluffy sky-high pancakes, the used bookstore that offers a generous discount to students, a one-screen cinema that shows classic films in 35 mm, three different antique shops that feud with one another, a provisions shop hawking twenty-five-dollar hunks of cheese and fresh-pressed apple cider, and Rex Taylor's, the lived-in coffee shop and bakery.

I started coming to Rex's when I was a freshman and realized that most of my peers preferred the diner or the provisions shop during off-campus outings and that I could come to Rex's for some alone time. His clientele is mostly locals, folks who live and work in Meadowbrook year-round, and I love looking at the corkboard, always advertising community events, mutual aid fundraisers, guitar lessons, and teenage babysitters.

It reminds me of Polly's, the coffee shop I would escape to when Mom came back to town and tried to mend things. I had no interest in placating her and was happier to spend time at Polly's, where the baristas would give me watered-down hot chocolate and day-old pastries for pennies while I did my homework in peace. That was where I discovered the free local paper, where I would read it cover to cover. It was a huge day for me when Polly's finally decided to subscribe to *The New York Times*, which they would spread out on the communal tables for folks to read throughout the day. The shop was right next to the public library, so on lazy afternoons, I'd bop between the two, visiting with staff and trying to read as much as I could before heading home.

I pull open the door to Rex Taylor's, and take a deep inhale, savoring the smell, which gives me a hearty dose of nostalgia and comfort. All cinnamon and coffee beans, sugar and melted butter.

The tables are small and metal, arranged around the big square room at odd angles, mismatched chairs pushed under them hastily. There are only a few people here, middle-aged parents in hiking gear, babies strapped to their chests as they take down iced coffees and breakfast sandwiches, a small group of elderly women playing cards in the back. Rex is behind the counter and as soon as he sees me, his face lights up.

"Wasn't sure we'd see any of you kids from the academy this week," he says, reaching over the counter to give my shoulder a sweet little tap.

Rex was born and raised here, just like his parents, and never left, inheriting the coffee shop when he was in his thirties. He told me it took him a few decades to turn it into what he really wanted it to be, which was a community gathering place, but he could never quite break into the Meadowbrook Academy scene, not that he really wanted to. He had no kids of his own, but his wife, Mildred, had been mayor of the one-thousand-person town for ten years, and the two of them were basically local royalty.

"I got special permission to come into town today," I say.

"You doing all right?" His brows pinch together with worry.

"I'm fine," I say. "Personally, I mean. The girl's roommate . . . she got placed in my dorm, so that's sort of unnerving."

A crash rings out behind the counter, and I lean over to see a tall Black boy wearing a dusted apron, fumbling with the espresso machine.

"Hey, Olly," I say, leaning over the counter.

He looks up and smiles, gleaming white teeth beaming back at me, and my stomach does a flip. Olly walks on over and Rex slaps him on the back.

"Final week here for my nephew before he starts a fancy new job over on your campus."

Olly blushes as he looks up at me. "Got a gig with the maintenance crew, but my start date's been pushed back after . . . you know."

"Oh wow. That'll be great for you." I mean it, too. One afternoon last year, it was just Olly and me here when he was cleaning up, and he told me he was dreaming about starting his own landscape business. A big job like that at Meadowbrook would be huge in setting him on that path. "Maybe I'll see you around campus sometime?"

A smile tugs at Olly's lips. "For sure."

Rex looks back and forth between us, and I cough, suddenly desperate to change the subject. "Is Joseph working today?"

"I'm gonna . . ." Olly darts back to the espresso machine and Rex lowers his voice, wincing.

"He's in the back finishing up the breakfast shift. But he's on edge. Most people around here are. But he was kinda close to them, you know?"

"Of course. Amy, his girlfriend."

"Well, at least she got you for a roommate. Are you . . . writing about it?" Olly reappears and sets down a cappuccino, sprinkling it with cinnamon. My usual. Rex pats him on the shoulder and retrieves a lemon poppy loaf for me from the baked goods counter, dropping it into a parchment wrapper.

"Trying to," I say. "Realizing it's harder than it looks."

"All things are," Rex says.

"Amen." I pull out my wallet.

Rex wrinkles his nose and waves his hand at me. "Not today. Maybe tomorrow."

I groan. "Come on, man. I can't have you going out of business. It's the only place in town I actually like."

Rex laughs but retreats, not giving me a response. I sigh and drop a few bills in the less-than-full tip jar. I lean over the counter to wave at Olly, but he's disappeared down the hallway with a bag of trash.

My shoulders relax, and I start to head toward my favorite table in the corner with the pillow-covered benches, but before I can grab it, Joseph darts out from the kitchen carrying two plates topped with bright yellow omelets, setting them down in front of two elderly hikers.

"Enjoy," he says, his voice lifeless.

"Hey," I say to him as he turns around.

He stops in his tracks, startled. "Oh. Hi, Liz."

"How you doing?"

Joseph nods, tucks the rag into his apron. "Fine."

"Amy told you we're roommates now?"

He looks up then and I see his gaze is fixed, more serious than the other local kids I've seen around Rex's, the ones who seem to gawk at our Meadowbrook uniforms, sneer at the bikes we leave locked on the street. More than once I've wanted to call after them and scream, "I'm not like the others. I'm like *you*!" But I know it would be no use, not when I'm wearing the pleated jumper, the Meadowbrook crest. And besides, I escaped Wisconsin so I *could* be like my classmates, so I could achieve what they had already been given. Only Joseph and Olly seem to see me as something in-between, something more like how I feel on the inside.

"Yeah, she told me."

"Right." He doesn't say anything else, so I try my luck. "How're you holding up? It's gotta be hard."

He cocks his head. "Come on, Liz. You know I'm not going to talk to you like that. I'm not trying to get quoted in your paper or anything."

My face flushes. "Sorry. I mean, with all this news about how Sarah and Amy fought the night before she died . . . it sounded bad. She's probably upset over it. That's all I meant."

"Where'd you hear that?"

"Kids at school. People talking, you know." He's staring at me hard, with an intensity that makes me uneasy. I break eye contact and take a sip from my cup.

He shakes his head and turns away. "Don't believe everything you hear."

Amy

Mrs. Oliver shuts the door behind me, so I'm trapped between her and Mr. Oliver, only a few steps away. My chest tightens and I will them to step back and give me space.

Mr. Oliver sidesteps me and busies himself by a bar cart in the corner of the room, while Mrs. Oliver stays put, blocking the door. Claustrophobia kneads at my stomach, but I will myself to push through the next little while. It will end soon. Everything does.

I've been in this suite before, last year during alumni weekend when my dad made his once-a-year visit to campus. The Olivers attended, too, and they stayed here, in their usual quarters, while Dad's room was right down the hall.

I look around and realize it's exactly the same as it was then, with the gingham upholstered settee and an antique hutch pushed up against the far wall. The curtains are pulled back and outside the window I can see the grassy fields, bucolic and expansive, that extend to the far side of the grounds, toward the boathouse, Sarah's favorite view. Fresh lilies stand at attention in a vase above the fireplace.

Mr. Oliver disappears into the bedroom behind the pocket door with his tumbler full of dark liquid and I'm left alone with

Sarah's mother, whose face wilts like a flower the more she looks at me. I notice a pitcher of ice water sitting on the bar cabinet next to four glasses. "Would you like something to drink?" I ask, motioning that way. But she doesn't respond.

It feels like we're in a détente and I know I should say something, but everything I can think of sounds trite.

Finally, she breaks the silence. "We saw Kayla yesterday," she says, sitting down. "The poor girl was crying so hard she could barely speak." She looks at me now, as if she expects me to burst into tears.

"It's horrible."

The door opens and Mr. Oliver returns to the room and refills his scotch. He paces around the room and then stops. "We've been told you're cooperating with the police in any way you can."

"Of course."

He nods. "We can't think of anyone who might want to do this to Sarah or Ryan." He pauses. "The Pelhams are beside themselves, as are we."

I look down at my hands, my red and bloodied cuticles.

"If there's anything I can do . . ." I start, though I'm not sure how I, the survivor, could do anything to help ease their pain.

They both look at me blankly and I know they're thinking the same thing. *Why our daughter and not you?*

There's a knock at the door. Mrs. Oliver jumps up, relieved, and opens it slightly, peering into the hallway. When she sees who's there, she steps back and her shoulders relax. "Peter," she says, giving him a soft kiss on the cheek.

I turn to him and see Peter for the first time since the party.

He's gaunt and pale, as if grief is an illness. He offers me a weary smile but follows Mrs. Oliver to the small sofa and sits by her side, his hand still wrapped in hers.

"I hope it's okay I stopped by. Ryan's mom told me which room you'd be in and I wanted to pay my respects."

Mr. Oliver clasps his hand around Peter's shoulder. "Good boy," he says. "Your father would be proud."

That would have been the right thing for me to do, too—to *pay my respects*. But instead, I had to be summoned, and now that I'm standing here, I'm only a reminder that I was not murdered in my bed, like Sarah was.

Peter's shoulders are slumped over, like he's hunched in on himself, so unlike the boy I've come to know. The kid who commands attention just by walking into a room, usually with Ryan by his side.

They moved through the halls of Meadowbrook like they had been born here, like they owned the classrooms, the grounds, the locker rooms. Their crew duffels slung over one shoulder as they roughhoused in the halls, ragging on one another like they were brothers.

Sarah liked to say that Peter only began to realize his potential once he got to Meadowbrook and met Ryan, that they developed some sort of competition to propel one another forward, make each other better.

Sometimes, in the early spring mornings, when frost still covered the grass, we'd go out to the boathouse and watch them race on the single crew boats, too out of breath to shit talk one another on the water.

Sarah and I would sit in silence, sipping mugs of coffee, and listen to the sounds of water splashing, of their guttural grunts echoing across the surface.

"Who's better?" I asked Sarah once.

She shrugged, keeping her eyes on both of them. "Depends on the day."

Now it looks like Peter would give anything to be back on that water, racing Ryan to the finish line.

"You kids have been through so much," Mrs. Oliver says. She turns to me. "One day, we'll discuss what you saw."

"Margaret," Mr. Oliver starts, but his wife holds up her hand.

"Not today," she says. "Of course not today." Her eyes are glassy and her hands start shaking as she reaches out toward me. "Today, we only wish to provide one another comfort. Isn't that right?" The question is directed to Peter, who looks down and sniffles, dragging his arm across his nose to capture a bunch of snot. "And to find out who did this. We *must* find out who did this."

Mr. Oliver drains his glass, his eyes on me, searching, and all I can think is that he's wondering why the hell someone killed his perfect angel daughter—the one who was surely bound for greatness, the one who had a boyfriend that everyone approved of, the girl who would go on to found a company or cure a disease or achieve any of the hundreds of things that were on her list of goals, a neat little note she compiled diligently on her phone— when *this* girl was in the other room.

This other girl, the one who had a totally fine, passable academic record, who was no soccer star, no genius, nothing notable at all. The one who had coasted by on her family's good name, the fortune in her bank account, the pretty-enough looks, and the well-taught table manners. *This* girl, the roommate—me. Well, she was not special. She was ordinary.

And if I learned anything from being Sarah's roommate it was that her father despised those who were ordinary.

Mr. Oliver keeps looking at me. "You didn't wake up." A statement, not a question. "You didn't hear anything at all."

I shake my head, realizing I'm going to have to lie now to the people who have to bury their only daughter. "No. It must have happened before I got home."

"Peculiar," he says. "You know, it's not uncommon for people who've been through trauma to suppress memories, to push them deep inside and only remember them much later or never at all. Perhaps you *did* hear something and you don't recall. Perhaps you *do* remember key details, things that might be able to help the police find the culprit."

Swallowing feels like sandpaper, but I force my shoulders to shrug, my head to nod. "Maybe," I croak.

Peter looks up, his eyes wide and hopeful, as if I might be able to solve the crime here and now in Fielding House. But before he can say anything, Mrs. Oliver lets out a strangled sound. "I still don't understand what they're saying, how there could have been so few witnesses aside from you, Amy. A dorm full of people and no one heard anything."

Peter drops his head into his hands. "If only your room had been closer to the others'." He turns to Mrs. Oliver. "Theirs is all the way in the corner, tucked away from the rest of the hall." He shrugs his shoulders up to his ears and his cheeks blush, like he's admitting a secret. "I stayed with Kayla that night," he says. "If only I had seen something." He chokes up, his words catching in his throat.

But I jerk my head up. Kayla hadn't told me that Peter had been on our floor, not that I had asked.

Peter turns to me, his voice breaking. "Sarah was so happy with that room."

On our first day back to campus last week, we had marveled at the placement of our suite. Sarah was excited to have some privacy for once, after feeling like our previous dorms were on top of the other rooms, sharing thin walls with our neighbors. But this year we had landed a spot in the corner, where we only shared one wall with a communal bathroom. Kayla and Hillary were closest to us and they were way down the hall, a whole emergency stairwell, the one that leads to the tunnels, between us.

Perhaps she and Ryan would still be alive if we had been assigned rooms in the middle of the hall, where someone might have heard them scream.

"Maybe Amy will remember something useful." Peter looks at me, hopeful. "Anything at all."

I gulp down my desperation, ignoring the warm feeling turning my insides into mush. "I'll do my best," I say, lying again. "Anything to help."

Liz

I'm halfway through writing a draft of my story when I almost miss the commotion outside. It's only when the young family at the table next to me gets up to peer out the window that I realize something's going on.

"It looks like a press conference," one of the parents says, the baby making sweet cooing noises against their chest.

I shove my laptop inside my bag and scramble to my feet, pressing my nose against the glass of the window. Across the street, outside Town Hall, a crowd has gathered in front of a wooden podium, and from my perch, I can see two cop cars idling by the stop sign.

My heart rate picks up and I gather my things, tossing out my trash before I dart through the doors and across the street, running into a shaggy dog that comes up to my waist. "Sorry," I say, barely looking at the owner.

There are about thirty people here, and they've all got press badges dangling from their necks in front of their rumpled button-down shirts, telltale signs that they're reporters from out of town. As I get closer, I spy a few news cameras setting up their shots, a handful of middle-aged folks holding notebooks and recorders, looking bored as they wait for something to happen, and a few photographers, testing out their shots. I elbow my way to the front of the crowd at the same time a man in uniform walks to the stand. I get up on my tiptoes and look around to see if anyone from Meadowbrook Academy is here. It's not that I was explicitly *forbidden* from showing up—and technically my off-campus pass covers this stretch of street—but after my conversation with Egan and Herschel at Fielding House, I can't imagine they'd be thrilled to know that I'm here.

And yet . . . there's no way I'm going to miss this.

"You dropped something."

I turn to see a woman who looks familiar holding out my Meadowbrook Academy pen. She's got dark wavy hair streaked with gray that hits her shoulders, and she's wearing a blazer over her faded gray T-shirt, New York News Network press credentials hanging near her stomach on a lanyard. It takes me a second to recognize her from the photo on the back of her book.

"Oh my god, you're Yalitza Luna."

She smiles and tips her head toward me. "Guilty."

I stick out my hand. "Liz Charles. Editor in chief of the *Meadowbrook Gazette* over at the school. I think I've read everything you've ever written."

She shakes my hand gently. "Let's hope not my middle school assignments." Her face is warm and friendly as she pushes her hair out of her eyes. "You broke the story, didn't you?"

"That was me."

"Tough to report on your own community, isn't it?"

"Oh yeah."

"Keep up the good work, then."

My bottom lip drops open as she turns away from me, notepad and pen in hand, her attention now focused on the podium in front of us. *Keep up the good work.* The words buoy me, fill my chest with the kind of validation I didn't know I needed.

A screeching metallic sound fills the air as the detective adjusts the microphone.

"Sorry about that," he says, his voice cracking. "I'm Detective Diaz, deputy chief of police here in Meadowbrook," he says. I glance at Yalitza to see she's balancing her phone on her notebook, the tip of her pen pressed to paper. But her gaze is locked on the man up front. I wonder if this is what real reporting looks like. Intense focus. Unbreakable determination.

"I am here to confirm the devastating news about the two deaths at Meadowbrook Academy. Both victims were students at the boarding school, and both were pronounced dead on arrival at Meadowbrook Memorial Hospital. Officers arrived on the scene shortly after eight in the morning. The families have been notified and the case is ongoing. We are grateful for the support and cooperation from the Meadowbrook Academy community as we begin this investigation into the deaths of Sarah Oliver and Ryan Pelham."

My heart pounds as I watch the other reporters around me. They're all scrambling to catch his every word, their heads turned down. Yalitza stays composed, her pen moving swiftly even though she doesn't look at what she's writing.

"While we are still reviewing the crime scene and interviewing any potential witnesses, we now know that there was no forced entry into the building."

That must mean that the killer was someone who had access to the dorm—who knew how to get inside Getty, get inside Meadowbrook.

"We are asking for anyone who has information to come forward," the chief continues. "Anything that you think might be relevant could help."

One reporter on the other side of the huddle shouts out, "Do you have any leads?"

The chief's mouth turns downward. "We are investigating any and all possibilities," he says. "But because of the nature of this crime, because of the . . ." His face grows pale and he shakes his head as if he can't go on. He inhales a shaky breath and continues.

"We believe this was not a random act of violence. It was not an invasion, not a burglary. No one else was harmed, nor even approached. Nothing seems to have been taken from the crime scene. Forensics indicate this was a crime of passion, committed for a specific reason by someone who had full access to and trust of the victims. Again, we are asking for the community's help in this investigation. Our tip line is open. Thank you, no further questions."

The crowd breaks up around me as some of the reporters run after the police, while others move away to fiddle with their shoddy hot spots so they can set up camera angles. But I'm firmly stuck in place, my limbs suddenly cold, my brain cloudy. My chest begins to tighten and I squeeze my eyes closed.

"Are you all right?" I flick my gaze open and find Yalitza Luna looking at me with concern.

I force myself to nod and let out a shaky breath. "First press conference, that's all. Didn't think it would be this hard to hear details like that." I press my lips together.

She winces. "Covering this stuff . . . it's not for the faint of heart."

I look down, suddenly embarrassed that I wasn't able to take it all in as facts like the other journalists here, that I let my emotions crowd my reaction. Yalitza probably thinks I'm not cut out for this, that I'd be better off pursuing a career where you don't have to confront life's ugly realities in order to uncover the truth.

"I'm the same, by the way," she says.

I glance up, blinking.

"It makes me a good reporter, I think. Empathy." She shrugs. "There are enough robots out there. Our profession needs people who feel things, who understand the human condition. At least that's my perspective."

Her face is warm and open, as if she didn't just hear the grisly words I did. *Crime of passion.* But maybe that comes with practice, the repetition of hearing horrible things and fitting them into narrative stories with beginnings, middles, and ends. Good guys and bad guys. Rights and wrongs. Truths and lies.

"I'll be here a while covering this story," she says. She reaches into her bag and pulls out a card, handing it to me between two fingers. "Email me if you ever need to talk. Us reporters have to look out for each other."

I take it from her as she heads to a small sedan on the other side of the street and when I look down at the piece of cardstock, I see her contact information right there for me to use. Maybe she's right. Maybe it's a strength to use this kind of emotion when reporting on these stories.

I hitch my bag over my shoulder and start walking toward my bike, ready to head back to campus. But as I'm unlocking it from the rack, I look over my shoulder back at Rex Taylor's. Joseph is standing outside, his grease-spotted apron hanging from his neck. His face is stoic, but he's turned to the police podium, as if he overheard every word, knowing, like I did, that the police had insinuated something distinct. That whoever committed these horrific acts of violence was close to the victims—Sarah and Ryan—that they had trust and access.

My brain is spinning, but all I can think of is the one person who had both: Amy.

Amy

Friday night dinner at Meadowbrook Academy is always a formal affair, and tonight is no different despite the circumstances. Everyone around me is shuffling into the dining hall, wearing matching blazers and slacks or skirts. Stitched-in patches sit above every right breast, and in front of me all I can see is a sea of maroon, marching forward, heads ducked down. The rest of the students should have arrived today, ready to be welcomed into the Meadowbrook fold, but campus is eerily quiet with only our class filling the halls and dorms.

It's been three days since I found Sarah and Ryan and the police have no leads, despite that horrible statement they put out yesterday—that they were killed in a "crime of passion," some ridiculous phrase that should only be uttered in trashy documentaries and slasher films.

But as news of the press conference drifted through campus and was blasted on every front page and local broadcast station, sending more reporters to campus, to our little town, it's clear everyone here is jumpy and scared, sticking to their own friends more fiercely, not going anywhere without a buddy. I mostly stayed in my room yesterday and today, and couldn't help but hear the click of Liz's door lock when she came home, bolting herself inside her room even when our suite itself was locked, too.

The hall is dimly lit, only illuminated by the dozens of candelabras lining the walls, flames flickering as the sun sets behind the floor-to-ceiling windows. Long, elegant taper candles sit on each rectangular table, too, cloaked in thick white tablecloths, place settings neatly arranged in front of each seat with a dozen or so pieces of silverware, each one serving a purpose. Making a point.

Friday nights are supposed to be for joy and revelry, when the already-excellent food is served with flair, and RJ, the cook, goes all out, filleting whole branzino or carving rib eye off the bone. Sometimes they're themed, like last year when we had tapas night and RJ had spent hours slicing jamón Ibérico so thin you could see the candles flicker though the fat when you held a piece up to the light.

I shuffle inside the room and see baskets full of fresh Italian bread on each table, a sign that a red sauce feast is upon us. The staff retreats behind the steam tables in the kitchen when more students appear. But RJ stays still at the steel counter, his eyes fixed on me, unblinking as I move into the room.

I shiver, suddenly cold, but I can't seem to break contact, not as his eyes track me. His mouth is a hard line, and my stomach seizes. If his intent is to unnerve me, he's achieved it tenfold.

Someone taps me on the shoulder from behind, causing me to jump and break the tether connecting me to RJ.

"Iris grabbed the table in the middle," Olivia says. "Come on."

I follow her over to the soccer girls, keeping my head down to avoid RJ, and slide into a seat at the end next to Liv. On her other side is Iris and I watch as their hands intertwine beneath the table. Iris leans over to peck Liv on the cheek and Liv leans into her shoulder. They've been dating since sophomore year, and seeing them together, so natural, always makes me wish that I had ended up with someone who also went to school here, someone I could sneak away with into the boathouse or the tunnels. It seems so much easier.

Iris's short dark bob hits her chin as she cocks her head in my direction, her mouth upturned on one side. She rests one hand on my forearm and I see her nails are chipped like she's been picking at them, flecks of bright blue polish speckled against her skin.

"How you holding up?"

"Been better." Iris lets out a quiet laugh, and some of the other girls turn to us. Kayla's on the other side of the table, but her face is unreadable.

"It's good for us all to be together," I say. I mean it, too. When it's only Sarah and me, I rarely give a thought to these other girls, but I can't deny that these are the people with whom I've shared hundreds of bus rides to faraway soccer games, all-nighters studying in the library, and movie marathons full of the caramel-coated popcorn Sarah always kept stashed under her bed. These are the girls who cover for one another when we go to the boathouse to party, who make up white lies to protect one another when someone is too hungover to run five miles at practice. We've been through three fall fairs and homecomings, countless sleepovers in the dorms, and too many sing-alongs on sweaty buses. That should count for something.

Egan takes the podium and says a quick welcome before asking us to bow our heads in a moment of silence. Then she departs, disappearing into the wings, and the kitchen staff begins to bring out our food. There are no student waiters tonight, no acts of service from our own. On Fridays we are served, and tonight everyone seems grateful to have someone else do the work.

Family-style trays of linguini pomodoro and chicken Milanese, chopped salads, and fried artichokes fill the tables. The smell of olive oil and roasted garlic takes over, and I'm ravenous, filling my plate with a little of everything, sprinkling spoonfuls of Parmesan cheese over my portions.

The sound of silverware clanking and muffled chatter takes over and for a second, it's as if this is a normal Friday night at Meadowbrook.

My phone buzzes in my pocket and when I pull it out, keeping it close to my side, I see a text from Joseph.

Just checking in. Everything okay?

I wipe my fingers on my cloth napkin, typing quickly. As okay as I can be. Sorry yesterday didn't work out. It was just too risky. Maybe tomorrow?

I stare at my phone, waiting for a reply, until Olivia elbows me in the side.

"Don't look at that. Seriously. It won't do you any good."

I stop and glance up.

"Those true crime freaks don't know what they're saying."

"What are you talking about?" Iris gives Olivia a look like she said something she wasn't supposed to and my heart rate quickens.

"She clearly hasn't seen it," Iris whispers.

Olivia winces. "Shit."

"What?"

"You really wanna see?" Olivia asks.

"Uh, now I do."

Liv whips out her phone and pulls up an article from some

fake-looking news website and spins it around for me to see. "It's bullshit," she says. "Obviously." But I barely hear her as I take in the headline, "Armchair Detectives Start to Piece Together Meadowbrook Murders."

I scroll down, seeing images of our school, class photos of Ryan and Sarah, and there, right in the middle of the page, a photo from last year's yearbook where Sarah and I are hugging in our soccer uniforms, our arms around one another after we won the regional tournament. The caption says, "No one's heard from Sarah's roommate, Amy Alterman, daughter of Silicon Valley tech magnate Derek Alterman."

"What the fuck." My chest seizes and for a second, I can't breathe.

"Inhale, it's okay," Olivia says, placing a hand on my back. "No one knows anything yet. Besides, they're just looking for someone to blame. You're an easy target, being the roommate and all, the one who found them."

Iris nods, somber. But then she gives Olivia a look and Liv pulls her hand back, placing it in her lap. The gesture is odd and all of a sudden, the food in front of me looks unappetizing, grotesque, and for a moment, my vision blurs. I swallow hard and finally find the words to speak.

"People think I . . ." I say, unable to finish my sentence.

Olivia and Iris exchange looks and a moment too late, Olivia shakes her head. "No, I mean . . . well, we don't."

Iris nods fervently. "Of course not, Amy. *Of course.* Those freaks will back off once the police come out and say the roommate isn't a suspect. Happens all the time."

An awkward pause lingers between us and the realization

passes over me: the cops *haven't* come out and said I'm not a suspect. They haven't told these internet goons to back off. Which could mean they don't believe I'm innocent.

I dip my head, shielding my face behind my hair, when I hear Kayla's voice rise above the others girls' at the table, now quiet and turned toward her.

"Peter brought it up first," she says. "That we could do a vigil sometime next week. Honor them, you know? Talk about them in a real way."

All around me, heads nod in assent, and Hillary places a hand on Kayla's shoulder. "You're so right," she says. "It's what Sarah would have wanted."

"How would you know?" I mumble the words under my breath, but based on the way Olivia stiffens next to me, I know she heard it. Heads turn and I realize the others did, too. My cheeks burn, but I know I'm right. Hillary would *never* have known what Sarah would have wanted. Behind her back, Sarah joked that Hillary wouldn't know how to get around campus unless Kayla told her which direction to walk.

Hillary's face is pinched, bright red, and her mouth is slightly open like a fish. No one speaks. No one says anything at all. Kayla leans forward nearly halfway across the table.

"What did you say, Amy?"

I know better than to double down, not right now when Kayla thinks her pain is worth more than mine, not when it's clear some of the other girls are growing suspicious of me and my movements. "Nothing."

Kayla doesn't retreat. "It sounds like you said that Hillary wouldn't know what Sarah might have wanted." Her voice is rising and heads all around us begin to turn. "You've been stalking around acting like you're the only person on this whole campus who's hurting. You're not the only person in pain."

"You didn't find them." My voice cracks, but I can't help it.

Kayla seems to soften for a second, but then her face hardens. "Maybe not, but I also didn't call Sarah a fucking *idiot* the night before she died. I didn't tell her to break up with Ryan." She smirks. "No, that was you."

The tears come fast and hot and I push my seat back from the table, desperate to get away. The legs of my chair squeak against the floor and more heads turn, a silence taking over the dining hall just as the waitstaff begins to serve dessert, tiramisu layered in large ceramic platters.

I push through them all and rush toward the door, but I can still hear the girls behind me, their voices carrying through the cavernous room.

"You shouldn't have riled her up," Hillary says. "You heard what the police said: someone close to them did it." I can only imagine what she wants to say next. *Someone like her.*

That's when I collapse right in the hallway, the sun setting through the window, blinking orange and yellow hues in my direction before I can't make out anything at all.

Liz

A chair knocks to the ground somewhere behind me and I turn around to see Amy fleeing from her table, the rest of the soccer girls staring at her.

"What the hell was that?" Kevin murmurs. Most people turn back to their food as the whispering continues, but I slip out of my seat, following Amy's footsteps until I come to the corridor between the dining hall and coat closet where we're all supposed to stash our parkas during winter. It's painted a dark blue, with wood wainscoting nailed up the sides. Amy's curled up like a snail on the floor, her knees tucked up under her chest.

"Hey," I whisper, crouching down beside her. I reach out to touch her shoulder, but Amy jerks away.

"Leave me alone," she says, hiccupping in between the words. But I don't move. She raises her fists up by her head.

"Breathe," I say. "You've gotta breathe."

She lets out a shaky exhale, then another, though she doesn't sit up. Not yet. I think of what Yalitza said—use empathy.

"This must be incredibly hard for you," I say.

"They think I did it," she says.

I bite the inside of my cheek. Those online sleuths certainly made a good case—that Amy was the only one who was in the room with them, that the police were being cagey about any in-

128

formation, that they hadn't said the roommate *wasn't* a suspect. All of that coupled with the fact that, according to Peter, they fought viciously that night did put a target on Amy's back. But looking at this wrecked girl in front of me, it's hard to imagine her doing something so violent. So vile.

"You didn't, though," I say. "Did you?"

Amy looks up at me, her shoulders tense and her bottom lip quivering. "No," she says. "Of course not."

"Then you don't have anything to worry about," I say. "Right?"

Amy sniffles and sits up. She pauses.

"What?" I ask.

Amy shakes her head. "Nothing." She stands and brushes off her behind, wiping her fingers under each eye. "I'm going back to Holbrook if anyone asks."

I open my mouth to say something, but she's gone before the words come, before I can ask her one final question: *What are you hiding?*

THE DAY THERE'S A
BREAK IN THE CASE

Amy

Four days. It's been four days since Sarah and Ryan died. Four days since everything changed. That's all I can think about as I jog around the Meadowbrook campus this morning. It's barely dawn, the sun still mostly hidden behind the horizon. I woke this early on purpose, to get a run in before the stares start, before people start asking me questions. Before I have to defend myself.

I take it slow around the perimeter of the grounds, following the metal gate that surrounds all of Meadowbrook Academy. It's a route I used to navigate with Sarah when we were working on our endurance. Coach always said it was the perfect trail because of the hills. Sarah liked to use it as interval training. I had to push myself to keep up with her, to match her pace and keep her stride. Runs with her usually left me on the verge of vomiting, alternating between being jealous of her natural ability and proud that I was able to keep up. But only sometimes, only when my body allowed.

Today, though, I run at my own pace, slower and steadier, focusing only on the birds chirping above, the breeze tickling my neck. It's a perfect Meadowbrook morning with dew on the grass and a slight fog rolling in over the pond.

Sarah loved mornings like these.

I look at my watch and see it's been three miles, that I've almost done the full loop, and when I glance up, I'm coming upon the main Meadowbrook gates, a massive iron archway that dates back to the school's beginnings in the 1800s. It's tradition to knock on the massive M carved into the iron as you pass it. Legend has it if you don't, you'll fail at least one final exam, and out of habit I tap my knuckles against it as I run.

But as I do, I'm startled by the sounds of voices rising up all at once.

"There she is!" someone calls out.

"Is that the roommate?"

The snaps of cameras go off and a lightbulb flashes in my face. I stop, the toes of my sneakers catching in mud, and turn to the gates, where I see a dozen people standing there, holding cameras and notebooks and cell phones. There are no security guards, no barking dogs. Just screws and metal that separate us and now seem too flimsy to deter them.

I stop in my tracks, stunned by the déjà vu. It's just like when I was ten. When the cameras sat outside our hedges, waiting to catch a glimpse of someone packing up my mother's closets, of a heartbroken tech CEO. Of me.

"Amy Alterman! Can we ask you a few questions?"

I lose my breath, a punch to the gut. A tingly sensation flows through my hands, my feet. They know who I am. They know my name. And there's nothing I can do to stop them from asking questions, from sharing my likeness. Nothing except run.

I take off sprinting back to main campus as my heart pushes forward, threatening to break out of my chest. I rush down the stone-paved path, through the arches that lead to the classroom buildings. I look back over my shoulder as the gate grows smaller in the distance, but I swear I can still hear them, their calls pulsing in the air.

My lungs are on fire, but I keep pressing when suddenly I run right into something hard and stumble backward onto the ground, landing in a soggy patch of grass.

"Shit," I say, my hands muddy as they break my fall. I look up to see Peter standing over me, his glasses askew and his cheeks red. He's wearing his crew practice uniform even though I know they don't have training today.

"Ah, sorry," he says, extending a hand to me. "Guess we ran into each other."

"No shit." I take his hand and pull myself to stand.

"You okay? You look awful."

I nod back to the gates. "Reporters. They're everywhere. Swarming campus."

Peter shakes his head. "My dad warned me this might happen. It's the biggest story in the country right now."

"Seriously?"

He toes his foot in the mud. "The media can't resist a 'beautiful dead white girl story.'"

A chill runs through me. I hate thinking about Sarah as a *story*. She was a person first. But so was Ryan. Peter seems to read my mind.

"Drives me crazy how the headlines always start with her. It's like, he's dead, too. Someone killed him, too." Peter's voice is rising now, the anguish boiling to the surface.

"Bullshit. All of it."

He nods.

"Have you talked to your dad about this? Asked him to get his reporters to back off or something?"

Peter rubs a hand on his forehead. "That's the thing. When I told him Meadowbrook was swarmed with reporters he said, 'Hopefully they're mine.'" He throws up both hands. "Said that if he dropped the story, they'd get beaten by all his competitors. Now he's trying to get me to feed him information, as if ratings and views are more important than his kid's goddamn well-being." Peter's voice cracks and he lets out a shaky breath. "Sorry," he says. "It's all so much."

Behind us the reporters begin yelling again, camera clicks filling the air.

Peter narrows his brow and tilts his head down. "I'll take care of this." He sets off toward the gates.

"Wait," I say. "You can't talk to them."

He turns back around. "You don't want them to write about *you*, right? Let me give them something else to cover."

Before I can say anything else, I watch as Peter approaches them. I can't hear him say anything, but I see the reporters nod, their attention fixed on him, his damp crew sweatshirt, his thick hair only slightly out of place. Even from the back he looks every bit the all-American prep schoolboy they want him to be, the survivor who can speak for us all. A few moments later he jogs back to me and they disperse, no longer the vultures they seemed. My heart rate slows and the tension eases from my joints.

"What did you say to them?" I ask, almost breathless.

"I told them that as senior class president, I'm just trying to make sure everyone on campus feels safe and that their presence negates that. Then they asked for a statement and I gave them one." He shrugs. "My dad always says the best way to get reporters to go away is to give them something usable. Guess that was one good piece of advice."

"Thanks," I say.

Peter pushes his glasses up on his nose. "Sure thing."

There's a quiet between us, a silence that extends for a beat longer than comfortable. We've found ourselves together often, with Sarah and Ryan, Kayla and the others, but so rarely on our own, just the two of us. He looks at me like he expects me to say something, but I don't.

He clears his throat. "I'm planning a vigil. Some way to honor them."

"Kayla mentioned it."

"Right." Peter rocks on his heels. "I was thinking maybe you'd want to help me?"

I lift my head. "You think that's a good idea? With everyone wanting to talk about the roommate?"

Peter's mouth shifts into a smile, so small I might miss it if I hadn't spent so many hours near him, hanging out in the boathouse, studying in the library, huddled around the same lunch table. "You were her best friend, Amy. It wouldn't be right to do this without you."

Warmth blooms in my chest and it's the first time I realize how much I need someone to validate my relationship with Sarah. His acknowledgment lands deep inside my core.

"Okay," I say. "I'd like that."

"Do you want to meet to talk about it? Maybe after dinner?"

I had made plans to see Joseph after dinner; he said his mom was going to bring him to campus with her while she worked on team strategy, but if there ever was a time to put Sarah over Joseph, it's now.

"Sure," I say. "That sounds good."

He nods, an easy smile taking over his face. "Come on. I'll walk you back to Holbrook."

Our footsteps sync up as we take the path back to the dorms, campus still quiet and calm, betraying the reality of what has happened. But suddenly, with Peter by my side, I finally feel a little less alone.

Liz

"This really is nice work, Liz." Mrs. Herschel is standing behind me in the office, looking over my shoulder at the article I just published, the one about Peter and the efforts the class representatives are putting into making us all feel safe.

I griped about her suggested headline—"Student Government Steps Up in Difficult Time"—but rolled over in the end, grateful I was able to publish *something*.

"See," she says. "Now you have an advantage no other outlet in the world has: access to Meadowbrook Academy students."

"Right," I say. "Maybe people will take notice." I scroll through the rest of the news that's come out about the murders. There are dozens and dozens of smarmy tabloid stories, creepy photos of the Meadowbrook dorms, weird conspiracy theories that have been blasted all over the web, and so many quick takes from reporters who've parachuted into town for a few days, thinking they know everything about Meadowbrook. One even got the name of the school wrong, calling it Meadowbrook Prep instead of Academy. "Everything else out there is garbage anyway."

"Guess we should start thinking of your next story, huh? Something Egan will be interested in." Mrs. Herschel wrinkles up her face as she types at her laptop, pecking each key before pausing. "I'll be right back," she says. "Nature calls." She sets her computer on the desk and darts into the hallway.

At first, I turn back to my own screen, refreshing the news about the murders, looking for more stories to appear. Mine sits close to the top of the search results. It may not be the gritty story, the one that tells of blood and horror, but it's one that could help students here and share our struggles with the outside world, explain what being here right now is *really* like. And in some ways, part of me thinks that transcribing our present, making sure it's honest and can be recorded in the history books, is more important than writing of violence and terror.

But something nags at me, a curiosity I can't quite shake. Amy hasn't been featured in any story, not her name or her background or her alibi. I should have stayed to talk to her this morning, but she was gone by the time I got up, and her door was locked when I got home last night. All throughout campus, everyone began whispering: *What if she did it?*

After all, Amy was the person who had unfettered access to Sarah's room. Perhaps there might be an explanation for the so-called crime of passion. Maybe she and Ryan were hooking up—or she and Sarah were together behind Ryan's back. Everyone seems to have an opinion, a take. But no one knew the truth.

I wish there was a way to convince Amy that coming forward might help her, might further explain what happened, what she knows.

I turn my head and the glare from Mrs. Herschel's laptop beckons me. She's got the *Gazette* pulled up in one tab, but her school email is open in another. Butterflies hum inside my chest as I roll my desk chair in front of her laptop. I know it's wrong, but my fingers seem to have a mind of their own, disconnected from my body, as they move over her keys, expanding her inbox.

I don't intend to snoop, but my eyes flit toward the doorway, knowing that the closest bathroom is so far from the newspaper offices, basically located in Siberia. Maybe, before she comes back, I can take a peek at any correspondence between her and Egan. Only to see if there's any sort of nugget of information I might be able to follow, an idea for the kinds of stories she might approve.

I hold my breath and try to push away the guilt swarming my brain as I type the word EGAN into her email's search bar.

Hundreds of messages appear in reverse chronological order and I scan the snippets—all-staff messages about the deaths, a few back-to-school notices—until I see one that makes me pause. Sent last spring, there's an email with the subject line: "Ryan Pelham academic dishonesty allegation."

I double click to open and try to read the chain as fast as possible:

From: Janet Egan <janet.egan@Meadowbrook.edu>
To: Disciplinary Committee <disciplinarycommittee@ Meadowbrook.edu>

Hello all: I received an anonymous letter alleging that junior Ryan Pelham cheated on his final precalculus exam, and that he may have had access to tests from previous years, where he was able to see answers. As per the Meadowbrook Academy handbook, I am sharing these accusations with the faculty members of the Disciplinary Committee, so you may choose whether or not this incident is worth investigating. Please see the letter attached, and keep me in the loop as this is a sensitive matter regarding an esteemed member of our community.

It doesn't take a huge leap to know that by "esteemed member of our community" she means "legacy kid we don't want to piss off." I lean in closer to the screen as I continue to read down the chain.

From: Geoffrey Flynn <geoffrey.flynn@Meadowbrook.edu>
To: Disciplinary Committee <disciplinarycommittee@ Meadowbrook.edu>

Ryan was in my precalculus class this year, and I did have my suspicions when he received a perfect score on his final exam after struggling on the midterm. He is close friends with Peter Radcliffe, who took precalculus as a sophomore and earned an A in the class. I don't want to make assumptions, but I would not be surprised if he found a way to study Peter's old exams.

From: Janet Egan <janet.egan@Meadowbrook.edu>
To: Disciplinary Committee <disciplinarycommittee@ Meadowbrook.edu>

As Mr. Flynn's allegations are not based in anything other than "suspicions," I implore all members of the Disciplinary Committee to keep their theories offline.

From: Sylvia Herschel <sylvia.herschel@Meadowbrook.edu>
To: Disciplinary Committee <disciplinarycommittee@
Meadowbrook.edu>

Janet: Would you like us to pursue a formal investigation? As
chair of the committee, I can spearhead the process.

From: Janet Egan <janet.egan@Meadowbrook.edu>
To: Disciplinary Committee <disciplinarycommittee@
Meadowbrook.edu>

No need, Sylvia. Let's drop the matter unless someone comes
forward with actual proof rather than a hunch.

The sound of footsteps squeaking in the halls jolts me upright
and I quickly move the mouse so the *Gazette*'s home page is
back on Mrs. Herschel's screen. I push off the desk and roll back
to my own computer, where I pretend to focus on whatever's in
front of me.

"Well, I'm off to a faculty meeting," Mrs. Herschel says, walking straight to her laptop and shutting it. "I'll see you at the *Gazette* later. Until then, don't do anything that might land you into
trouble."

I turn around and see she's looking at me with a narrowed
gaze. "I won't."

She disappears out the door and I press my palm into my forehead. If Ryan did cheat off Peter, maybe there's something here,
the kernel of a news story. Egan would never approve a story that
investigates Ryan's academic dishonesty, but what if these cheating rumors had something to do with his death . . .

I squeeze my eyes shut, trying to think, but I know there's no use in mulling this over on my own. I need to talk to Peter.

I press my lips together and push myself back from my chair, heading out my office and down the hall to the student government's room. It's packed with the rest of the student council, milling about, typing on laptops and eating donuts. They all look up, surprised, but I ignore them and scan the room until I see Peter's sitting behind his desk, alone.

I walk right though his open glass door. "Is there a chance that Ryan stole your precalc exam and cheated off you last year?"

Peter jerks his head up. "Excuse me?"

The audio from a news clip blares from his computer speakers and I switch focus to the screen in front of him. My stomach tightens into a knot as I see what's there: Peter standing in front of the Meadowbrook gates wearing workout clothes. A girl stands behind him wearing a Meadowbrook Soccer T-shirt, but her face is cut off in the grainy footage. Off-camera voices are shouting at one another as I watch Peter shush the crowd and commands their attention.

"Liz, what are you talking about?"

But I don't answer him, can only watch as he gives them a statement.

"What the hell?" My voice breaks, but I can't help it. "You gave another interview? After you said mine was exclusive?"

Peter stands up and squints at me. "I was protecting Amy. They were harassing her. It was the only thing to make them stop."

I cross my arms over my chest and realize the girl behind him must have been Amy. "Were they saying she did it? Asking her what she knows? Because honestly, they're not crazy to think she's hiding something."

Peter opens his mouth, but then snaps it shut as his gaze lifts from my face and moves over my shoulder. I spin around to see Amy standing in the doorway with a plastic cup of iced coffee in her hand. "That's what you really think," she says. "So glad you were there to comfort me last night in the dining hall. Real fucking nice."

She pushes past me so our shoulders collide and I wince, reaching my hand up to hold my upper arm.

"Amy's here to talk about the vigil," Peter says, his cheeks red. "Maybe it's best you leave, Liz."

I open my mouth, but then snap it shut. There's nothing to say. Nothing to make this right. I turn around and head for the door, but Peter clears his throat and I stop in my tracks. "No one cares about an exclusive when two of our friends are dead, Liz."

I don't turn around, don't stop. I keep my head down and keep going out the door because I hate that deep down, I know there's someone who does care, even now: me.

Amy

"You didn't have to do that." I pull out my notebook and take a seat across the table from Peter, which makes this feel oddly like a job interview or like he's a teacher. I should have suggested we meet in the library or the senior social space.

Peter drums his fingers against the desk. "She was being an asshole."

I look up from my pad in surprise. It's not often you hear Peter Radcliffe talk shit about someone. The last time I witnessed that was at a boathouse party last year, the one time I've ever seen him drunk. It was right after the Meadowbrook rowing team won the independent school regatta and someone on the team had scored a few handles of Banker's Club with a fake ID.

They had almost lost the race when Ryan missed a call from the coxswain and messed up his stroke for a few moments. Peter was posted up in a corner of the boathouse while Ryan was off with Sarah, debriefing with another teammate. "Man choked," Peter said, shaking his head. "If he wasn't my best friend, I'd shove an oar down his throat."

The next day, I spotted Peter and Ryan having breakfast together in the cafeteria, laughing over egg sandwiches and mugs of coffee.

"So, the vigil's going to take place next week," Peter says. "Egan says we have the whole auditorium. We can give out those fake candles. Maybe go outside after and release some balloons in the air. Maroon and white to honor the school."

I nod along but find it hard to concentrate.

"Sorry, is this too much?"

"How can you be so calm, planning this? Every morning, I've woken up and had to remind myself that they're dead. Every day, it's like relearning the worst news of my life."

Peter blinks. His Adam's apple bobs up and down. "Having things on my to-do list helps me move forward," he says. "It's the only way I can keep going. Stay busy." He taps his fingers against the wood desk and then stops. "I guess that's called avoidance. I'm sure I'll unpack it in therapy one day."

I choke back a laugh. "Yeah, I guess." We're both quiet, the silence sitting between us, when I remember what I overheard Liz say about Ryan. "What was Liz talking about? Ryan cheating in precalc?"

Peter raises one eyebrow. "I have no idea."

The class was never an issue for Peter. He and Sarah took it sophomore year, while Ryan and I toiled away as juniors. We both lamented how hard the final was going to be and that we both needed eighty-fives to pass. I eked by but only because Sarah stayed up late to help me. Ryan shocked everyone by getting ninety-five, acting all sheepish and blushing when I made him show me his paper.

"Really?" I ask.

Peter looks around like he's trying to make sure we're alone. "I guess it doesn't matter now," he says, lowering his voice. "I could never prove it, but I'm pretty sure he yanked my final exam from when I took it. Knew Mr. Flynn wouldn't change the test."

"Damn."

"I never narced on him or anything, obviously, but I'm not surprised Mr. Flynn was onto him." He licks his lips, nervous. "I was so mad at him at the time. Seems dumb now, right?"

"Incredibly."

"He was always trying to one-up me. But never could in math. History, maybe but . . ." Peter shakes his head. "Anyway, please don't tell anyone, okay? I'd hate for his reputation to be ruined now that . . . you know."

Tension eases from my limbs. "Of course," I say. "I'd do the same for Sarah. Not that she'd ever need to cheat."

Peter offers a weak smile, a quick nod. My phone buzzes in my lap and I retrieve it, seeing a text from Joseph pop up.

Holy shit, he writes. Have you seen this? Then he sends a link to a message board for Meadowbrook, the kind where local busy-bodies post classified ads selling old chairs and lamps, or where handymen share that they're looking for new decks to repair. But the post he sent is nothing like that.

It's from a woman named Sharon, who wrote, I live next to RJ Gilman, the cook at Meadowbrook Academy. Cops came this morning and put him in a squad car!! I asked one of them what was going on and they said something about the murders at that school. I always knew he was a creep! Stay safe out there, folks.

"Oh my god."

"What?" Peter asks.

I spin my phone around so he can see. "It looks like RJ was arrested."

"No way." Peter snatches the phone from my grasp and starts reading, covering his mouth with this hand. "No fucking way. That's not possible."

Outside Peter's office, Melody gasps and I turn around to find the rest of the student government leaders are all staring at a phone, too. I leap up from my seat. "Is it true?"

Melody shakes her head. "I don't know." She points to a post from a reporter online. "They're saying he was taken into questioning." On the screen is a photo of RJ with his Meadowbrook Academy uniform, a white chef coat and black-and-white gingham pants, walking into the police station, uncuffed, eyes down and stoic, away from the cameras.

"He always gave me the creeps," says Peter, shivering. "The way he looks at people . . . it's not right."

I grimace, remembering his gaze the other night, how it stayed on me even as I moved through the room. A horrifying thought bubbles up in my brain: *What if I was next?*

I sink down in a desk chair, overcome with a wave of relief. If they caught who did this—RJ—then that means this ordeal might be *over;* we will have justice and answers and maybe even closure.

Melody scrolls down as the rest of the group crowds around and then she stops halfway down the screen. "Oh my god," she says. "It says he has a criminal record from his twenties."

Peter squints, his face now next to mine. "I don't think one DWI leads to double homicide," he says, reading the page.

"Does it say they found evidence or something?" I ask.

Melody shrugs as she continues reading. "Apparently the town's cameras caught someone running out the service entrance a little after the time of the murders. They say the person matched his physical description, that his car was seen parked near campus overnight."

Joseph. He left campus in the middle of the night, no doubt sneaking through that same entrance.

Melody's eyes are trained to the screen. She blinks as she gets to the bottom of the article. "That's it. Nothing else."

The rest of us are quiet, waiting for something—anything. I know this moment should feel good. They caught someone. There are answers. But all I feel is fear.

I get back to my dorm and lock the dead bolt behind me, pressing my back against the door. It's a relief to be inside, away from everyone in the quad talking about RJ, Sarah, and Ryan like they're the most recent stars of a documentary—a soap opera. I could hear the reporters from the gates as I raced back here, could feel my stomach drop into my shoes.

But then I hear the sound of someone clearing their throat and remember my room isn't mine alone. I blink my eyes open to see Liz standing in front of me next to a pile of boxes.

"Doc Kolner dropped these off for you. She said they were extra things from your room." She pauses. "Your other room."

"Yeah, I got that."

"She said she'd bring back more when she can."

"Helpful." I scan the stack and see four big filing boxes made from cardboard. The last thing I want to do is go through them, especially in front of Liz. She stares at me, expectantly.

"What?" I ask. "Are you trying to figure out how to apologize for insinuating I'm a murderer or are you going to ask me if Ryan cheated in precalc now that he's dead?"

Liz jerks her head back. "Neither. I mean, come on." She pauses. "I *am* sorry."

"Apology not accepted. And you better not go looking into Ryan either. Who cares if he cheated? Who cares if he did *anything* wrong? He's dead, Liz. They're both dead."

The air is tense between us, almost like Liz is holding her breath, waiting to see what I do. She's still, staring at me, and a ping of fury springs to attention inside my chest. I can't fight what happens next, an instinct, an impulse. I raise my right foot, the one I've used to kick a thousand soccer balls, and swing it back then forward with momentum, making contact with the stack of boxes in front of me. Papers and pens, books and trinkets fly out of them all over the floor.

I expect Liz to make some ugly remark about how I'm messy and disrespectful and this is *her* space, too, but instead, she drops to her knees and begins to gather my things, gingerly stacking and sorting items to be placed back inside cardboard.

I'm overcome with a deep, desperate bout of shame and I drop down beside her, my belongings feeling strange and foreign in my hands.

"Did you have any idea it was RJ?" Liz drops a pen inside the box.

I shake my head. "No."

"He gave off a weird vibe but never like this," she says.

"Yeah, well, people do all sorts of terrible things."

Liz doesn't say anything and we're both quiet, picking up items and putting them back in the box. She turns to me and holds up a black leather notebook that I've never seen before. "I love Moleskines, too," she says. "Best way to keep track of ideas."

She holds it out to me and I take it, running my fingers over the soft cover. I flip it open and my heart drops. The handwriting is bubbly and loopy instead of tight and small. It's not mine. I scan the rest of the pile. None of it is.

Doc Kolner brought me a box that Sarah had been storing in my closet, the items she said she would unpack and figure out where to keep once she got her room sorted, the stuff she would never see again.

"Sarah," I croak. "This is all Sarah's."

"Oh." Liz stops touching everything, steps back. "Shit."

Seeing her handwriting, looking at her stuff in Liz's hands . . . it's all too much. No one should see this, least of all a stranger. I shove everything else back in the box and grab it by its sides.

"Do you need any help?" Liz asks, but I ignore her and instead go right into my room, slamming the door behind me.

Liz

The common space is full of Amy's stuff, still piled high where Doc Kolner left everything. Well, everything except Sarah's box, now safely inside Amy's room. A few remnants are strewn on the floor. A pale pink scrunchie. An extra pair of tie-dyed shoelaces. Markers and pens tucked neatly inside a soft fabric pouch. One Polaroid of Sarah and Ryan posing in their homecoming outfits from last year.

Two perfect-looking people, though no one's perfect. Not in real life. I press my front teeth into my bottom lip, thinking about what I saw on Mrs. Herschel's computer, Ryan's alleged academic dishonesty. Peter wouldn't confirm it, not to me, but there's got to be another way to find out. Talk to Mr. Flynn, Mrs. Herschel. If it's true, people deserve to know. At least, that's what I always thought. Now, in death, I'm not so sure.

I pick up the photo and hold it close to my face, seeing Sarah's arms draped around Ryan's neck, his suit rumpled but still sleek.

I hadn't gone to the dance that night, but I saw them as I was leaving the *Gazette* office at eleven, after putting the finishing touches on a special edition of the paper that would come out in time for alumni weekend.

I was walking back to the junior dorms when I saw Sarah and Ryan running across the lawn, holding hands as Sarah's dress train trailed behind her, catching on the fallen leaves. I stopped and watched them take off, laughing to one another, until they stopped behind a bush, hiding from a security guard walking in the other direction. I'd adjusted the shoulder straps of my back-pack, suddenly feeling so young, so different from them. There was an intimacy between them that I had not experienced at Meadowbrook, hell, maybe ever. A glimpse into what could happen if I found a way to penetrate this world, lay claim to a few of its inhabitants as my own.

As the guard walked on, they giggled and fell into one another, their kisses swallowing their laughter, and I forced myself to look away, to keep moving back to where I belonged, in my room alone. But once I got there, the place that had previously felt safe only underscored the fact that while everyone else was dancing somewhere on campus, I was on my own, an unanchored boat that had drifted out to sea without a captain or a crew to even notice it was gone.

I set the photo down on Amy's desk, but then her door swings open and she stomps out of her room, pulling on a jean jacket.

"Where are you going?"

She grunts but doesn't say anything and in a second, she's out the door, slamming it behind her.

"Asshole," I mutter under my breath.

I drop down onto the couch and start scrolling through my phone, muscle memory directing me to all the regular news sites I check. But then I get a text from Peter:

No hard feelings from earlier, okay? Consider this your personal invitation to a boathouse party.

A link comes through and I see it's an invitation to Melody's app. My heart rate quickens as I click accept and make an account, logging into a chat called "Meadowbrook Seniors Let's GO!"

Party at the boathouse tonight. Come thru everyone!!!!!

Aren't we still on lockdown?

Not now that RJ is in custody.

What a messed-up thing to say. He hasn't even been charged. We don't know he did it.

R U SERIOUSLY DEFENDING A KILLER??

We need to blow off steam and you know it.

I watch as the texts stream in, debating the merits of throwing a party under circumstances like these, and I press my tongue to the roof of my mouth.

My phone pings and I see a private message from Peter: You in?

A small smile forms on my lips and I stuff my phone in my pocket. I bet that's where Amy was headed when she left in a hurry. And you know what? I'm going, too.

I've only been to the boathouse once before, when I was a freshman tasked with covering a regatta for the sports editor. When

I leave my dorm, I worry I'll get lost, but that proves ridiculous since all around me, other seniors are drifting in the same direction, hoodies pulled up tight over their heads even though no one seems to care that we're all technically sneaking out.

I walk along the lit footpath to the edge of main campus until I reach the athletic fields. If you keep going this way along the official path, you'll get to the boathouse eventually, but I follow the others, taking the back route where there aren't any cameras. Where no one looks for you.

I hang a left and veer down the dirt road covered in footprints and keep going until I reach the Japanese maple tree. Here, everyone sprints for the weeping willow at the bottom of the hill, where a red boathouse comes into view, just beyond the grove of cherry trees. It's illuminated only by the moon and one window, through which I can see the warm twinkle lights casting a glow inside. Behind the building is the pond and rows of crew boats, stacked neatly in their wooden racks.

Someone enters before me and I slip inside, taking in the scene. It's a vast wooden structure with vaulted ceilings and dozens of oars lined up against the walls. The whole place smells vaguely of seaweed and sweat. A keg is set up in one corner and I watch as a bunch of basketball boys hoist one of their own up by his ankles while he chugs beer. I wince as it dribbles down his face.

Opposite them, a handful of lacrosse players are flipping plastic cups upside down, throwing their hands up in the air as someone downs whatever's left in their glass. And to their left, I see the soccer girls—Hillary, Kayla, Olivia, Iris—huddled in a group, talking close. It takes me a second to spot Amy, who's in their vicinity, but just outside their conversation. She's got a glazed look on her face, clenching a cup in her hand. She slugs from it, looking at no one. Nothing.

All around the room, I see familiar faces, people I've known since I first got here, to Meadowbrook, but none of them stop and say hi. No one welcomes me into their conversation or offers me a drink and I stand awkwardly near the entrance wondering what to do with my hands, where to go from here. Three years in and no one seems to notice me at all.

I walk toward the makeshift bar, grabbing a cold seltzer from a cooler. But as I open it, I hear a loud commotion, the sound of falling boxes and wood cracking as gasps ring out into the air.

"You're wasted." Kayla's towering over Amy, who's sprawled on the ground, cardboard boxes overturned all around her.

Amy pushes herself to stand and I push closer to see what's going on.

"If there ever was a time to get drunk, I think it's now." Amy sways a bit, clutching her cup.

Peter emerges from the crowd and starts to take Amy's elbow, but she shrugs him off. "You should probably head home," he says.

"Yeah, wouldn't want anyone else to end up dead," Kayla says, not quite under her breath.

"Oh shit," someone says. "She said it."

Amy looks at Kayla, incredulous. "Are you serious right now? They have someone in *custody*. You're really going around telling people I did this?"

"I mean . . . anything's possible."

Peter steps in between them and turns to Kayla. "Can you cool it? At least be relieved that we finally have some answers?"

Kayla presses her lips together, holding his gaze. But Amy

shoves Peter out of the way, getting so close to Kayla, their noses almost touch. "How dare you," she says.

Kayla doesn't back down. "We all saw your fight with Sarah the other night. We all know you were there when they were killed. All I'm saying is that it would be nice if we knew for certain that a killer *wasn't* walking around, hanging out with us here, at a party."

Amy steps back as if she's been slapped, her eyes wide and her mouth in the shape of a circle.

Something inside my stomach spasms as I watch Amy stand alone in this room full of people she knows so much better than I do, people who have been her friends for years. Olivia and Iris avert their eyes and the rest of the soccer girls congregate behind Kayla, choosing sides so obviously.

None of it sits right with me, the way Amy's lip wobbles, the way her face contorts into a look of horror. I've been around liars my whole life and nothing about the way Amy is acting makes me think she's lying.

I push through the crowd and when I break into the middle of the circle, I reach for Amy. But as I do, she bolts for the door, fleeing the boathouse in a panic, running into the dark.

No one follows her.

The music gets louder and the circle breaks up as Peter turns to Kayla. "Come on, Kay," he says. "You really think she did it?"

Kayla's eyes narrow and she grips his forearm, ducking her head toward his. "RJ's creepy, but murder?" she says. "I don't buy it. Besides, Joseph . . ."

Peter arches an eyebrow. "What are you talking about?"

But then Kayla's gaze turns to me and her cheeks flush as she realizes I'm right there. "Come on," she says to Peter, pulling him into the corner to finish their conversation so I'm left alone in the middle of the room, wondering what the hell Joseph has to do with any of this.

Amy

I stumble through the woods, my heart pounding, as I reach for my phone, dialing Joseph as fast as I can.

"Amy." He picks up on the first ring.

I let out a gasp, tears wetting my cheeks. "Can you come get me?" I ask, my voice shaking. "Now? The turnoff near the lake?"

The sound of keys jangling drifts through the phone and I picture Joseph springing up off the couch, reaching for his wallet, heading to the car. "I'll be there in five. Stay put, okay?"

I wipe my face on my arm. "Okay."

I look out at the lake, so clear I can almost see my reflection, not a ripple in sight. The turnoff is through the grove of elms to my right and I set off, leaving the party behind, using my phone as a flashlight. I stumble ahead, realizing I've had way more to drink than I should have, than I usually would. But I had been so relieved to know that RJ was in custody. So overwhelmed by seeing Sarah's handwriting. I had wanted comfort from my friends. But now I don't know if I have any of those left.

Kayla's words replay in my head, getting clearer as I repeat them to myself. *We all saw your fight the other night. We all know you were there when they were killed.*

I come to the clearing where the turnoff begins and slump down next to a tree, waiting for Joseph. I press my forehead to my knees, hugging my shins. That fight. That awful fight. It all started because I came late to the party. I had blown off getting ready with Sarah to see Joseph. He had just gotten off the late shift at Rex Taylor's and I wanted to hang out with him. It was as simple as that.

We met here, in this very same spot, where the only cars that pass belong to service workers for the school, where deliveries never happen after work hours. It's guaranteed privacy, easy for someone like Joseph to go undetected.

We were together for that short hour, alternating between rolling around in the back seat of his car, sweaty in the September heat, and giggling about nothing, our foreheads pressed together. After, I smoothed my shirt, made sure my mascara hadn't run down my face in his flip-down mirror. He left me with a bag of homemade popcorn, tossed with sriracha and nutritional yeast, and flashed his headlights as he disappeared down the road.

When I got to the boathouse, I lingered around the periphery, talking to Iris and Olivia, plotting how we'd decorate the soccer locker room for the underclassmen's arrival. Out of the corner of my eye, I watched Sarah and Peter on the other side of the room, deep in conversation, his hand reaching out to hold her hip in a familiar sort of way. She flinched and moved away, drifting to another conversation with Kayla and Ryan. Olivia and Iris headed to the keg, and I went over to Sarah, throwing my arms around her, delighted by the night already—the fleeting feeling of being a senior with my best friend in my favorite place, my loving boyfriend smelling of home in his car. I pressed the bag of popcorn into her palm. "From Joseph."

"No thanks." She turned away, dropping it on the ground so kernels spilled over the floor. Her eyes flicked past me to where

Peter was standing, and then she moved back to her conversation with Kayla. I didn't get it. Not then. And I slipped away, toward Liv and Iris, who let me into their huddle, where they were sipping fresh cups of beer and comparing friendship bracelets they had braided on the quad.

Sarah's dismissal stung so I avoided her, but at the end of the night, I reached for her hand. "Do you wanna leave? S'more cookies in bed?" I'd snuck a few for us from the dessert platters at dinner.

Sarah raised both eyebrows. "Oh, so now you want to hang out?"

"Seriously?" I asked, confused. "You've been ignoring *me* all night."

Sarah turned to me, her mouth a tight circle. I knew the look she was giving me, the one she reserved for betrayal, like when she heard an unsubstantiated rumor that Ryan had hooked up with someone at his sailing camp.

"You really want to get into it right now?" she asked.

I stood there, dumbfounded, and she continued.

"We have *one* senior week and you've spent all of it with Joseph. Don't you understand how precious this time is? You're supposed to be hanging out with *me*."

This, coming from the girl who had promised we would go to the sophomore soiree together but then ditched me when Ryan wanted to pregame just the two of them, the girl who snuck out four nights a week last fall to hook up with Ryan instead of watch movies with me in Getty.

"I never gave you shit when you chose Ryan over me."

"It's not the same."

"Why? Because Ryan goes here?"

Sarah pursed her lips. "Because he's your friend, too. I don't even know Joseph."

"Like you want Joseph to be your friend. Stuck-up snob."

Sarah's nostrils flared and I could tell a crowd was forming, but I didn't care. I couldn't stop, couldn't help myself. "Final game of the season last year, I wanted to stay in and stream the new Taylor Swift album and you went into town with Ryan instead. Junior spring, you lost your soccer sweatshirt and I spent four hours looking for it, only to find out you left to go hook up with Ryan while I was digging through every lost and found on campus. Freshman fling, I suggested the whole team have a sleepover in our suite and you snuck out to his dorm—"

"Stop!" Sarah threw her hands in the air. "Just stop it!"

I stood there, taking her in until something clicked inside my chest. "You're jealous," I said. "You're jealous that finally I have someone of my own who's not you."

"Jealous? Of you?" She let out a mean snort, one that lodged itself in the back of my brain, carved its way deep into my heart, fracturing it in half. "Your grades are mediocre at best. You're barely good enough to stay on varsity, and your boyfriend is some random townie. Jealous?" She sneered. "I pity you."

For a moment, I couldn't breathe. Couldn't see. Could only smell the stale stench of beer, the faint odor of a joint floating from the lawn.

I searched her face for regret, but all I saw was satisfaction, a curled lip, and cold eyes. She had wanted to hurt me, knew how to find my soft spots and press hard until I bruised. She had succeeded. I swallowed, refusing to let the tears fall, to let her know how much anguish she had caused.

"Guys, come on." Ryan approached us with his mussed-up hair and cheeks flushed from a few beers. "Relax, this is supposed to be fun."

I didn't wait to hear what anyone else had to say. I pushed past them both, ran out the door, and called Joseph to come to pick me up, just like I did tonight. And I made the mistake of taking him back to Getty, of violating the one rule we always said we wouldn't.

But I can't think about that.

Bright lights emerge from the brush and I stand up, running to where Joseph slows on the gravel in front of me. I throw open the passenger door and climb in, looping my arms around his shoulders. He holds me tight as I begin to cry into his shoulder.

"What the hell happened?" he asks, his voice warm.

I press my forehead deeper into him, not wanting to come up for air. "Kayla accused me," I say, hiccupping. "Insinuated I was some sort of jealous, crazed killer."

Joseph pulls back and looks at me with his eyes wide. "You can't be serious. They caught the guy. The cook."

"But what if he didn't do it?"

Joseph chews on his bottom lip.

I take a deep breath and blurt out what I've been thinking. "We need to tell everyone the truth," I say. "That you came back with me and stayed in the room. I fell asleep and you snuck out. I was with *you* when they died. I can't keep lying like this; it's making everything worse."

Joseph drops his hands from my waist and shakes his head. "Amy, I—" He pauses like he's trying to gather himself, find the words. "We can't."

"Why?"

"Because they said the town's cameras caught someone leaving campus that night."

"So?"

Joseph's quiet like he's waiting for me to put the pieces together, and all of a sudden, I do.

"That footage might be of you."

He nods. "Like I said, it's a simple story. I'm easy to blame."

My head swarms from all the booze and the confusion of the night. I squeeze my eyes shut. "It's not like you have a motive or anything. You'd only hung out with Ryan and Sarah a few times. Barely knew them."

Joseph licks his lips, his eyes flitting around the car, and suddenly a pit opens up in my stomach.

"That's the truth, right?"

Joseph tilts his head, quick but in agreement. "Right."

Liz

I wake up in the morning to find Amy sitting in our common space with a mug of coffee, watching some old movie I don't recognize.

"Hey," I say, rubbing the sleep from my eyes. "You okay?"

She doesn't take her eyes off the screen. "Yep."

I make myself a cup of coffee from our little auto drip and sit down beside her. "Last night was really messed up, what Kayla said. We can talk about it if you want."

Amy turns to me slowly, her jaw tight. "I don't want to talk to *you* about anything."

My chest tightens. "I'm just trying to be nice to you when it's clear no one else is. You don't have to be such an asshole about it."

"I'm the asshole? You're the one who's writing stories about my friends as if they're tabloid fodder, then trying to insert yourself into every little thing going on that has nothing to do with you."

"Tabloid fodder? Have you even read any of my articles?"

Amy's quiet, her eyes glued to the TV.

"Why won't you let me be nice to you? Don't you ever let anyone in?"

I must hit a nerve because Amy snaps her mouth shut and

turns off the TV. She stands on shaky legs and sets the remote down on the table as she heads into her room.

"Yeah, walk away again. Go slam another door." I wave at her back, suddenly so over this entire interaction. She's not the only person at this school who's hurting. I'm about to tell her that, too, when there's a knock on the door.

"Girls?" Doc Kolner calls through the door. "Open up."

Reluctantly, I swing open the door and greet our advisor with the calmest face I can present. "Good morning, Doc."

She smiles thinly, but then frowns when she looks at my pajamas. "You're not ready."

"For what?"

"The outing. Did you not check your email?"

I shake my head. "I just woke up."

Doc Kolner clucks her tongue. "Seems like *most* of you girls slept in this morning. Perhaps there were some extracurriculars that took place last night?"

I snap my mouth shut and she holds up her hand.

"Actually, don't answer that. I don't want to know." She cranes her neck to see Amy standing in her doorway behind me. "Head Teacher Egan organized an excursion into town for half the class this morning. The other half will go in the afternoon. She thought it might be nice for everyone to get off campus now that some questions have been . . . answered."

I straighten my spine. "Does that mean they've officially arrested RJ?" I hadn't seen anything when I did my morning scroll and didn't get a response when I texted Brenda from the Meadowbrook PD for any updates. But perhaps Doc Kolner knows something I don't.

She shifts her weight from foot to foot and I hear Amy step back into the common room, waiting for an answer.

"Let's leave that up to the cops, shall we? In the meantime, get dressed in your uniforms. Bus is leaving in ten."

Doc leaves to go knock on the next door, and I can't help but let out a groan.

"What? Too cool to be seen wearing Meadowbrook maroon?" Amy asks behind me, sarcasm dripping from her voice.

I don't deign to give Amy a response and now it's my turn to slam my door behind me as I get dressed. But as I'm pulling on my white polo shirt, tucking it into my skirt, I realize that going into town might give me more than an opportunity to get a perfectly made cappuccino from Rex. It might also give me a chance to snoop around for information about RJ and the case.

Our yellow school bus pulls into the public parking lot behind the library and everyone files out onto the sweet little Main Street. It's quiet today since it's a Monday, but the folks that are out stop to stare at the dozens of kids wearing matching outfits, spreading themselves out around the sidewalk. A few townspeople whisper to one another behind cupped hands.

I take off from the group, shouldering my backpack as I walk the two blocks to Rex Taylor's, smiling as I catch sight of the empty window seat covered in plaid pillows. The chime on the door rings when I push through to find the place nearly empty, save for two guys talking close together in the corner. They seem older, maybe in their thirties, but don't look up when I come in. No one else is behind the coffee bar except Rex, not even Olly or Joseph.

"Hey, Rex." He looks up but doesn't smile, motioning toward the pastry shelf. "Just you today?"

"Mm-hmm," he says. "Gave the boys off amid . . . everything. Want your usual?"

"That'd be great." Rex nods and moves behind the espresso machine. "You okay?" I ask.

After he locks the coffee in place, he grabs me a lemon poppy slice, setting it on a small plate. "I can't believe everything going on. Can't wrap my mind around it."

I shake my head. "Pretty wild. But at least we're starting to get some answers. Did you hear about the cook?"

Rex presses his lips together. "I don't believe anything they say about RJ."

I look up, surprised. "Do you know him?"

"*Know* him? We live two doors down from him. He's been coming over for dinner every week since his wife died a few years ago. She and Mildred were like sisters." His eyes grow glassy. "There's no way in hell Roger Jack Gilman did this. No way in hell." He clenches his fist, which is sitting on the counter in front of me.

"I guess some people lead double lives."

Rex shakes his head vehemently. "Not this time. He was at my house for dinner *that night*. Fell asleep right there on the couch after we fed him lasagna. He always does that, passes out after a big meal."

"He was at your place all night?"

"Well, he sure as hell was there in the morning when I woke up."

I stand up straighter, my shoulders dropping down my back. "So, he has an alibi. The police will probably release him soon, then." Though I don't say what else I'm thinking—that if RJ is innocent, someone else is still guilty.

Rex shakes his head. "I was at the station for hours yesterday telling them all this. They just kept saying that he could have slipped in and out when we were asleep, orchestrated the whole thing to make it seem like he was with us the whole time." He swipes the back of his hand across his face, leaving a wet, teary trail behind. "Tried to make it seem like we helped him or something, like we were accomplices."

"That's awful." I break off a piece of the lemon poppy loaf, feeling it crumble in my fingers. "I read his car was near campus all night."

Rex sighs. "He'd had a few drinks after dinner service with the other cooks, he said. Rode his bike to us and said he'd get his car in the morning. It's a goddamn witch hunt." He rubs his fingers over his temple.

"Oh, Rex." Part of me wants to believe everything he's saying, but maybe the cops are right. Rex didn't say anything about the fact that someone matching his physical description was seen leaving campus in the middle of the night, or the fact that RJ has access to most buildings on campus. "I'm so sorry."

He sniffles and tilts his chin up. "Guess I'll just have to pray that they catch whoever *really* did this."

"You know . . ." I pause, trying to figure out the best way to say what I'm thinking. "If you ever feel like you want to share this story widely in order to help RJ, I'm always here as a reporter. Of course, I'd never say anything otherwise. I just want you to know, I'm here."

Rex seems to consider this as he hands me my cappuccino. "I'll think about it, kiddo."

I nod and slide a five into the tip jar before settling into a table near the other two guys, who still don't seem to have noticed me.

Right as I set my plate on the table, a clanging of silverware rings out from the people next to me. A mug spills and a puddle of milky coffee starts pooling on the floor around my shoes.

"Oh crap," the first guy says. He's white with a dark beard, little flecks of croissants caught in his facial hair.

The other man, Black with tortoise-rimmed glasses, leans over and starts mopping up the spill. "You're jumpy as shit, Julian." He turns to me. "Sorry about that."

"It's fine." I press a napkin to my sneakers. "Everyone around here is a little anxious."

The second man buses their dirty dishes, but the first is staring at me, his eyes on the Meadowbrook Academy patch sewn onto my blazer.

"I'm a senior there," I say, pointing to my chest.

"Uh-huh," apparently-Julian says. I look at him closer to see his hands are twitching. He looks off to the other man, makes a signal with two fingers, and then starts to pack up a few notebooks, stuffing them into a worn backpack. He's wearing leather Chelsea boots and a flannel button-down even though it's still warm outside. With the beard, he looks like an artisanal cheesemonger or a woodworker, one of those guys who probably moved up a few years ago from the city.

"You don't have to go," I say, suddenly uncomfortable.

But this Julian person doesn't say anything, only zips up his bag and heads for the door, following the other guy outside onto the street and in the other direction.

I sit for a second, dumbfounded by the interaction, but when I look back over at his table, I see there's a small photo stuck under the napkin holder, like it had been left by accident. I reach over and retrieve it, pulling it out from the metal. I turn it over and have to blink twice before I register whose faces are staring back at me.

Right there, I see Julian, that man who was sitting here, standing in front of a hydrangea bush and a home clad in weathered gray shingles. He's wearing a chambray button-down and khakis, looking more Kennedy than Brooklyn. But he's not alone. Standing next to him, just under the crook of his arm, is Sarah Oliver.

Amy

The last time I came to town on a trip like this, Sarah and I headed straight to the diner, our arms linked as we grabbed one of the booths in the corner, Hillary, Kayla, Olivia, and Iris crowding in around us. The boys took the one behind us and we spent a few hours swapping seats, nibbling on fried zucchini sticks, and drinking so much Diet Coke that my hands shook from all the caffeine.

At one point, Sarah was perched on Ryan's lap, his hands wrapped around her waist, hugging her to him so tight she had to stretch to reach me across the table. She grabbed my face in her hands and pressed my cheeks together. "Do it, do it!" she shrieked.

"Chubby bunnies," I said, the words sounding like gibberish as they came out through my squished mouth. We both erupted in laughter, a nonsensical joke formed in the depths of freshman winter that no one else found funny.

Yet, Sarah laughed so hard soda came out of her nose onto Ryan's grilled cheese in front of her, which only caused her to laugh even harder.

I left soon after that to see Joseph at Rex Taylor's, where he fed me a panzanella salad right there at the counter. Each bite felt like a gift, perfectly assembled to my preferences, swapping basil for mint and tomato for peach. Olly waved at us from behind the counter, not saying hello before he darted out the back, hanging his apron up on a peg in the hallway.

"You didn't fill up at the diner?" Joseph had asked. There was a hint of disdain in his voice. He was critical of the diner, where he had worked for a few years before quitting when they wouldn't let him cook off-menu or try anything new. At Rex's, he could make whatever he wanted.

"Never." I ate the whole plate, pausing only to make yummy noises and plant small kisses on his lips, wondering if he could taste the mustard vinaigrette he had so lovingly whisked.

When it was time to go, I noticed Liz hunched over a table in the corner, with a stack of magazines in front of her. She didn't even look up as I left. On Main Street, I tried to find Sarah but couldn't. She had taken the earlier bus home without letting me know. I should have understood that for what it was: a warning.

Now, I press the heels of my palms to my eyes, wishing she were here now, willing to give *anything* to be sitting across from her at any table in the world. Instead, I'm sitting on a bench outside the deserted bait and tackle shop at the very edge of town, only because I know no one else in their right mind would ever come here.

I reach into my backpack and pull out my phone to see if Joseph has responded to my texts about coming into town, but there's nothing there. With a pit in my stomach, I reach farther into my bag to find the real reason why I came to this spot: Sarah's notebook.

It felt like a betrayal to go through it on campus, in Holbrook. Like she might come through the walls and rip it from my hands. It was a strange thought, though. She was never protective over her belongings. By October of every year, our closets would become so intertwined I would forget which sweaters were mine and which jeans were hers. We dumped our makeup into one big bin, our books moving from her nightstand to my shelf, our soccer uniforms only identifiable by our numbers Coach insisted we keep separate. Fifteen for her, twelve for me.

I clutch the notebook in my hands so tightly I think I might rip it apart. Sarah never kept a journal. Not that I know of. So, it's probably just a random scratch pad, something she used to write down assignments or keep track of our schedule. And yet, it's all I have left of her, at least right now.

I crack open the book, hearing the spine give way, the pages soft and worn under my fingers. On the first page she'd written her name followed by *junior year.*

I flip and find dates written at the top of each page, peppered with little notes to herself, scribbled in the top right corners: *game v. Hotchkiss, AP calc, dorm clean duty.*

On each page, there are notes that look like she took them in class, but they're all for different subjects. I turn each page and see lessons for math, history, English, Spanish. Nothing cohesive. Each page is formatted the same, the subject written at the top of the page, followed by a bulleted list of notes, like she'd rewritten dozens of lectures over and over, as if writing them down might emboss them on her brain. I frown and grip the edges of the notebook as I realize it's another place she kept assignments. It means nothing, reveals nothing.

I keep flipping until I'm in the end of the notebook, on a page dated to May of last year. But on the page isn't only Sarah's handwriting. Someone else had written there, too, her loopy letters side by side with small, scrunched ones.

You left this behind today, so I wanted to leave you a note to say how AMAZING you are. Can't wait for this summer. J.

I look up, my head spinning around me. Who the hell is J?

By the time I get back to the pickup spot to meet the rest of the group, I'm still in a slight daze, reciting that note over and over in my head. I follow everyone else onto the bus, the Moleskine safely inside my backpack. By now I've memorized the message and the only conclusion I can come up with is that Sarah had hooked up with someone named J. Someone she saw back in May, when the school year was still going on. Someone who called her *amazing* and had plans to see her over the summer, even though Sarah spent most of that time on Cape Cod at her family's compound.

I sink into a seat in the back of the bus and grip my knees. There are loads of people in our class whose names start with J, people like the lacrosse midfielder Jordan Kenley or the saxophonist Jessica Richards. But in what world would Sarah cheat on Ryan so blatantly, so obviously? A sickening thought flashes through my mind—*Joseph*—but I quickly discard it. An impossible idea.

I close my eyes and try to picture his handwriting, but my mind is blank. He's never written me a card, never scrawled something on a piece of paper and slipped it in my pocket. All of his recipes are typed and printed onto index cards, kept in an old Rolodex.

There's no way J is Joseph. They barely knew each other.

Someone sits down next to me and I wince, pulling my bag

up onto my lap. But when I swivel my head to see who it is, my stomach spasms.

"Seriously?" I ask Liz. "There are a million other seats."

"Yeah, well, tough titties." Liz buckles her seatbelt and turns to me. "I have to ask you something."

"What?"

"Did Sarah know anyone named Julian? Tall older guy? Lives in town?"

"What the hell are you talking about? No." I rest my forehead against the window, but she doesn't let up.

"Well, the weirdest thing just happened. This guy named Julian was in Rex Taylor's and he seemed all freaked out when he saw my Meadowbrook uniform, and then he left *this* behind."

Curiosity gets the best of me and I slowly turn my head to see what she's pulling out of her pocket. When I register the photo in her hand, I yank it away.

"Hey," she says.

But I hold it close, not believing what I'm seeing.

"Do you know this guy?"

I blink, wondering if I keep staring at it, will he turn into Ryan or Peter or Jordan goddamn Kenley, someone I *do* recognize, someone I know? I flip the image over and see in the corner, there are a few numbers scrawled, 7/31, a date. July 31. I rack my brain, trying to remember what was going on around that time. I was stuck at home in Palo Alto. I'm sure of it because at one point in June, Sarah had suggested I come visit her in Hyannis. We looked at our calendars and found the only time that worked for both of us was the last week of July. We set the date, planned my flights, and everything.

But then she called me the week before telling me she needed to cancel, that her family was going to a friend's house in Nantucket and she couldn't get out of it. "Next summer," she said over the phone when she broke the news. "Promise."

I was disappointed but understood. I had no reason to suspect she was lying, and instead I spent that week lazing by the pool, learning every lyric to Liz Phair's *Exile in Guyville*, and FaceTiming with Joseph, who was working double shifts at Rex Taylor's, perfecting a corn chowder recipe.

Sarah never brought up the trip that could have been, and neither did I.

Liz taps the photo with one finger. "Guessing that's a no."

I peer at the image, trying to place his face, trying to recognize anything. Then I see the hydrangeas, the weathered house. Somewhere in New England. Cape Cod. Nantucket. "He's probably a family friend or something." But as I say the words, I'm not sure I believe them.

"I dunno," Liz says beside me. "He was so strange at Rex's. Basically bolted out of there. Don't you think he would have said he knew her? Asked me about her? He seemed scared."

I flick my eyes up to Liz. "Scared?"

She nods. "The weirdest thing."

"What did you say his name was?"

"The guy he was with called him Julian."

My stomach sinks and I reach into my backpack, pulling out Sarah's notebook. I flip to the last page, where the note is still there, written in thin ink. I read it again.

You left this behind today, so I wanted to leave you a note to say how AMAZING you are. Can't wait for this summer. J.

Whoever wrote this in June knew they'd spend time together on the Cape. They knew they'd see her this summer. And, of course, their name starts with a J. Julian.

A flutter of relief fills my chest. *Not Joseph.*

"What?" Liz asks. "You look like you're going to puke." She leans over my shoulder to look at the notebook and I'm too slow to shield it from her eyes. Liz gasps beside me and I know she's seen it.

"Holy shit," she says. "This guy Julian totally wrote that. What if he killed her, too?"

"This doesn't have to mean anything." Though I'm not sure I believe my own words. "They have RJ in custody. They think he did it."

Liz shakes her head. "Rex said RJ was at his house *all* night. They haven't even arrested him yet. What if . . ."

I don't want to hear her say the rest of the words, not as we're pulling back into the Meadowbrook Academy gates. Because what she's going to say—*What if they're wrong? What if the killer is still out there?*—could mean that this nightmare isn't over. It's only just beginning.

Liz

"What the hell do you think you're doing?" Amy stands over me in our dorm room as I pull out my laptop, loading up a web browser. The town of Meadowbrook only has a few thousand people in it, and Julian isn't as common a name as something like John. Chances are, I'll be able to find him pretty easily.

"I'm looking for this guy. Obviously."

I turn back to the screen and start with all the most popular social media sites, typing in "Julian + Meadowbrook, CT."

Amy slams my computer shut.

"Hey," I say, suddenly angry. I stand up to face her. We're about the same height and I look right into her eyes, so hard she steps back. "Are you scared of finding out that your best friend was keeping secrets? Because she one hundred percent was."

It was obvious from the way she was looking at that photo, at that note in Sarah's Moleskine, that she had no idea who that guy was or why someone might have that book in the first place, might spend time with Sarah during the summer at all.

"People *lie*. It's what they do. Sorry your life has been so perfect up until now that you didn't realize that." I drop back down to the couch and reopen my computer, but Amy shuts the top again.

"You don't get to talk to me like that."

"Why? Because my daddy's not a gazillionaire? Joke's on you because I haven't seen my dad in more than a decade."

Amy's mouth drops open just a bit, but then she snaps it closed. "I love how you're making this all about *you*. You have no idea what I've been through."

I let out a laugh. "All I know is that you're trying to pretend that you two had this picture-perfect best friendship. But I think you're forgetting that someone else was killed, too. Don't you think Ryan deserves justice as well? Don't you think if we have any leads on who could have done this that it's our duty to actually follow up on them?"

"They have RJ." Amy crosses her arms. "Besides, I'm pretty sure that's what the police are for."

I shake my head and reopen the laptop again. "Yeah, well, look what a crack job they've done so far. Rex Taylor said RJ was at his house all night."

"You don't know that's true."

I look up at Amy. "I believe Rex."

She's quiet and doesn't make a move for my laptop, so I start searching again, this time in various databases. A few dozen pages appear, and I scroll down the first one fast, stopping to take note of a few obituaries for a man who owned a cattle farm nearby but died in the nineties. But then something catches my attention: a post on Down the Road, one of those neighborhood watch websites, where folks can post freely about anything and everything having to do with their hometown. I frequently visited the page on Meadowbrook last year when I was reporting on how neighbors were furious that the school had planned to break ground on a new row of faculty housing units, which would cause a whole bunch of noise pollution for the neighbors.

Amy perches on the couch next to me. I can feel her gaze on my screen and I angle it toward her but only slightly since I'm still pissed.

The snippet on the search engine just says, "Julian was incredibly helpful . . ." and I click to find a notice from a woman named Melinda. I zoom in on her photo and see a middle-aged white woman who looks like she could be just about anyone. She has written a short notice, one that reads, in full:

> I never do this, but I'm here to recommend a tutor in
> the area, Julian Polk. He teaches at the county community
> college but is working with local high school students
> to help in areas like English and history. I hired him after my
> son almost flunked out of US history (come on, Conrad!).
> Julian was incredibly helpful and by the end of the semester,
> Connie was at the top of his class. If your teens are
> struggling, hire Julian!!! Pricey, but worth it to give your
> kids a leg up, especially when they're competing with those
> Meadowbrook Academy students for spots in college.
> Yeesh.

She signed off with Julian Polk's phone number and a few more lines ranting about how this summer's tomato season was a wash thanks to root rot.

There's a fizzy feeling in my stomach, one that only appears when I know I'm getting close on a story, racing to the finish line. I type "Julian Polk + Mountain Creek County Community College" into the search engine and it only takes a second before I'm redirected to a faculty page bearing the name Julian Polk as well as the headshot for the very same man I saw at Rex Taylor's, the same guy in the photo with Sarah.

Amy lets out a grunt beside me.

"What?" I ask.

"He looks old," she says quietly, pointing to his undergrad credentials from Princeton.

I do some quick math. "He's twenty-eight." My stomach flips and I know that Amy's thinking the worst, because I am, too.

I keep reading, seeing that his course load includes a bunch of survey classes like American history of the Revolutionary War and Civil War to Reconstruction, as well as a seminar in pre–Revolutionary War America. The same phone number that was listed on Down the Road is here, right under his photo, as is a college email address.

"Welp," I say. "It's pretty obvious what's going on."

Amy turns to me, one eyebrow arched high on her head.

"He was tutoring Sarah. Probably in town or something. And it seems like they got pretty close and . . ."

"No way." Amy's shaking her head. "Sarah didn't have a tutor."

"Okay, well, she knew this man. Why else?" I leave out the obvious explanation: *she was seeing him.*

"Sarah was valedictorian without even trying. Besides, I'd *know* if she had a tutor."

Now it's my turn to raise an eyebrow at Amy. "I think we already established she was lying to you."

Amy doesn't say anything, only frowns. But I have a plan. I need to hit up Julian and begin gathering proof. I need to report. I grab my phone and start typing in the number on the screen.

Hi Julian, I saw your information on Down the Road and am looking for a tutor. Do you have availability?

Amy reaches for my phone, but I yank it away. "You can't do that," she says.

"Why not?" Technically, I'm not lying. I *could* use a tutor, but more likely in a subject like music theory or physics than something like English or history.

"Because . . ."

"Because you're scared of knowing the truth about what Sarah was hiding from you? What if her secrets got Ryan killed, too?"

The V in Amy's brow deepens. "You didn't know her," she says, gritting her teeth.

"Yeah, well, maybe you didn't either."

Amy stands, her fingers tense, and for a second, I think she's going to reel back her hand and smack me across the face. But she doesn't. She just walks right on out the door, leaving me alone in our room.

I read over the text, knowing it's wrong. Knowing it is a *lie*. But it's a lie in search of the truth, one I know I would never get from him if I came out and told him I was a reporter. Maybe sometimes it's okay to lie in order to get at the greater truth. I inhale and close my eyes. I do it. I hit send.

I set my phone down on the table but keep watching it like it's about to jump up and come alive. It only takes a minute before he responds.

I have some openings for new pupils between 1 and 3 p.m. tomorrow. I do sessions at the Meadowbrook Public Library if you want to meet there?

We go back and forth a little, firming up the plan and discussing his rate before he signs off with a message that causes my shoulders to tense: Looking forward to meeting.

If my hunch is right, maybe, just maybe, RJ is innocent after all.

Amy

Campus is nearly empty since half the class is now in town, meaning I pass no one as I follow the dirt trails along the outer skirts of campus over to the tennis courts, past the academic buildings, the locker rooms, the auditorium.

It's one of those perfect September days, when the air is crisp but the sun is high and bright, a reminder that it's still technically summer, and all I can think is how furious I am that the weather is so nice when everything else around me is awful.

I pick up my pace, clutching Sarah's notebook in my hand. She lied to me about *so* many things. About whoever this Julian person is, about that week on the Cape . . .

A familiar feeling of apprehension sinks into my stomach. After the whole incident with the paparazzi back when Mom left, Dad began to get paranoid. He installed dozens of security cameras around the house, put tracking devices on all his cars and my laptop, in my backpack. Our conversations had grown stilted and practical and he spoke to me at length about how to keep myself safe, how to make sure *no* one would ever take advantage of me.

That was right around the time when I stopped trusting my friends at Palo Alto Prep, the ones who spoke behind cupped hands about my mother, their whispers traveling through the hallways, making their way to me. I had never had a real *best* friend up until that point, but I moved seamlessly between groups, fitting in with the soccer players, the theater kids, the gifted students. It was easy to belong when you were just like everyone else, when your dad was a tech star just like their parents, when your houses looked the same, when there were dozens of other Jewish kids who all stayed home on the High Holy Days, who ate their sandwiches on matzah instead of bread during Passover. When there was nothing to distinguish you from the others.

But when Mom left, when the cameras came out, it became harder to blend in. I stopped being invited to sleepovers and hiking trips. I was left out of group texts, bat mitzvah invite lists, and weekends in Lake Tahoe.

When I confided in Dad one night in eighth grade, desperate for answers as to *why* this was happening and how to deal with the loneliness, Dad looked up from his laptop at our black granite kitchen table. His fingers never left the keyboard.

"How about you look at boarding school for next fall? You might like my alma mater."

His words felt like a blast of hope, a preordained prophecy revealing itself to me. I didn't hesitate. I applied the next week, was accepted soon after, and within months I was deposited in New England, shocked that a girl like Sarah Oliver liked me enough to choose me over Kayla as a soccer drill partner, that when I told her about my mom—a test to see if she would share that information, if she would discard me like the girls back home—she kept it between us without judgment or hesitation. She earned my trust.

But now . . . now all of it feels like a sick joke.

I stop when I reach the tennis courts, the ones on the far side of campus where just beyond the fence lie the woods that lead down to the boathouse. The pond is visible in the distance and I can hear cars driving past just beyond the wooded gate.

There's no one around, no one in sight, so I plop down on one of the benches facing the water.

But I'm not alone for long. There's a rustling in the trees and my stomach lurches. "Hello?" I ask. No one responds. "Hello?" I ask again, feeling foolish. Maybe it's a rabbit or a squirrel.

But then, there's more noise, the cracking of branches and the crunching of leaves and all of a sudden, someone tumbles out of the brush.

I let out a shriek and jump to my feet, but when I see who's there, I hinge forward. "Joseph?"

He rolls over and holds his side with his hands, wincing in pain. Little twigs are stuck in his hair, which is now mussed and peppered with dirt. "Shit," he says, pushing himself to stand gingerly.

"What are you doing here?"

He runs a hand through his hair and looks around, his eyes darting between the trees and up to the main buildings. "I thought I dropped something the other night. I came to see if it was here."

"What did you drop?"

Joseph doesn't look right at me.

"Joseph, what? You're freaking me out."

He takes a step closer to me and lowers his voice. "The night that Sarah and Ryan . . ." His Adam's apple bobs up and down as he swallows. "One of my knives is missing. The one I gave you last week."

The paring knife I had left on our coffee table in Getty. I hadn't thought about it since the morning I found Sarah and Ryan. I had borrowed it from Joseph earlier in the day to slice peaches at soccer practice. He handed it over from his kit, the one he brings to and from Rex's every day. I took it home with me by accident, leaving it on our coffee table to return.

I shake my head. "You must have grabbed it that night on your way out. Dropped it or something."

Joseph shakes his head. "I went out the window, remember? Didn't go back through the common space."

"You didn't leave it at Rex's?"

He sucks his bottom lip into his mouth and for the first time I see real fear in his eyes, the kind of panic that only comes with knowing that something has gone horribly wrong and not knowing how to fix it.

"I don't have it." His words are hard and definitive, not up for debate.

"Do you think . . ." I start, but Joseph shakes his head, not letting me finish.

"Don't say it."

His eyes find mine, dark and frightened, and I don't finish my sentence even though I know we're both asking ourselves if the killer—RJ or Julian or someone else entirely—used that knife to kill Sarah and Ryan.

Liz

"This is so ridiculous." I'm walking down the stairs of Holbrook House with Rachel, the sports editor, carrying one of the pillows from my bed, wearing a matching set of Meadowbrook pajamas, just like every other person in my dorm.

"I guess they're trying to make us feel normal," she says, shrugging as we follow the rest of the group down the stairs, toward the door that leads to the tunnels below the dormitory, the maze of passageways that will put us in the auditorium.

"Throwing us a movie night is not going to make everyone forget what happened. Besides, I just posted a piece on how local businesses are reacting to the influx of reporters in town. I should be tracking responses to it right now in the office." I don't tell her that I can't stop thinking about how Egan put a stop to Ryan's cheating allegations before that investigation even started—what else the administration might be covering up.

Rachel sighs. "Can you try to let us forget about the murders for a few hours?" She shuffles ahead and my cheeks burn.

I launch up on my tiptoes to find Amy, but I haven't seen her since she stormed out of the dorm earlier this afternoon. The chatter gets lower as we descend through the tunnels, lit only by single light bulbs overhead.

We're not allowed down here by ourselves, but Doc Kolner leads the way, walking fast in front of the group until she reaches a big red door marked THEATER.

"Right this way, girls," she calls in a singsong voice. We walk through and end up inside the lobby of the auditorium, where the rest of our class has gathered, everyone wearing their pajamas, holding pillows, blankets, and bags full of candy.

Usually, movie nights are scheduled on the class calendar well in advance, giving everyone enough time to decide who they're going to sit with and where, who they might try to steal some alone time with under the cover of darkness. But tonight's was thrown together in an hour, a signal to relax, finally.

There's a heightened energy in the air as everyone files into the theater, filling the velvet seats, the same ones where Egan held the assembly only a few days ago. All around me, people are buzzing about RJ, hungry for morsels of information even as the lights dim in the theater.

"Hey, Liz." I spin around to see Owen, the captain of the baseball team, leaning down in the seat behind me. "Have you heard anything else about what's going on?"

He's sitting with a bunch of other baseball players, guys who are looking at me with intense, curious gazes, eager and hopeful that I know something they don't.

I shake my head. "Nothing yet."

"Damn." Owen leans back in his chair, away from me.

But then my phone buzzes with a push notification, and around me I hear other people's phones going off, too. When I look at my screen, I see a news alert: "No Arrest in Meadowbrook Murders after School Chef Produces Airtight Alibi."

My heart starts pounding and I tap the article so it takes up my screen. There, right at the top, is a photo of RJ walking away from the station. Rex Taylor stands behind him with one hand on his back.

Roger Jack ("RJ") Gilman was released from police custody after eighteen hours of questioning regarding the double homicide that took place at Meadowbrook Academy, the Meadowbrook PD said this evening. Gilman, who has been the head chef at the boarding school for the last twenty years, was able to produce an alibi that placed him nowhere near the school at the time of the murders, despite video footage that showed an unidentified person leaving the premises through a service entrance.

Photographic and video evidence taken from local security cameras in the neighborhood prove he was at the home of local business owner Rex Taylor, a friend and neighbor.

"RJ spent the night at my house after dinner and a few too many glasses of wine. We stayed up late playing dominoes, as we've done for the past decade, before he fell asleep on the couch."

According to police, another neighbor's security camera picked up footage of Gilman entering Taylor's home at 7:00 p.m. on Tuesday night and didn't capture anyone leaving until twelve hours later, when Gilman was seen exiting the home, hopping on his bike, and taking off in the direction of his own home two houses down.

"Gilman has officially been cleared of all wrongdoing," said police chief Fitzpatrick. "We appreciate his cooperation."

In regard to the double homicide that has rocked this small town, he said, "We are still investigating all leads, evidence, and possibilities as to who killed Ryan Pelham and Sarah Oliver. This is the most brutal slaying in the history of our community and we will not stop until the perpetrator is behind bars."

Everyone around me begins talking, drowning out the showing of *The Princess Bride* on the screen in front of us.

"What the fuck?" Owen says behind me.

"I knew he was innocent," someone else says.

"They're never going to find who did this." Iris sniffles in the row below me, leaning her head on Olivia's shoulder next to her.

"We should be happy RJ didn't do it," Hillary says.

But then Kayla clucks her tongue. "Only, this means someone else did."

I follow her gaze as she looks down to the other side of the auditorium, where I finally spot Amy, sitting alone with her soccer sweatshirt pulled up over her head, her number stitched into the arm. Her feet are pressed up against the seat in front of her and she's shielding her face from the rest of the group.

I pull my backpack up and sling it over my shoulder, heading toward the aisle.

"Ouch!" someone says as I step on their foot, but I don't slow down until I reach the end of my row. I make my way to Amy, sliding into the seat next to hers.

She doesn't look up, but I reach for my phone and pull up my text messages with Julian, sliding it over to her.

"I'm going to see him tomorrow," I say. "You can come if you want."

Amy looks up then, her eyes rimmed with red as her bottom lip shakes. She grabs the phone and reads the messages.

"He could have the answers. He could have done this."

Amy swallows, her neck wobbling as she hands me back my phone. "Okay," she says. "I'll go."

THE DAY
OF THE ARREST

Amy

"This is never going to work." Liz is staring at me with her backpack slung over one shoulder, a bike lying on the ground in front of her.

"It is if you hurry up," I say, frustrated as I pick up my own bike by the handlebars and start walking it over to the dirt road near the pond. "Besides, this was your idea anyway."

"Which you *agreed* to." She grunts but then wheels over to me. We both stand there staring at the line that divides Meadowbrook Academy from the rest of town. After yesterday's revelation that RJ was innocent and the killer is still out there, Egan shut down campus again, forcing everyone to stay put until further notice. No one's allowed into town or anywhere outside bounds, and we're certainly not supposed to go off and actively *look* for whoever did this.

I should have said no, let Liz hang herself. But after finding out that Joseph's knife is missing, everything in me rejected the idea of sitting back and doing nothing. Knowing that Sarah kept something from me . . . it's only making me want to find out the truth, even if it gets me into trouble. When Liz suggested we take the bikes through this exit, where there's just a narrow pathway and certainly no cameras, it seemed like the only option.

"Tell me the plan again," I say.

Liz blows a stray piece of hair off her face. "I put the 'Do Not Disturb' sign on our door and sent an email to Doc saying we were both feeling fluish. She already responded, saying she'd check in after lunch. That gives us three hours to get this done."

"And here I thought you were obsessed with telling the truth."

Liz bristles. "That's what we're doing. Isn't it?"

I don't have a response and I don't know what else to do so I follow Liz's lead and hop on the seat, pedaling down to the road where the turnoff begins. I hold my breath, but no one stops us. No alarms go off. And so, we ride into town, Sarah's notebook bumping against my back the whole way there.

We arrive at the library ten minutes early and Liz pulls out her Meadowbrook Academy ID, which gives us access to a variety of public services around town, not that anyone takes advantage of things like the Meadowbrook Compost Collective or the renowned goat therapy farm.

I haven't ever been here before, never needed to, since the library on campus is a three-story brick building the size of a full city block. It was refurbished a few years before I got there and is fully state of the art with a high-tech movie screening room, a temperature-controlled rare books room, and approximately fifty times more volumes than there are people in all of Meadowbrook.

Walking in there always gives me a reverence that forces my heart into my throat. The building is so emblematic of everything I associate with the East Coast—old and storied, with hundreds of years of history. So different from the places I was familiar with back home, big airy boxes built in recent years, chrome and shiny, crafted with the latest technology for those who create it. That was what amazed me about Meadowbrook, how devoted everyone seemed to be about upholding the legacy of the school, though after three years I'm not quite sure what that actually means.

Liz and I are both quiet as we walk through the first floor, cozy and full of disorganized stacks of books. I look up to find big wood exposed beams supporting the vaulted ceiling, the second floor wrapping around the perimeter like an open loft, with a big old ceiling fan whirring around overhead.

The wide wood floors creak as we walk through the space. Julian said for us to meet him upstairs, but since we're early I want to take my time with the space, wondering what Sarah must have thought if she ever came here to see him. *Why* she came to see him.

It all seems so improbable, Sarah getting extra help. She was the one who helped *me* when I told her I was barely passing Spanish and that Señor Gilbert said I'd have to do an enormous extra credit assignment just to get an average grade. She had stayed up late with me that night, helping me with translations and reading comprehension I never thought I'd understand, guiding me to the answers gently, without judgment.

Most of the tables on the first floor are empty save for two retirees holed up in the spirituality section and what looks to be a few new parents gathering near the board books display with babies strapped to their chests. When we reach the far corner, Liz whispers to me. "Come on, let's go."

We come to the narrow staircase and when I look up, it seems dark, like there aren't many windows up there, like there's only one way out.

"It'll be all right."

"You don't know that," I say, an edge to my voice.

"Well, you don't know that it *won't*."

I groan as she starts to climb the stairs, my stomach dropping further and further with each step. When we reach the top, I peer around, seeing bookshelves jutting out into the middle of the floor, dark curtains obstructing the windows.

"There." She points over my shoulder to a round table in the corner where Julian is sitting, scrolling on his phone, an open notebook in front of him.

I press my hands to my sides, grip my skirt. "What's the plan, again?"

"Ask him how he knew Sarah."

"That's it? You don't have some script or a list of questions? Aren't you supposed to be a journalist?"

Liz purses her lips, defensive. "I want to feel him out first."

"Are we going to give him our real names?"

It's too late. Julian looks up, right at us, and waves in our direction.

"Come on." Liz pulls me by the elbow and drags me over to him. "Julian Polk?"

He stands and extends a hand, a warm smile spreading on his face. "Nice to meet you." He looks to me and knits his brow. "I didn't know there would be two of you. My rate is usually double when it's a twofer."

I open and close my mouth, then turn my gaze to Liz, hoping she realizes I need *her* to answer.

"Yes, hi. I'm Liz. This is Amy." Julian's gaze lingers on me as we both drop into the flimsy chairs, and I wonder if Liz shouldn't have used our real names. "I must have forgotten to tell you she was coming. I'm so flighty these days—"

I kick Liz under the table and she winces. "Sorry," she says. "I talk when I'm nervous."

"That's all right," Julian says, patting her hand, which fires off all the red flag synapses in my brain. "You girls look so familiar," he says, his gaze darting between us.

I never thought there was a possibility that Sarah showed him my photo, but maybe I was wrong, and, shit, there's a chance he recognizes Liz from Rex Taylor's. We were so foolish to think we could pull this off.

Liz shrugs. "It's a small town."

"Of course." Julian smiles and opens the notebook in front of him. "Should we begin by going over your summer assignments? Helping you prepare for the start of school next week? If you're in Meadowbrook High's junior English, you should have an American lit section, is that right?"

Neither one of us corrects him and before we can say anything else, Julian's launching into a lesson about how to construct a straw man essay. Liz starts nodding like she's paying attention, but I can't stop staring at his face—a strong jaw hidden by a neat beard and an angular nose, dark eyebrows, chapped lips despite it being just past summer. I wonder how Sarah knew this man, if she ever touched any of those features, here in the library or alone in the dark somewhere. I wish I knew what went through her mind when she invited him to Cape Cod, why she didn't tell me, if she thought I would judge.

There are so many things I wish I could say to her now, so many things to apologize for. I blink, realizing my eyes are wet, and I wipe the back of my hand across my face, hoping neither Liz nor Julian notice.

But suddenly he stops talking. "Do you girls want to take notes? I find it's helpful to write things down as we absorb them."

"Um, yes," Liz says. She reaches into her backpack and pulls out a notebook and pen, but all I have is Sarah's Moleskine and

I'm not about to present that. Liz realizes, and tears a few sheets from her spiral notebook, handing them to me with another pen. "Sorry," she mumbles, motioning for him to continue talking.

Julian begins again and we both start taking notes on this lesson about something we learned in Mr. Judd's freshman year English class, but suddenly he stops, and I can feel his eyes on us, searching.

When I look up, I see he's staring at my pen, bobbing up and down against the page. My stomach drops. It's a maroon-and-white Meadowbrook Academy pen, the kind that has our school insignia emblazoned on it. Anyone in town would know where it came from.

"Where did you girls say you went to school?" he asks.

"Um . . ." Liz stumbles, and I snap my mouth shut.

Julian's eyes search my face like they're putting together a puzzle and in an instant his complexion grows pale.

"You said your name was Amy?" he asks slowly.

I open my mouth, but nothing comes out, and that's all it takes for Julian to push his chair back, the legs squeaking against the floor.

"Wait," I say, standing. "I can explain."

"This was a mistake," he says, frantic, gathering his things as quickly as he can. But then he pauses, peering at Liz, leaning in as if seeing her for the first time. "You're the girl from the coffee shop." He doesn't wait a second longer, dashing down the steps of the library and toward the door. Liz jumps up from her seat, the chair falling back behind her, and she starts running through the stacks, following his footsteps.

There's nothing left for me to do but follow them out the front door of the library into the hot September afternoon. My heart beats fast and I surprise myself by how badly I want to catch this guy, how desperately I need answers. I stop and look around the street, trying to spot him, until finally I see him near the bike rack, trying frantically to twist a code into his lock. "There!" I call.

I make it to him just as he releases the wheel, and I clamp down on the handlebars so he can't take it anywhere.

"How do you know Sarah?" The words tumble out.

He looks at me, his eyes frantic and glossy, like he's about to cry, and his top lip trembles. "I—" he starts. But he can't finish and instead lets the bike go from his grasp and drops to the grassy knoll.

Liz finally catches up, her breathing heavy, and stops when she sees him on the ground, me standing at his bike.

"Who are you?" I demand. "What did you do to her? To Ryan?"

Julian shakes his head. "Nothing," he says through gulped gasps of air. "Nothing, I swear."

"Then why are you running?" Liz asks.

"She told me all about you, Amy," he says, his gaze meeting mine. "Amy Alterman." All the air rushes from my lungs, an indication that I should be worried, that if this man really did kill Sarah and Ryan, then maybe he might do something to *me*. To Liz. I step back, my hands out in front of me.

Liz must read my mind, because her voice pierces the air, nervous and warbling. "I could call the police."

His shoulders heave up toward his ears and he curls over. "Go ahead," he says, the words a hiss. "I've already been cleared."

"What?" My voice is shaky, a whisper.

Julian runs a hand through his hair, licks his lips. "Sarah didn't want anyone to know about us."

A pit forms in my stomach. That phrase—*about us*—as if he had convinced her to become a trope, a cliché. An old washed-up teacher who used her. An ache runs through me, a gaping wound only Sarah could heal. I wish I could hear the truth from *her*.

"She found me last year. One of those DNA tests."

Liz lets out a rush of air behind me. "You're related."

I snap back to that moment in our dorm last autumn when we swabbed our cheeks, hoping in vain to be sisters. We had brushed off the results, content to continue being two only children in a sea of massive families. To have something that kept us bonded, different from all the others.

"What, are you cousins or something?" I ask.

"We have the same dad," he says softly. "I had no idea until Sarah messaged me out of the blue last November, right around Thanksgiving. I was living up in Vermont with Gus and . . . she found me."

I glance at Liz and she's got a shocked look on her face, too.

He looks up at me. "My mom always told me she and my dad had an arrangement. The checks came every month, but his identity was a secret. She was his assistant when he and Sarah's mom were engaged. I guess . . ." He trails off. "My mom never wanted to confirm the details, but Sarah and I pieced it together. Mom never went back to work after I was born. Moved us up to Portland, Maine, to be near her family."

"You two are siblings," Liz says, blunt and a little dejected.

"Does Mrs. Oliver know?" I ask.

Julian wipes his wrist across his face and all of a sudden, he looks so young, like one of us even though he's a decade older. I peer at him, trying to find Sarah in his face. Her huge doe eyes, her pointed mouth. There's a faint trace of her, but only if I squint, make my vision go soft. I can imagine him with Sarah, their heads pressed close to one another, trying to figure each other out, find their similarities, their differences, all the things that had been missing in their lives from being only children. I know they did this, because she and I did it, too. I thought *I* was her sister.

Julian shakes his head. "Not yet."

"I don't understand." I press my hands to my temple. "How are you here? Why?"

"After she found me, I realized how much I missed out on, not having a sister, not having *her*. Gus's job is remote and I was looking for work, so I said screw it, let's try moving close to Sarah for a year. We came down, and I got an adjunct gig at the community college."

Liz steps closer to him, her eyes narrowed. "But you said you were cleared by the police? Why would they even suspect you?"

"When the news broke, I went straight to the cops. Told them everything, showed them all our correspondence." He shrugs. "I figured they'd find out at some point and I wanted them to hear it from me, not some email from her computer and then come track me down."

"You wanted to produce an alibi." My voice is flat, the truth washing over me.

"Gus and I were up in Vermont that night, visiting friends." Julian's eyes well up. "She was supposed to come over for dinner to celebrate the start of a new semester this week. Gus was going to make a tomato galette." His shoulders heave up close to his ears. "And then I got the news . . ."

Liz leans in. "So you weren't even in the state. You didn't try to hurt her or Ryan."

His face pales. "I tried to protect her."

"Protect her?"

He looks at me, a ghost, and shakes his head. "The Olivers are so . . . uptight, obsessed with her being perfect. Her grades, her boyfriend . . . it was too much pressure for one person. I wanted her to know that she was wonderful the way she is. Was."

Doubt creeps in. "Prove it," I say. "Who's to say you're not full of shit?"

He juts his chin out like he doesn't want to prove anything to two teenage girls, but then his shoulders go slack and he fumbles on the ground for his phone that flew out of his pocket. I watch him slide his thumb up and down the screen until he stops and turns it around to face us. An email from Sarah, dated last November, with the subject line: "Hello from a stranger (who may not be such a stranger after all)."

I skim the words fast enough to know it's the truth. Her formal writing, her perfect grammar. Even signing off with the phrase "Best, Sarah." She was professional and poised even when confronting a secret brother at age seventeen.

Julian turns the phone around again, his brow furrowed, and taps a few times until he flips it to us so we can see a photo on the screen. I peer at the image of him and Sarah, just like the one Liz found in the coffee shop. They're standing arm in arm in front of a weathered home, hydrangeas sneaking into the frame. He swipes and now another man—Gus, likely—has entered the photo with an arm around Julian, his head leaning toward the two of them.

"Is this on Cape Cod? The Oliver compound?"

Julian looks at the image, a small smile forming on his mouth. "Provincetown. Gus and I were there in July for a week and Sarah drove out to see us. She told her parents she was taking a biology seminar in Woods Hole so she could escape for the day." His eyes become glassy and he blinks a few times. "We took her to drag brunch and ate lobster rolls on the beach."

There's an unsettling feeling pooling in my stomach, a mixture of relief and frustration. The man in front of me isn't a killer. He didn't murder my best friend and her boyfriend. He only wanted to know her.

And that means that the person who took her from me, who murdered Ryan, is still out there and we're no closer to finding out. Eliminating a name off a suspect list means nothing. It doesn't help or make things right. It only leads to more questions, more confusion.

"Wow." Liz is quiet behind me, stunned for once.

"So, you're cleared," I say.

He nods, but then looks at me, his face searching. "You," he says. "They wanted more information about you."

Liz

Julian's words hang in the air and I turn my gaze to Amy. Her mouth falls open and her head jerks up.

Julian pushes himself to stand. "I have to go. I shouldn't be talking to you." His hands shake as he unlocks his bike, and neither Amy nor I make any move to stop him. Together we watch him ride away, the only sounds coming from the birds circling above.

I press my palm to my forehead, but when I lower my hand, I catch the time blinking back at me on my watch. "Shit," I say. "Lunch is about to end. We gotta go."

I reach for my bike, righting it and popping up the kickstand, but Amy stays put, a dazed expression on her face as she watches Julian ride off.

"Come on," I urge. "We *have* to go. We can debrief back on campus."

"Not if your debrief involves ways to turn this into a story."

I ignore her though I can't deny I had that thought. A secret sibling would make an unbeatable headline, a wrinkle in the case. But is it news or just plain gossip?

There's no time to dissect all this now. If we don't get back *fast*, we'll be caught. And being caught means major trouble for both of us.

Amy slides onto her seat and together we begin to move, pedaling furiously toward campus. I focus on the wind in my hair, Amy's deep breathing beside me, anything that blocks out the realization that if RJ didn't kill Sarah and Ryan and neither did Julian, then we're no closer to figuring out who is responsible, and that this mission into town could all have been for nothing.

We cut through a side street until the back entrance near the lake comes into view. I slow as we get closer. All we need to do is get two feet on campus and ditch the bikes. Then hightail it to Holbrook as quickly as we can. That's all we need to do.

The entrance looms, and I scan the grounds, searching for anyone who might see us. "Come on!" I call. We're so close to being officially on campus, to dashing through the open field near the pond and getting back to Holbrook. Then we'll be safe. I tear through the gate at the end of the driveway and hop off my bike, letting it fall to the ground. I turn around to see Amy pedaling slowly, tears shining against her face.

"Let's go, let's go, let's go," I mumble under my breath.

Finally, she pulls up, and as soon as she gets past the final gravel hump, she lilts to one side, falling off her bike and into the bushes.

"For fuck's sake." I rush over to her and reach for her elbow, jerking her to stand, but behind me I hear chattering, the unmistakable sound of voices coming from the pathways that lead back to the dormitories.

"Hurry." Amy stumbles and I spin both of us around. But when I see who those voices belong to, I stop short. Doc Kolner and Mrs. Herschel are walking toward us, their words growing louder.

There's no time to do anything except duck behind the brush

and clamp my hand over my mouth, motion for Amy to do the same.

"I'm beginning to worry," Doc Kolner says.

"It's too early to freak out." But Mrs. Herschel's wobbly voice betrays her suggestion. Fear cuts through the air.

"With the news . . . I don't want to think the worst."

I can't hear them anymore and raise my head to see them retreating in the direction of the main quad. "Come on," I whisper to Amy, who's still crouched down. "If we sneak around the back to the tunnels, we'll be fine."

Amy looks up, dazed. "What did she mean? 'The news.' What news?"

"I don't know—all of it, probably. Let's go."

Amy pushes herself to stand next to me, clumsy like her limbs are made of stone, and I grab her hand, pulling her with me to the back of the science hall, where an unmarked metal door will lead us through the tunnels back to Holbrook. I look around to see no one's there and fling it open, pulling Amy into the darkness with me.

"What the . . ." she murmurs as it slams shut behind us.

Light bulbs are positioned overhead every few feet and I make a break for it, running left at the fork. Back when I was a sophomore, I did a big story on the history of the passageways. We even had an AP art student draw a map of the intertwining system to be displayed next to the article. I thought that information was taking up useless space in my brain until now, but in this moment, where we come to a four-way cross, I'm grateful that I know exactly which way to go, which door will open up to the laundry room inside Holbrook.

I'm breathing hard, my lungs straining, and I can hear Amy panting behind me. When we get there, I throw my shoulder up against the door and push it open so we're inside the stairwell. It's full of hot air, and I look up to see a skylight pouring sun down into the shaft.

Only three flights of stairs to go, but I worry my lungs might give out. My legs, too.

Amy pushes me forward, her breath urgent in my ear, and I move up the stairs, taking them two at a time. She's right behind me and finally we get to the top. I'm about to burst through, but Amy stops me, reaching for my elbow.

"Hold on," she says. "Is anyone on the other side?"

"We don't have time."

"Someone might be interested in ratting us out."

Amy shoves me aside and presses her ear to the door. It's thick and metal; she won't hear a thing. But then she nods like the coast is clear and ekes it open ever so slightly.

She looks out and then motions for me to follow her, a hand behind her back, and so I do.

As we step into the dorm, the light from the hall so much brighter than it was in the dim stairwell, I hear the static of TV.

My heart rate slows. We made it.

Doc Kolner comes around the hall, her cheeks flushed from her own brisk walk. "There you are," she says. "I just knocked on your door. No answer."

"We were getting out for some air," I say. "Feeling much better now."

Amy nods. "Better."

Doc's gaze shifts from Amy to me and for a second, I think she might see right through us, our lies, but she tilts her head toward us once. "Good."

The TV from the lounge gets louder, impossible to ignore, the words *Meadowbrook* and *murders* floating through the air.

I sidestep past Doc Kolner and head into the room, now crowded with other girls from our dorm, huddled around the TV, blankets and pillows strewn about the couches, open cans of soda on the coffee table.

"Amy, wait—" Doc Kolner reaches for her, but it's too late. Amy is already in front of the screen and the other girls get quiet, no one looking at her, their eyes on the ground or the images in front of them.

It's all so confusing, but when I peer at the TV, I realize why. Joseph is right there in high-def, so realistic it feels like I could reach out and touch his arms, which are pinned behind his back, clasped together with silver handcuffs circled around his wrists.

A newscaster's voice comes through the speakers, clipped and precise. "Eighteen-year-old Joseph Stone was arrested this afternoon after Meadowbrook Police raided the home he shares with his mother, Pamela Jensen, a soccer coach at Meadowbrook Academy. Police say Stone is wanted for his involvement in the Meadowbrook murders and his arraignment will be held tomorrow. This story is still developing."

The room is quiet as the news cuts to commercial, a jingle for fast food too jolly in the background.

Amy's face goes white. Her gaze is far away, stunned, but then she blinks and, as if realizing where she is and who is around her, she turns on her heel and sprints out of the room.

"Amy!" I follow her, trying to catch up as she heads to our suite, throwing open the door. I'm quick behind her and manage to get inside before she slams it shut and falls to her knees. Her chest rises and falls faster than it should and her breathing grows frantic, out of rhythm.

I kneel down beside her and try to rest a hand on her back, but she pulls away. I search for something else to say, something comforting that carries the weight of what we learned, how her life has changed in only a few minutes.

"You didn't know." It's all I can muster, all I can find.

Amy jerks her head up, her face red and splotchy, saliva pooling at the corners of her mouth. "You don't understand. I was *with* Joseph that night."

Everything in my body freezes. "What?"

Her bottom lip trembles as her mouth drops open. "In our dorm room. Right next to Sarah and Ryan. He stayed here."

I fall back on my heels, trying to understand what she's saying. Her eyes grow big and everything clicks into place. Amy lied about what happened that night—about what happened after the party. And if Joseph was there, inside Getty, then not only is Joseph definitely guilty but Amy might have been an accomplice.

I inhale sharply as the truth settles in.

Amy Alterman just blew up the whole case.

Amy

I can't believe I told Liz. Of all people, I shared my biggest secret—the secret I swore I would never tell anyone—with the nosiest person in school, who just so happens to have a platform where she could do real, serious damage.

"You can't tell," I whisper, shaking my head. "Please, you can't write about this in the *Gazette*."

Liz backs away from me ever so slightly. There's fear in her eyes. Real fear.

"I had nothing to do with this. I didn't . . ."

"You've been lying to everyone. Obstructing the case."

"He's innocent." The words come out small and feeble and Liz's face contorts, her lip pulled up to her nose like she's smelled something funny.

I look at my phone, expecting a text from Joseph to appear, to say the whole press conference was a misunderstanding. But there's nothing there.

"What makes you so sure?" Liz keeps her voice measured.

"He would never."

"That's not going to hold up in court."

"Thanks. Helpful."

Doc Kolner's voice echoes in the hallway. "Afternoon snack

will be in the dorm lounge instead of the cafeteria. Self-service, girls."

Liz stands, but her legs shake as she makes her way to the door. "I'm going to eat," she says, looking at me expectantly.

"Liz," I start. "Please don't say anything. Don't write anything. Not yet."

She looks at me, her lips pressed together. "We'll talk about it later." She shuts the door behind her, leaving me finally, firmly alone.

I squeeze my eyes shut and hug my knees to my chest. I haven't dared go back to that night in my brain, not yet, but now . . . now I need to. I need to think, really think, and figure out if there is a chance that Joseph could have done what they say he did.

He met me down by the gated entrance, folding me into his arms as I cried, getting his Henley all wet.

But when I pulled away, I felt bold, like it didn't matter what came next, where we went, or what was said.

"Come on," I urged.

Campus was warm that night, the air still sweating like it was summer, and our hands were clammy as we clasped our fingers together, running through the trees until I got to the tunnel entrance at the science hall.

"What the hell is this?" Joseph asked as he pressed up against me from behind, sending tingles through my legs.

"They built the passageways a million years ago. Perfect for sneaking around."

Joseph exhaled, his breath tickling my ear as I opened the door. My want for him was pulsing, electric, and I thought about turning around and kissing him right there in the dirty, dusty hallway. But I wasn't about to waste time in a space that didn't deserve it, so I raced through the maze of tunnels, making a few wrong turns until finally I found the door that would lead us to Getty. Joseph was quick behind me, but as we climbed up the stairs, still hand in hand, Joseph paused.

"Isn't this risky?" Joseph asked. His hair was disheveled and his cheeks were flushed from the run. I laid my hand on his chest and pressed my lips to his, softly at first and then harder, hungry. He kissed me back, moving his hand inside my sweatshirt against the small of my back.

My stomach lurched and I pulled away. "The security cameras aren't up yet. The chaperones are barely on duty. It's our one shot before the semester starts."

I didn't know if any of that was true, but it was what we told ourselves that week, granting one another permission to be our wildest, freest selves. Perhaps it was a mistake. Perhaps it came with a price.

Joseph nodded and I pushed the door open, rushing down the hall to our room. Sarah's door was already closed, and I couldn't hear a thing. Part of me wanted her to barge into the common room and see me with Joseph, know that her words didn't stop me from seeking him out. I wanted to flaunt him in her face and say, *Look! Look what I've done!*

But when she didn't come out, I kept going, didn't let it sting me. I didn't bother with the lights, knowing my way to my room by feel. I led Joseph inside, closing the door behind me, and flipped on my bedside lamp.

I watched him look around the room, taking in my dirty soccer cleats in the corner, a drawing of our dog on the corkboard, a photo of Sarah and me on my desk.

His gaze lingered there. I remember because I moved my body in between him and the frame, propping myself up on the desk. I wrapped my arms around his middle and tilted my chin up to him, giving what I could of myself to him, and he took the opening, leaning forward until our lips met and our bodies found one another.

Under the covers of my tiny twin bed, it was hard to avoid him—his soft skin, the tickle of his underarm hair, the guttural noise that seemed to come all the way from his toes when I found the right place to touch. But I didn't want to avoid him. I wanted to devour him and have him erase everything that had come before.

"Amy," he whispered, running his fingers in my hair. "I can't believe I found you."

After, I watched him dress, pulling on his T-shirt and stepping into his chinos. He kept pausing to look at me, a small giggle emerging from his throat, and when he was ready, he leaned down and kissed me again, softly, his hair feather-light against my forehead.

"I'll see you soon," he said with his hand on the doorknob.

"Wait," I said. I rolled over and pushed open the window next to my bed. "Go out this way, just in case Doc Kolner is roaming around. There's a trellis you can climb down."

He peered out the window into darkness but followed my finger as I pointed out his route. Nothing stands behind Getty, just an iron fence that leads all the way back to the boathouse, where his car was parked. "Follow the fence and you'll be fine."

"Aye aye, captain."

I gave him a playful shove and watched as he shuffled out the window and disappeared into the night.

Sleep came easy, and I didn't wake up until morning.

I had told the cops the truth—I hadn't heard a thing. Not a scream nor a peep. Not the opening of a door. He couldn't have done it. I would have woken up. I *would* have.

But what if I'm wrong? What if I had given him an opening, shown him the way into our dorm? What if he came back after, when I was asleep, when his knife was still on the table?

The door to our suite slams shut and I jump up from my seat to see Liz barreling through. "Hey," she says.

"You scared the shit out of me."

"The school made a statement. I thought you'd want to see."

By the tone of her voice, I know it's not a good one. Liz clears her throat and begins to read.

"'We are grateful to the Meadowbrook Police Department for apprehending a suspect swiftly and for taking precautions for keeping our community safe. We hope this brings our students, faculty, administration, and families peace. Please respect our institution's privacy at this time.'"

She looks at me, with one eyebrow raised. "They're making it look like an open-and-shut case. You really think he's innocent?"

I blink a few times, staring at the floor. "I believe him." Of course I do. The alternative is impossible. Unbelievable.

"So, what are you going to do?"

I widen my eyes. "Does this mean you're not going to report on this?"

Liz shrugs, but I'm taking that to mean no, that she realizes this is my truth to share, mine to explain. A plan solidifies in my mind and suddenly I know what I need to do. I reach into my pocket and find the business card Detective Diaz gave me when we spoke for the first time. It's crisp, the edges still pointy and pristine, a reminder of how my world changed only a few days ago.

"Please tell me you're calling a lawyer," Liz says. "At least they could give me a statement to work with."

I think about it for a second, knowing the answer should obviously be yes, but there's no time. Innocent Joseph is sitting in a cell, and I'm out here. The one person who knows where he was, knows he couldn't have killed anyone. "Lisa Brock can't help us," I say. "I'm calling the cops."

Liz hesitates, but she doesn't fight me as I dial the detective. His voice is deep and serious when he picks up, and he doesn't sound surprised when I tell him I have more information to share.

"We'll send a car for you to come in," he says. "And we'll tell the administration you're on your way."

I nod, relief and nerves mixing together in my stomach. I'm going to get Joseph out.

Liz

Dusk has settled in by the time we get to the police station, which is totally different than it is on all those procedural shows. It's small and quaint, in a redbrick building just off Main Street. Out front, there's a mailbox and a Little Free Library packed with well-loved paperbacks and even a few hardcovers. At first glance it could be an old one-room schoolhouse or a daycare center. But when we step inside, I see linoleum tile and bright lights, an American flag hanging proudly on the wall. Detective Diaz stands near the reception area with his arms crossed over his puffed-out chest. He rocks on his heels as Amy walks toward him.

"Right this way, Miss Alterman," he says, pointing down the hall.

Amy throws me a look over her shoulder and I ask her once more, "Are you sure you don't want me to call a lawyer?"

Amy shakes her head and I bite my tongue, knowing it's the wrong call. I've read enough true crime stories and seen enough news to know you *always* call the lawyer, but before I can push it, she disappears into a conference room.

I sink down into an uncomfortable metal chair in the make-shift waiting room and shake my head. "Unbelievable," I mumble to myself. It doesn't take long for me to find Amy's lawyer, Lisa

Brock, online and only a few minutes later I'm patched through to her assistant.

"She's in questioning now," I whisper. "Can Lisa come?"

"Oh," the assistant says, surprised. "Um, it may take a couple hours?"

"As long as she gets here."

We both hang up and I try to push away my nerves as I scroll on my phone, looking for updates about Joseph and the murders. Part of me thinks that I should have stayed on campus and gone to the newspaper office, where I would have brainstormed ideas for my own story. But then Amy would have been all alone.

Over in my texts, there are a few unread messages from Mom, the most recent one consisting of all-caps emotions: SCHOOL SAYS THEY CAUGHT THE GUY WHO DID IT!!!!!! U OKAY???

I tap away. The last thing I want right now is to answer her. If she really knew me, really understood who her daughter was, she wouldn't have asked if I was okay. She would have read my stories and asked about those, wondered how I was handling the paper through all of this and what my next angle would be.

But, hell, she never cared about the truth. Maybe she thinks working at the *Gazette* is a silly little hobby I'll grow out of, like her stint in California growing weed.

I move to my email inbox, refreshing it to find a message from Egan with the subject line "Return to Normal." As if that could ever happen.

To our beloved Meadowbrook community . . .

I scan the screen, my eyes glazing over the platitudes about justice and unity, until I stop at one line. The rest of our Meadow-brook family will be joining us the day after tomorrow, and we will resume classes. It's high time we proceed with our school year as planned. Please know that you are safe here with us.

But what if we're not? What if Amy was right and Joseph is the wrong guy? She sounded so sure of herself, so sure that he could *never* hurt someone.

I throw one leg over the other and bounce my foot up and down. A crooked clock on the wall tells me Amy's been in there for twenty minutes. To my left, I can see the bullpen, where a few officers are still stationed. No doubt the rest of them left on a high after making such a huge high-profile arrest and, based on the grease-stained pizza boxes sitting near the trash, throwing a little party to celebrate.

No one seems to be paying attention to me, the unassuming girl in the corner. Come to think of it, no one seems to even know or care that I'm here.

I stand up slowly, waiting for someone to come over and shove me back down into the seat with a meaty paw on my shoulder, but no one does. Gingerly, I start walking around the room, and still, no one tells me to sit.

I don't know if I was expecting a conspiracy-style corkboard with red string leading them to Joseph, but there's no trace of the investigation here, out in the open. Instead, I get a closer glance at the cops still here: there are only a few night officers waiting around, presumably for traffic incidents or DUIs. Most of them seem to be playing games on their phones or scrolling through social media, stopping to laugh at the occasional dog video. I reach the water cooler and fill a triangle paper cup, and still, no one no-tices. Not even as I wander into the hall.

My plastic sandals squeak against the linoleum floor so I take my steps softly, heel-ball-toe-ing past a row of closed doors. I don't hear anyone inside and try to ignore the flickering fluorescent lights overhead.

Halfway down the corridor, I come to a door that's ajar, illuminated by a sliver of light. I look around, making sure no one else is here before I elbow it open, peeking inside. It's a standard conference room, small with an aluminum table and four metal chairs at the center. But there is a dry erase board on the far wall and when I see what's there, I cover my mouth to suppress my surprise.

Ryan's and Sarah's class photos are taped up, staring back at me, smiling wide. I swallow the lump in my throat and force myself to look at everything around them: a map of campus with Sarah's room starred in highlighter, two photographs clearly taken inside Sarah's dorm—a bloody sock next to a ruler and the doorknob, dark red smudges against the metal. My stomach flips and I avert my eyes, grateful there's not more gore to take in.

But that's when I notice what's on the table: a Ziploc bag holding a photo the size of printer paper. I glance around again and see I'm still alone, and I make my way into the room to get a closer look.

I stop when I see the photo, an outline of a small paring knife, the kind my grandma might keep, sheathed, in the glove compartment of her car in case she wanted to slice an apple or needed to cut off a loose string. But this one is smudged with the same dark brown stains that are on the sock and the doorknob, and the wooden handle is stained, too.

It's sitting in the trunk of a car, though the scene is dark and hard to place. I lean in and see there's handwriting at the bottom of the photo, time-stamped and dated from earlier today, the words *2009 HONDA ACCORD* written on the bottom, followed by numbers and letters, enough to make up a license plate. I'm reading the characters again, trying to commit the sequence to memory, as footsteps pick up behind me, voices calling out.

I slip out of the door, checking that the coast is clear, and make my way to the bathroom near the waiting area, just as the officers walk by, not taking a second glance in my direction.

I recite the license plate over and over under my breath until I get back to my chair and pull out my phone, type it into the public database we use at the *Gazette* to look up personal information and records. It only takes a second before the search engine spits back the car's owner: Joseph Stone.

Amy

"You did the right thing coming forward," says Detective Diaz, who nods at me as we both stand up from the chairs.

"Can he go, then? This is all a mistake." That's what I tried to stress over the past few hours, that Joseph was *in* the dorm but that he couldn't have done it, that he left before anything happened. How I watched him wedge through the window, snake down the trellis, and run off into the distance, disappearing into the darkness.

Diaz coughs, stuffs his fists into his pockets.

"I get if you have to hold him overnight, but tomorrow he can go, right?"

"We're very grateful you came in, Miss Alterman, but we still have a few things we need to explore. We don't arrest people for no good reason."

My stomach churns. "But he didn't do anything. I told you."

"We're not at liberty to discuss this with anyone, let alone others involved in the case."

"You mean me."

"You were a witness and . . ."

"And what?"

"We're investigating all potential leads and aids."

I open my mouth to say something, but someone clamps down

hard on my shoulder. I spin around to find my dad's lawyer, Lisa Brock, staring at me with fury in her eyes.

"How did you—" But she cuts me off.

"That's enough." She turns to Diaz. "She won't be answering *any* more questions. And I take it you understand that if you intend on using anything she just said, I'll be moving to suppress all of her previous statements. It's totally unethical of you to interview a minor without a guardian or lawyer present."

"She came to us—it's not like we could have stopped her from talking."

Lisa shakes her head, her expensive haircut sharp against her chin. "Bullshit," she says. "This is a total violation of her rights, not to mention the Constitution."

"Well, it kind of isn't. She didn't ask for a lawyer. It's not illegal to talk to a seventeen-year-old."

They're goading one another, and Diaz is acting like I handed them a gift wrapped in a bow. Except I didn't. I pointed out how they *didn't* do their job, how they had made a grave mistake.

Lisa turns to me, her jaw tense. "Can you wait with your little friend for a second? I need to remind these detectives that I went to law school with the district attorney. It would be so sad if she had to call these bumblefuck detectives to inform them they had suddenly lost their jobs."

My cheeks burn, but I follow her instructions and walk to the front of the station to find it empty save for a few officers on their phones, some empty pizza boxes, and Liz sitting in the corner, her hands folded in her lap. She stands when she sees me, her eyes wide.

"Did you call her?" I ask, suddenly realizing how Lisa could have known I was here.

"I had no choice," Liz says, her voice a low hiss.

"I told you not to. How did you even get her information?"

"I'm a reporter. And you were in there forever." Liz shrugs. "Couldn't hurt."

"Totally unnecessary," I say. "They're going to think he had something to do with it. They keep calling him the suspect as if he's some monster, but I don't get why they won't believe me. He's *innocent*."

Liz shakes her head. "He's not. I didn't want you to incriminate yourself by accident."

"I told you he was with *me*. Of course he's innocent." Frustration builds in my stomach and I don't understand why no one will believe me, why I'm all of a sudden so unreliable or why everyone wants to turn on Joseph.

"They have the murder weapon," Liz says.

"So? That doesn't mean anything."

"They found it in his car. A knife."

My stomach seizes and for a second, I can't breathe.

"Slim paring knife with a wood handle? Gold Honda Accord from 2009?" Liz asks.

My hands become jelly.

"I saw the photo," she says. "I looked up the plates."

I shake my head. "You're wrong."

Liz frowns, casts her gaze downward. Something nasty rises in my throat, a torrent of pain I want to unleash on her, but before I can, Lisa hustles from the hall, anger written all over her face. "Come on, girls. I'm taking you back to the dorms."

I look up at her, this woman I've known for my entire life, who is trying her best to protect me even when I won't let her.

"Did I just fuck up?" I sound like a child, but I can't help it.

Lisa leads us to her car, a shiny black Volvo SUV that smells new. She climbs into the driver's seat and motions for me to sit beside her. Lisa rests her hands on the steering wheel and takes a deep breath before looking right at me. "Yes," she says. "You fucked up."

THE DAY THE TRUTH COMES OUT

Liz

A fog rolled into campus this morning, blanketing the quad in a thin layer of gray mist. No one was out when I woke up early and made my way to the newspaper office, when I opened the blinds inside and peered out the window.

And now that I'm here, sitting in front of my computer with a cursor blinking in front of me, I have no idea where to begin.

Well, that's not exactly true. I do know where, and it's with an email.

> Dear Head Teacher Egan,
> In light of yesterday's news, I would love to write an article for the *Gazette* about . . .

But that's where I stop. I don't know what my next story *should* be about. I could follow Mr. Flynn's suspicions about Ryan or write all about Julian and how Sarah's final few months were complicated by the discovery of her brother. That's not right though. Both of these ideas seem less like news, more like gossip. Nothing that involves the case.

But if I were to write about what I *really* know, that the police have proof—real proof—that Joseph Stone killed Ryan and

Sarah, and Amy may have just thrown her whole life away trying to defend him, I could risk doing real damage, especially if Joseph does turn out to be innocent. For the first time since rooming with Amy, I realize I have real power to hurt her with the facts she entrusted to me—and right now, I'm not quite sure if it's worth it.

I reach my hand in my pocket and my pointer finger catches on a piece of cardstock. I pull it out to reveal Yalitza Luna's business card, the corners now rounded and soft. Her name is big and bold and right under it sits her email address, given to me with an invitation. Maybe now's the time to accept.

I close out my message to Egan and instead begin to write a different one.

Dear Yalitza,
I'm not sure if you remember me, but I'm the student journalist who met you at the first press conference in Meadowbrook. I was wondering if I might be able to take you up on your offer to chat. I'm struggling with how to cover this story and would love your perspective. If you're still in town maybe we could meet?

Sincerely, Liz Charles

I wheel away from my desk and busy myself in the main room, quiet and smelling like freshly brewed coffee.

When I get back to my seat, I refresh my email and my pulse jumps when I see Yalitza Luna's name in my inbox.

I hold my breath as the message loads.

Of course. I'm actually on campus today. How does 11:00 a.m. sound?

There's a buzzing in my fingers as I reply, letting her know where she can find me in the office. Then I stare at the clock wondering how the hell I'm going to fill the next three hours.

"Liz, hi."

I look up from my computer to see Yalitza smiling at me from the doorway. She has on a similar outfit to the one she wore to the press conference, simple slacks and a blue button-down shirt, her feet stuffed into beat-up leather clogs. She's wearing little makeup, only a swipe of mascara, and she looks younger than I remember. She shifts the weight of her shoulder bag and sits down across from me. But as soon as she does, the power dynamic feels all wrong. I'm not the one who should be behind a desk, like I'm interviewing her. I roll my desk chair around the side so we're face-to-face, no formal barrier between us.

"I can't believe you responded."

Her smile widens, showing a few bottom teeth, and she shrugs. "I got my first internship at the *Houston Chronicle* because a guest lecturer at my college invited me to coffee to talk about an assignment I totally bungled. It only had one source! She brought me with her when she moved to New York News Network. I like to pay it forward." She pauses for a second. "Plus, it's probably smart to get in with the school newspaper editor when I'm trying to write a story about what happened here."

She talks in a warm, bubbly cadence, even when admitting that she showed up not only out of the goodness of her heart but also because it benefits her professionally to get to know me. The honesty disarms me in a way that makes me want to tell her everything I know. This must be her superpower.

"I'm surprised Egan let you on the grounds."

"We had an off-the-record conversation," she says. "Part of reporting stories like this is negotiating with those in charge before writing a word."

I think about my conversations with the administration and can only imagine the kind of sweet-talking Yalitza will have to do to get Egan on board with anything she's about to write.

"So, what would you like to talk about?" she asks.

Now that she's here, I think of all of the questions that have been swimming in my head: How do you stay confident when people don't want to talk to you? How do you *get* them to talk to you in the first place? How do you maintain your sanity when reporting on unconscionable violence? How do you report something everyone thinks is true when you're not sure if you believe it? When the facts don't back it up?

But there's only one question that forces its way forward.

"I don't know how to report on this stuff without . . ."

"Feeling things?" she finishes.

My face flushes, like I've been exposed, and in some ways I have. I've admitted, even inadvertently, that the violence, the terror, the closeness of it all, it affects me.

"That's a good thing," Yalitza says. "It means you're human. It would be strange if you had no emotions about two of your classmates being killed."

"But you never let emotions get in the way of your work, not when you reported on the Catskills Killer. 'It's like a wall goes up. After I file, that's when I get to grieve.' That's what you said in a *Vanity Fair* interview." I think back to the glossy spread that came out around when the book was published. It showed a photo of Yalitza sitting on a boulder outside the state park where some of the victims' remains were found. She looked pensive in a blouse and jeans, like the only thing she cared about was getting the facts right.

Yalitza taps a pen against her thigh. "I guess I did say that." She breaks eye contact and looks around the office. The walls are covered in yellowed newspaper clippings from when there was a print edition, stories that were published decades ago, and photos of the school and the *Gazette*'s staff tacked to the wall with push-pins or straight nails.

"You know, I came up in school papers, too," she says. "Covered campus crime in college."

"Oh yeah?" I ask, even though I knew this, studied her resume and read interviews with her dating back decades.

"When I was a junior, my roommate, Megan, died in a hit-and-run. Horrible. A frat boy was drunk driving. They caught him a few days later after some of the campus security guards saw his dented car, ran the plates. My editor made me cover the story even though it was a total conflict of interest. Would never fly in a professional newsroom."

"Wow."

She presses her lips together, leans back in her chair. "I was so close to it. She and I weren't best friends or anything, but I *lived* with her. I knew her family. Had her sister's phone number."

"How did you handle it?"

Yalitza runs a hand through her hair. "Callously. I was desperate to be a *real* reporter, to tell the story no matter the human cost. I did all the things I thought I was supposed to, bombarded Megan's family and friends, reported on things that weren't related to the case—like how much she drank, the people she dated. Megan became a story, not my roommate."

A ball of anxiety knots in my stomach.

Yalitza sighs. "Even if those things were true, it doesn't mean I needed to write them down for anyone to read."

I swallow the lump in my throat, blink to stop the tears.

"Being a student journalist can sometimes feel like an oxymoron," she says. "You want to be part of your community, but also document it. You want to expose indiscretions, but you still have to live and work with the people who you might be hurting by telling the truth."

"What happened? With Megan, I mean."

She looks out the window to where students are lounging on picnic blankets, uniforms slightly askew, laughter floating through the air for the first time in days. Someone's blasting old rock from a small speaker in the middle of the quad, and a group of kids are playing cornhole with burgundy Meadowbrook bags, landing in soft *thwacks* on the wooden boxes. If either one of us were to look at this view out of context, we might think we were watching an idyllic scene, one full of promise. Seniors about to embark on their final year in a storied institution, one that will challenge them and build them into the adults they were destined to be.

But we both know that what we're watching is a wave of relief. An exhale.

"I ran gratuitous coverage, published nonessential photos of the crime scene. Ran salacious quotes from random people who said Megan shouldn't have been walking home alone when she was drinking. Wrote descriptions of her family in the courthouse . . ."

She shakes her head. "I was so desperate to prove to people that I was unbiased. That even though she was my roommate, I could see the story with clear eyes. I wanted people to view me as a journalist."

"But in doing all that, you weren't."

Yalitza offers a thin smile. "Exactly. We have a million judgment calls to make every day, in every story. We can't get them all right, but we need to try. We need to do better."

"So, what would you do in my situation? Editor of the paper. Roommates with the prime suspect's girlfriend, the girl who found them. What should I do?"

She throws her hands up. "There's no golden rule and anyone who tells you there is one is full of shit."

"Well, that's annoying."

She shakes her head. "We work in the gray areas. All I can say is that you're never going to satisfy everyone. Someone is always going to think that your coverage is biased or unfair or misleading. All you can do is try to tell the story as best you can within your means and values." She leans forward. "What's *your* highest value?"

"To tell the truth," I say. "Honesty. It's the only thing that matters."

A small smile forms on Yalitza's face. "Well, then you have to do that. But it's up to you to determine which truths matter."

My brow furrows. "They all matter."

She smiles. "Do they, really? Every single truth?" She clasps her hands in front of her. "Just because something is a fact doesn't mean it's newsworthy."

I suck on the inside of my cheek. Her words hang in the air and I think of Ryan and Sarah, how at ease they looked with one another in the hallways, how Sarah had cried at last year's awards ceremony when she won high honors in chemistry, English, and calculus. How Ryan led our class in never-ending waves during all-school assemblies. Those moments so many people will never know but that make them human, make their memories real.

But the other moments were real, too: the fact that Sarah had discovered a family secret, that Ryan probably wasn't the most honest student. For the first time since I started reporting, I begin to realize that these types of truths may not be the ones that deserve public consumption.

Yalitza stands and rests her hands on the doorknob, preparing to leave. I want to ask her to stay, to beg for her help, for more. But I don't. Instead, I grip my hands into fists and ask one final question. "What's yours?" My voice is urgent, desperate. "Your highest value?"

Yalitza turns around and cocks her head. "Dignity," she says. "For myself and the people I cover. When I'm ready to publish a story, I always ask myself one question: Could I defend it to the people I'm writing about? Could I see them at a coffee shop and have them yell at me and know, deep in my heart, that what I wrote was fair? Did I treat the subject like a person? If the answer is yes, then I've done my job. And you'll do yours, too."

Amy

I draw my hoodie tight over my head and fight the nerves swimming in my stomach. I shouldn't be here, at the back door to Coach Jensen's house—*Joseph's house*—cupping my hands to the window to see if I can spot Coach inside their mudroom. But I couldn't help myself.

All the lights are off in the small craftsman home, but I can see her van in the garage, meaning she's definitely still home. Joseph's car, though, that's gone.

"You got any spare batteries? I'm almost out of juice."

I duck instinctively, even though I know the reporters are in front of the house and that they can't see back this way, that they don't know most of Pulley Lane's homeowners come through the back entrances since all the garages were built to feed into the alley in the fifties.

It's the sweetest street in all of Meadowbrook, though Joseph recently complained that half of the homes have turned into short-term rentals over the past few years. Now he calls it Lovers' Lane because most of the places, like his, are only big enough for two people, so they attract couples from the city looking for a swoony weekend where they can cosplay country folk. They're all painted different colors—sage green, bird's-egg blue, rust red.

Coach and Joseph's is a pale lavender with black window trim, all made brighter by big raised planters full of dahlias.

The first time I stepped inside their home, I understood the appeal. With exposed wood beams and wide oak flooring, the space is cozy and inviting, a place that beckons you to curl up by the fireplace and watch snow fall out the picture window.

I rap my knuckles against the door again, peering inside to see Joseph's boots under a narrow bench, dried mud caked onto the toes. I wonder when he'll get to wear them again.

Lisa Brock filled me in on everything last night after reprimanding me for talking to the police without her consent or presence. She says she'll be able to get them to throw out my statement, but I can't tell if that's just her big-city confidence trying to convince the both of us.

She'd kill me if she knew I was here, especially since she told me to stay put in the dorm, only leaving to go to sanctioned school events, though she didn't have an answer to my question: *Until when?*

I give it one last shot and knock again.

A floorboard squeaks inside the house. A pause. "You shouldn't be here." Coach's voice is faint but stern, the same one she uses when she tells us she's disappointed after a defeat or when she's trying to impress upon us the gravity of what it means to be captain.

"I don't know who else to talk to." My words are a whisper.

The dead bolt moves ever so slightly, metal sliding against metal in a slick sound that makes me shiver. Finally, the door opens a few inches. Coach reaches her hand out toward me and grabs hold of my wrist.

"Come in," she says. "Quickly."

I step inside, bumping up against the door, and find myself in their small tiled mudroom. Coach's cleats are next to Joseph's boots on the floor, coats and sweatshirts hanging from a peg rail on the wall. Coach walks ahead of me, saying nothing, down the hallway, and I quickly slide out of my sneakers and follow her into the kitchen.

But as I walk through Joseph's house I want to stop and take in everything. I don't want to forget the details: a framed photo of him and Coach wearing matching fisherman's sweaters, a Mother's Day card stuck to the fridge with a magnet, a handwritten note still on the sticky pad next to the sink that says *love u mom*, a stack of floral plates sitting on a wooden floating shelf above the counter, dozens of cookbooks, their edges stained with tomato sauce and olive oil. I smell Joseph in here, can picture him at the stove caramelizing onions while a pot of stock burbles on the back burner.

I had planned to spend Thanksgiving here with him and Coach. He promised me he'd show me how to make pie dough, though I didn't care about learning myself. I just wanted to watch him press the butter into the flour, see his forearms flex as he rolled it out on the counter.

"You have to go back to campus." Coach leans against the far wall, her arms crossed in front of her chest, and if I don't look too closely, she might seem like she has for the past three years—ready for battle. But her face is sallow and there are dark circles under her eyes. Her ponytail is sloppy and her nails are bitten to the quick. She's wearing a white T-shirt instead of her usual tracksuit, a small tear near the neckline.

"I didn't know where else to go." But the truth is now that I'm here I don't know what to say.

Coach sighs and motions to the kitchen table. "Let's sit." But she doesn't. Instead, she starts boiling water and pulls down mugs in the shapes of farm animals. Sheep for her, a cow for me. Joseph always grabs the horse. "They told me what you said. That you brought him to the dorms. Your room."

"I watched him leave. Right out through the window. He didn't do anything."

Coach spins around, a deep crease between her eyebrows. "Of course he didn't do it."

I nod, fiddling with a rattan placemat on the table. "The police didn't seem to care what I said."

"You placed him at the crime scene." She says this in a matter-of-fact manner with no trace of judgment or opinion. But she's looking at me with a different gaze than she did yesterday, than she ever has. It's one that tells me we may not be on the same side anymore.

"I was only trying to help."

The hot water kettle makes a hissing sound and she turns her back to me.

"It's all a misunderstanding. It has to be. He didn't even know Sarah."

Coach drops her spoon on the floor, a clattering ringing in the air.

I crack my knuckles, the silence between us awkward and full of questions neither one of us has the answers to. All I want is to be close to him. "Can I grab a sweatshirt from his room? I think I left it here." The white lie comes out quickly, too fast to take it back.

Coach motions toward the stairs. "Hurry, okay? You really shouldn't be here."

I nod and dart up the narrow hallway, making a right into his small bedroom. It looks unaltered from when I was here last week. A twin bed pushed up in the far corner, a hunter-green plaid quilt covering neatly made white sheets. On the wall, he'd hung a map of New England, with little pushpins identifying the farms he wanted to visit, color coded to note if they sold fruit, veggies, meat, or flowers. He had so many still to see, so many ingredients to experiment with.

Against the far side of the room, he'd assembled a small wood desk, stacked high with guides on foraging mushrooms and old cookbooks with feathery pages. One time, we sat together on the floor as he thumbed through an ancient French tome, pointing out which recipes he wanted to try. Coq a vin and steak au poivre, a croissant made from scratch.

I run my fingers across the book covers, dragging dust along the edges, and perch on the edge of the desk, looking out at his room, his space. *He should be here.*

A dull ache sets in my chest as I force myself to stand and open his closet, looking for my navy Palo Alto Farmers Market sweatshirt, an oversized favorite that Joseph was always borrowing. I never left it here by accident, only handed it over when I wanted him to have something of me here. It's folded on top of a pile of hoodies, sitting beside a stack of T-shirts washed so many times the hems are as thin as tissue paper.

I press my sweatshirt to my nose and close my eyes, inhaling the scent of his laundry, fresh and simple. But when I open my eyes, I look down at the pile still on the shelf and see a piece of clothing so familiar, I have to blink to make sure it's real.

A maroon sweatshirt folded into quarters with the words MEADOWBROOK ACADEMY VARSITY SOCCER embroidered in the corner. I drop my own sweatshirt and reach for this one, my pointer finger finding the tag along the neckline.

Each player gets one when they make varsity, our jersey numbers stitched onto the sleeve. But I'd worn mine the other day to movie night. This one must be Coach's.

I reach for the sleeve and pull it from its folded position, laying it flat so I can make out two neat numbers, sewn into the fabric with white thread.

Right there on the sleeve are the digits one and five, numbers only one player wore all four years, numbers no one will again. Fifteen. Sarah Oliver.

I drop the sleeve and stare at it, trying to make sense of its presence here in Joseph's room.

Last fall Sarah had lost hers and asked me to help her look for it. It was one of the things I yelled at her about the night she died, how she had ditched the search to go hook up with Ryan, leaving me sifting through dirty old clothes. She never got a new one.

But all this time, it was here, sitting in Joseph's room. Every time I was in here, every time we kissed . . . her sweatshirt was here, sitting just below mine for reasons I'm not quite sure I want to know.

My legs wobble as I force myself out of Joseph's room, holding the sweatshirts in one hand. I grip the railing tightly as I make my way downstairs, where Coach is still standing there, clutching a mug of tea.

"Why is Sarah's soccer sweatshirt in Joseph's room?" I hold it up, the numbers visible for Coach to see.

Coach looks away, out the window toward the paparazzi out front. "I think it's time for you to leave, Amy."

"But . . . he didn't even know her. Why is this here? Why does he have this?"

Fear flashes in Coach's eyes. "It's best you go back to campus," she says again. "Now."

Her words slam into my stomach as shame fills my chest. There's still so much I don't know about Joseph and Sarah, and based on the way Coach just reacted, she's not about to tell me.

Neither one of us says anything as she opens the door and ushers me outside into the late summer heat, the air still heavy and humid, the sun shining high up in the sky. A lock turns behind me and I retrace my steps until I'm near my bike on another street, ready to pedal back to Meadowbrook. But before I can hop on, I glance at my phone to see a news alert from *The Boston Globe*, a headline blaring back at me: "Break in the Meadowbrook Murders Case Reveals New Details about Suspect."

I open the link and scroll, my stomach flipping at every paragraph as I scan the article for unknown details, facts he never told me, surprises. But the thing that jumps out at me halfway down the page is my own name staring back at me.

Joseph Stone had been dating Sarah's roommate, Amy Alterman. Sources say Alterman brought Stone into their shared suite the night of the murders.

There's only one way this could have happened. Liz told.

Liz

I never pictured myself spending much time in the senior social space, a loungelike room roped off specifically for seniors that most Meadowbrook Academy students waited three long years to gain access to. It always seemed like the sort of place where you might walk into a land mine, where you'd say the wrong thing by accident or offend someone without even realizing it.

But when Peter sent out an email to our entire class, saying anyone who might want to grieve and be together to support one another should meet in the social space before lunch, I found myself walking there, my backpack in hand, Yalitza's words replaying in my brain.

Could I defend this story to the people I'm writing about? Could I see them at a coffee shop and have them yell at me and know, deep in my heart, that what I wrote was fair?

These are the people in the coffee shop. These are the people who deserve fair reporting.

I pick up my pace as I get closer to Phillips Hall, which houses the auditorium and the student lounges, and head up to the top floor, following other seniors with the same plan. I've never been up here, never even attempted to get a look since it was so obviously reserved for seniors. But now that I'm standing in front of a set of glass French doors, which open to a massive room with floor-to-ceiling windows and a rooftop lounge that overlooks the campus, I can understand why this place is so desirable, so special.

All around me, my classmates are splayed out on couches and lounge chairs, taking up space and talking loudly at one another. A group of theater kids huddle up on the shag carpet, their limbs draped over one another's as they suppress laughter, as if we're not supposed to do that yet. Over by the bay window, across from a few vending machines selling refrigerated snacks like cheese sticks and apples, Peter is perched on the edge of an L-shaped couch with a bunch of his crew teammates and members of the girls' soccer team. The sun streams in behind them.

I wonder if they're talking about *The Boston Globe* article, the one that named Amy. I couldn't believe it when I saw it, that someone had leaked that detail. Probably one of the police administrators or a clerk at the county jail. I thought about texting her, but I didn't even know what to say. *Sorry your entire life is falling apart* doesn't really seem like the most appropriate option even though it's the truest.

I approach Peter's group to find him and the others listening attentively to Kayla tell a story about how Sarah once led the soccer team in a two-hour sing-along on the way home from a tournament up in Boston. I wait until she's done and the rest of the group starts laughing uproariously.

I take a seat on the floor next to Iris, who's covering her mouth after laughing so hard. When she registers me sitting there, she lets her hand drop. "Amy's not with you, is she?"

I shake my head. "I haven't seen her today."

Iris nods. "Good."

Hillary turns to us from her perch on the couch. "She needs to be locked up immediately."

"Well . . ." I start, but Hillary cuts me off again.

"I can't believe he was *in* the dorm." She nudges Kayla with her foot. "We were right there."

Kayla nods quickly and leans her head on Peter's shoulder. "I'll always regret that I didn't hear anything."

The group had been boisterous and full of joy only a few moments before, but now, as if they're remembering what's happened, the reality of the situation, everyone's quiet like they're unsure of how to proceed.

I tamp down my nerves and tap my pen against my notebook, remembering why I came here in the first place, to hear what these people have to say. "What do you think happened?"

Iris and Olivia exchange glances, while Hillary looks to Kayla for guidance.

The room is quiet and suddenly I realize that everyone else in the social space has turned to look, to watch and wait for Peter to make the call. For all Mrs. Herschel's talk about how Egan has control of this place, how the administration and the board run Meadowbrook Academy with influence that might as well be held like bargaining chips, I know for certain it's students like Peter and Kayla, Ryan and Sarah who wield *real* power. They're the ones who can determine if people will talk to you or help you, not just for a student newspaper article, but in the future. They're the ones who, when we're vying for postcollege internships and country club memberships, might choose to say, "Oh yeah, I knew her in high school," an acceptance or a denial on the tips of their tongues.

Power can be earned. It can be stolen or seized. But privilege is something you're born with, something you can wield like a scepter. People like Peter and Kayla know that.

Peter puts his hands in the air. "Off the record?"

"Sure," I say. At least for now.

"It's not for me to say. That's why the police are on it."

Kayla lets out a puff of air.

"You disagree?" I ask.

Before she can answer, a door slams from the other side of the room, and I turn to see Amy running through the entrance, her hair falling loose from her ponytail, her eyes rimmed in red. I feel an urge to reach for her and ask what's wrong, but then I realize she's running right toward me, rage and fury on her face. "How could you?" she says, spit flying from the corners of her mouth. "I *trusted* you."

I stumble to stand. "What are you talking about? What's going on?"

"You're so full of shit." She turns around to face everyone else and throws up her arms. "You say you're a journalist, but all you're trying to do is out everyone's secrets. Ryan's, Sarah's, mine. You're just like all those other tabloids. Trash."

"What the hell are you talking about?" I stand and step toward her, but Amy spins around and pushes me, her palms colliding with my shoulders so I stumble back into the chair behind me. Peter steadies me by grabbing onto my elbow so I don't fall.

"Oh, so you didn't run off and help *The Boston Globe*? You didn't tell everyone what I told you in private?" She spins around to the rest of the room. "You're not plotting to tell the world about Julian? Not worth hiding it anymore, I guess."

"Who the fuck is Julian?" Hillary whispers to Kayla.

"You think I'm the one who leaked your testimony?" I lean in close to her and lower my voice to a whisper. "There are a dozen cops who could have done that."

She steps back as if I slapped her. "Like you *didn't* make sure this news got out, huh?"

"I had nothing to do with this." I shake my head. "It doesn't even make sense. Why would I want to help another news outlet get traction on this story?"

Tears well up in Amy's eyes. "See?" She turns to the rest of the room. "To Liz, we're all just part of some story." She jabs her thumb back at her chest. "These are our *lives*. It's not our fault no one likes you enough to include you in shit, so you don't understand what it's like to lose a best friend. You have no idea how it feels to know the people closest to you were lying. To have someone you love accused of . . ." She stops, choking on her words.

Someone drops their backpack, a thud echoing through the room. Amy lets out a laugh, surprising and terrifying. "You all know anyway. What's the use in hiding it anymore?"

Peter stands, a pained look on his face. "Come on, Amy. I'll walk you out." He reaches for her elbow, but she tenses, pulling away from him. Still, she lets him guide her out the door, glancing over her shoulder to throw me one more look of betrayal.

Amy

Peter keeps a steady hold on me as we walk down the stairs to the third floor, where the junior class social space is empty, not even a poster taped to the wall. "Get off me," I say, trying to wrench myself away.

He drops my elbow immediately, but I stumble out of his grasp and have to steady myself against the far wall.

"I'm sorry," Peter says softly. "I really am. But maybe it's best if you take a beat and let everyone digest all this information, okay?"

"You don't think I'm trying to process, too?"

Peter shoves his hands into his pockets. "But, Amy, not all of us have boyfriends who were . . . involved."

My jaw clenches and I press my teeth together before getting the words out. "He's innocent." My voice breaks as the final word comes out, as I think back to what the police found, *the knife*, and the sweatshirt folded in his room like it belonged to him.

"I'm not sure you should help out with the vigil anymore."

"She was my best friend."

"I know, but . . ." He looks back to the social space. "I don't know if people want to hear from you right now. You might take attention away from Ryan and Sarah."

I stare down at my shoes, press my heels deep into the ground.

"We'll get through this, Amy. We will. But we all need time." Peter turns and starts back up the stairs, taking them two at a time as he heads back to the rest of our class.

It's only once he disappears that I'm able to fully realize what's happened—that I've become an enemy here. I spin around and duck my head, letting the tears fall as I walk away from the social spaces. But as I get to the quad, I realize there's nowhere left to go. Not the soccer field, or my dorm room, or even into town.

All I can do is wander and so I let my feet take me anywhere on campus, anywhere away from my classmates, who are probably discussing my culpability behind curtains of hair, eyes wide as they dissect what they know about my relationship with Joseph, with Sarah, with Ryan. Whatever they say they'll be wrong, I know it.

"Amy!"

I jerk my head up and look around, trying to find where my name came from.

"Amy, over here." Over to my right I see a young Black man in a maroon T-shirt and dark pants standing with a wheelbarrow full of firewood, moving logs from an enormous pile to a rack near the campfire circle.

"Olly," the guy says as I get closer. "Olly Bolten. Joseph's friend."

"Olly, of course." There's surprise in my voice until I realize what he's doing here. "Joseph mentioned you got a job here. I . . . I forgot."

Olly sets the wheelbarrow down and wipes his forehead with

a gloved hand, leaving traces of dirt on his skin. "First day. Only supposed to be here one semester before I transfer to UConn."

"Helluva time to start."

"The school delayed all of our work this week, but once they announced the rest of the students were coming, I guess they realized it was time to mow the lawn or whatever." Olly crosses his arms over his chest and lets out a puff of air. "How are you? Seems like a ridiculous thing to ask."

"Not great." I study his face, his downturned mouth and the circles under his eyes. "You?"

"Been better."

A bird caws overhead and we both look up, watch it circle the grounds, unaware of the horrors that have unfolded here. For a moment, I'm jealous.

"I read what you told the police," he says. "That Joseph was with you."

"He was."

Olly nods. "I know. He told me. Texted me when he got home, said he couldn't believe how lucky he was to be with you."

My heart pounds in my chest. "Really?"

"Yeah." He stomps on a mound of dirt underfoot. "I showed the texts to the cops. They didn't seem to care. Said it only placed him at the scene of the crime." Olly crosses his arms over his chest. "You know he didn't do it."

I bite my lip. I want to say *I know*, but as the words form on my lips, I think of the sweatshirt. *Sarah's* sweatshirt, folded with care in his closet. The knife stowed in the trunk of his car.

"Can I ask you something?"

Olly shrugs.

"I found something in Joseph's closet. It was . . ." I take a deep breath. "It was Sarah's. Her soccer sweatshirt. Had her number embroidered on it and everything."

Olly clears his throat, looks up at the sky again, squinting.

My stomach seizes. "Do you know why he might have had it? They barely knew each other."

"I don't . . . it's none of my business." Olly turns back toward the woodpile. "I gotta get going."

"Wait." My heart is in my throat as I reach for him, my fingertips landing on his arm. The backs of my eyes sting as panic runs through me. "Please. I need to know."

Olly turns back around and juts his chin. He opens his mouth like he's deciding what to say.

"He knew her, didn't he?" My voice shakes, the words true as they land in the air. "Sarah."

"She came by Rex's a lot last year, right after Thanksgiving break."

"But Sarah preferred the diner."

Olly shakes his head. "She would come in with some guy. Scruffy city-transplant-looking dude."

"Julian."

"You know him?"

"Her brother."

Olly nods. "They were around a lot, early in the morning right after we'd open, before Joseph and I would head to school. Usually getting pancakes or lattes or something."

She must have gone when she told me she was in the library or on a training run before breakfast. "I didn't know."

"The guy was often late, so she'd talk to me and Joseph. More Joseph, really, since I was on opening cleanup duty. I told him not to fall for her, that she seemed like the stuck-up private school kind of girl who would treat him like trash." He looks up. "No offense."

I wave my hand. No one has time to be offended right now.

"But he didn't listen. Got her number, texted all the time, apparently."

My heart launches into my throat. "She was with Ryan."

Olly nods. "Yeah, I mean, they never hooked up or anything. Just talked a lot. He was totally smitten." He shakes his head. "It was ridiculous. They barely saw each other, but I don't know . . . she told him she had a boyfriend at some point. Joseph was so upset, saying she played him."

"How long did this go on?"

"I don't know." He furrows his brow. "Stopped coming by Rex's around March, maybe."

"March," I say. "He and I got together in April. That's when he started hanging around our soccer practice."

Olly rocks back and forth on his heels. "It wasn't like that."

"Like what? Like he was trying to get back at Sarah by asking me out? Like he was using me to make her jealous? Like he *lied* to me about everything?" But as soon as I say the words, I realize it means Sarah lied to me, too. Something else she didn't tell me. I rest my hand on my stomach, squeeze my eyes shut to stay standing.

"I don't know, Amy. I think he started hanging around his mom's work to make Sarah mad but then met you. He really liked you. *Likes* you."

"Why wouldn't she tell me?"

Olly opens and closes his mouth. Of course there's no way for him to know. But suddenly, so many of her actions begin to make sense: the way Sarah was so dismissive of him, the vitriol she unleashed whenever I spent time with him over her. Her reactions seemed so outsized, but maybe they were marred by jealousy, fury over me having something she couldn't, even if she didn't want it anymore.

"So, what, did he steal that sweatshirt or something?" I ask.

"To be honest, I didn't know he still had it. Sarah left it at Rex's one day. Rex found it under a table and gave it to Joseph. He said he'd return it next time she showed up. Guess he kept it."

"Hey!" Olly and I both turn toward the firewood, where one of the head groundskeepers is arriving on a golf cart. "Let's go. We're on the clock, bro."

Olly holds up a hand and turns in that direction, but before he jogs off, he looks back over his shoulder. "Don't lose faith in him, okay? He needs us."

I watch Olly return to his supervisor and stack logs, his head turned down. I keep watching him as I contemplate what it means that the two people closest to me lied about knowing one another and that they kept something from me on purpose.

I lose my balance, falling forward as I press my hands into the ground to catch me. My breathing picks up as the truths begin to come into focus, my worst fears beginning to take shape. If Joseph had secretly wanted Sarah this whole time, if he blamed Ryan for keeping them apart, if he had, despite Olly's insistence, used me to get back at her, then Joseph had a motive.

And was at the crime scene.

And had the murder weapon.

And is the main—the only—suspect.

Without warning, a burbling erupts from my stomach and I vomit onto the ground, a sticky mess appearing between my hands, as I realize what I've been missing. What I've been too blind to see.

Joseph killed Sarah and Ryan. And I gave him all the tools to help him to do it.

Liz

After the outburst everyone drifts off into different corners and I'm left alone with my phone still recording. I shoulder my backpack and make one last-ditch effort, walking over to Melody, who's sitting in a bay window with the student government secretary, Farah Zaman. I clear my throat and they both look up.

"So," I say slowly, shifting my weight from foot to foot. "That was a little intense, huh?"

They stare at me, not saying anything.

"I wanted to see—"

"Sorry, Liz," Farah says, tucking a dark lock of hair behind her ear. "No comment." Her voice is icy and firm, no hint of budging. Melody looks down at her fingernails.

"Right. Well, if you change your mind, you know where to find me."

"We won't." Farah turns back to Melody and my cheeks warm. The two begin whispering to one another, and I take a step back, watching the way their foreheads nearly touch, how they pat one another for comfort. It's an intimacy that feels foreign and I try to ignore the stinging in my chest, the one that reminds me *you don't have that. Not here. Not anywhere.*

I grip the straps of my backpack to keep me grounded while

I leave. Halfway down the steps, I see Peter coming back up, his forehead furrowed as he grips the railing.

"Hey," I say, not bothering to pause. It's not like *he's* going to want to talk to me more than the others. But to my surprise, Peter stops.

"Woof," he says, shaking his head and raising his eyebrows.

I stop, hold my bag tighter. "How is she?"

He looks over his shoulder. "Shaken," Peter says. "I told her that I don't think it's a good idea for her to help with the vigil. Not with everything going on with Joseph."

"Wow." I look down the stairs, wondering where Amy is.

"I heard Egan approved coverage of the event for you," Peter says. "That you can write about it in the *Gazette*."

I nod. Her email came through this morning.

Peter rubs his palm on the back of his head. "I was thinking, why don't you shadow me around during prep and execution tomorrow? You can get an inside look at what we have planned, and I'm sure everyone there will be more willing to talk about Sarah and Ryan than they are here."

I blink my eyes open wide. "Really?"

"Yeah," he says. "Maybe that way people will want to tell stories about them."

"I don't know. Melody and Farah basically just told me hell no."

Peter smiles. "I think I can convince them."

A spark of hope flares in my chest.

"Meet me in the auditorium around five?"

"If you say so." I grip my backpack straps a little tighter.

"Great," Peter says. He starts to turn around, but before he does, he pushes his glasses up his nose and his bottom lip drops open. "That thing about Ryan, what Amy said. How you were going to out a secret or something? Was that about the cheating thing?"

I shake my head. "I don't even know if it's true."

Peter's shoulders shrug up around his ears. "He stole my exam right from my binder. I knew all along."

"And you never said anything?"

"He was trying to catch up to me for years. Always coming up just a little short." A small smile forms on his lips. "Anyway, what does it matter now?"

"I wasn't going to write about it."

Peter nods. "Good," he says. I watch him jog up the rest of the stairs, making his way back to the soccer girls, the crew team, his colleagues on the student government. As he ascends, I study his back, how his shoulders stay low and relaxed, how his button-down shirt rumples in an on-purpose sort of way around his waist. I wonder what it must be like to be him. To have been given so much power, so much adoration, that when your peers are faced with danger and pain, they turn to you for comfort, for guidance. That you can persuade people. Offer suggestions that are really more of commands.

Grandma liked to say that the greatest leaders are the ones who do it by example, not the ones who make prophetic speeches and disappear inside walled-off rooms and backdoor meetings. Sure, she said this after our town commissioner went on a whole campaign to mandate abstinence-only education in the public schools but then was found to have two different secret families in two different states.

But the notion holds up, especially now as I see how the other students follow Peter's lead, taking cues from the way he acts. Calm but devastated. Hopeful yet heartbroken.

He disappears behind the double doors and I skip down to the ground floor. Once outside, I'm hit with the brightness of the day, so sunny it blinds me. The air is hot and heavy, the last gasp of summer, and up above I hear voices floating through the window. I turn around and look up, seeing Hillary opening the window to the social space, her torso leaning out the glass.

Behind her, Kayla's face comes into view, her forehead etched with creases and her eyes red with tears, clouded by pain. These people may have everything—wealth, clout, and opportunity—but none of those advantages will be able to fix what has happened here at Meadowbrook. None of the prestige will wash away what they have experienced. There are some things money and status cannot fix, and grief is one of them.

I turn away, my face back up to the sky, and as I walk toward the *Gazette* office, an unrelenting sense of unease takes hold of my stomach. My classmates, the ones who were close enough to Sarah and Ryan to know their middle names and their parents' pet peeves, they're the ones who have lost something I can only imagine, and in a turn I never thought possible, I pity them.

Amy

Joseph's arraignment is called for today at four in the afternoon, and though I didn't even know what an arraignment was last week, it's all I can think about. The whole way back from Coach's house, I couldn't stop wondering what he was thinking, how I could talk to him—ask him why he lied to me about Sarah, if he . . .

But every time I got close to that big question—*Did you do it?*—my mind refocused away from the possibility. Because how could I keep going if he did?

I pull my knees up under my chin and readjust my seat on the blanket I've brought out to the dock on the pond.

I close my eyes and turn my face up to the gray sky dotted with puffy white clouds. A gust of wind rips through the trees and I shiver. I should have brought a jacket. Sarah would have remembered to layer up, that the weather in September can go from a calm and warm day to crisp and biting in minutes.

This was supposed to be the best year of our lives, ten months made up of lasts: last soccer games, last dances, last sing-alongs in the communal bathrooms. A year of final moments only to bring about a new chapter, one marked by firsts. Every so often, when we were in the midst of a totally normal activity—opening our lockers, leaving history class, swiping Parker House rolls from the cafeteria—Sarah liked to grab my hand and hold me in place.

"Remember this," she'd say. "Remember the little stuff. Because this won't last forever."

She was right, of course. But I never could have dreamed she'd be right like *this*.

"Hey."

I look over my shoulder and see Kayla holding one elbow in her hand, wearing leggings and a big New Canaan Tennis T-shirt. Her long hair is tied into a greasy knot on the top of her head.

"We need to talk."

I close my eyes and hold my knees tighter as the dock shakes, her footsteps getting closer as she sits down beside me.

"If you're here to scream at me, don't worry. I hate myself enough for the both of us right now."

Kayla slips out of her sandals and drops her feet into the water. "This isn't about you."

A spasm hits my stomach. "Why are you here?"

Kayla's quiet for a second and I hear a click, the sound of teeth breaking nails. I press my cheek to my knee and look at her, see her gaze focused on the one tree that has begun to change colors, its leaves burning into the horizon on the other side of the lake. "You let him into our dorm."

"I didn't know." My voice breaks.

"So, you *do* think he did it."

I shake my head. "It doesn't make sense. None of it makes sense."

"Explain it, then. How does it *not* make sense? What happened in your room that night?"

"You really want me to tell you?" I ask.

"Please." Kayla's voice is tense, strangled, but she's listening. She's quiet and waiting, as desperate as I am for answers.

"Fine." I sit up, straightening my legs and dipping them into the lake. The water's freezing, but I force my feet to stay still, to acclimate next to Kayla's. "I brought him back to hook up, and after, Joseph climbed out my window and never came back in. I didn't hear a single thing." I pause. "Doesn't that mean someone snuck in *before*, not after?"

"You could have helped him." Her voice is small, a whisper.

"If you really believed that you wouldn't be here." My toes are numb, but I keep them submerged, a punishment. Kayla grunts, kicking her feet beside mine. "You didn't hear anything either."

Kayla shakes her head. "I was pretty wasted," she says. "After Peter and I got back to my room . . . I barely remember anything. Hillary didn't come home until morning, slept over in Iris's room to give us some privacy. So . . ." She shrugs. "I blacked out. Maybe you did, too."

I shake my head. "I was drunk but not like that." I know this for certain. If Sarah and Ryan were killed when I was there, I would have heard it. "There's no way Joseph could have done this before we got there," I say, more a reminder to myself. "He was with me from right after the party until we went back to the room. Sarah and Ryan were still in the boathouse when I left. There wasn't enough time for them to get back there, have that happen, and then for Joseph to come meet me."

I glance at Kayla, who looks so young sitting here, like the girl she was in middle school, jumping with Sarah on the trampoline in the Oliver backyard. The girl who Sarah told her secrets to, who Sarah sought out when her parents fought viciously in front of us at junior drop-off, saying Kayla was the only one who could understand.

At the time I was so hurt, devastated she wanted to confide in someone who wasn't me. But that's how Kayla felt most of the time, when Sarah chose me, when Sarah branched out without consulting Kayla.

They had a shared childhood, an understanding of what went on in each other's home during the dark hours of sleepovers and what snacks were kept in the kitchen pantries. An intimacy that can only bloom with time, that can't be understood unless you were there, too.

If Sarah had told anyone at Meadowbrook about finding her brother Julian, about knowing Joseph, it would be Kayla.

"She kept secrets," I say, the final word a hiss on my tongue.

Kayla snaps her head toward me. "What do you know?"

I mull over the truths, where to start, which one would betray her the least. But Kayla beats me to it.

"You found out about Julian, huh?"

"You knew."

She nods. "I promised her I wouldn't tell. Her dad . . ." Kayla shakes her head. "He threatened her. Said he'd disown her if they went public."

"She told you that?"

Kayla pulls her feet out of the water, her skin red where it had been submerged. "She saw him on the Cape."

"Provincetown."

Kayla turns to me, her face a question mark.

"I met him. Liz and I confronted him about what he knew."

Kayla nods. "Yeah, P-town. She came back to Hyannis and told her dad everything, asked if Julian could come over. If they could get to know him as a family."

"Can't imagine Mr. Oliver liked that."

"Nope. Said Julian had been a mistake that he had been paying for over the past twenty-eight years. His mother signed some sort of NDA." She stills her feet. "So twisted. Mrs. Oliver still doesn't even know. Sarah said her dad threatened not to pay her college tuition if she told."

"I bet Sarah was pissed."

"Furious."

We're both quiet, just long enough for a storm cloud to enter my brain. "Do you think . . . do you think her father would want to shut her up?"

Kayla's eyes widen. "Mr. Oliver?"

"I don't know."

She shakes her head. "And kill Ryan, too? Not a chance." She cocks her head. "You don't want to believe Joseph did it."

"Would you?"

"The truth will come out, Amy. It always does."

"It already has," I mumble.

She shoots me a look. "What does that mean?"

The wind whips at my bare shoulders and I think of Sarah wearing her Meadowbrook Soccer sweatshirt for the last time, shedding it in Rex's because of the warmth, leaving it behind. I wonder if she knew that it was stuffed inside Joseph's closet all this time, that he kept it as a reminder of the bond he thought they had.

"Nothing."

"Tell me." Kayla's voice is soft but urgent, as if every piece of information counts. Which, of course, it does.

"Did Sarah ever talk to you about Joseph? Did she ever mention him?"

"Just that she thought you guys were a weird match." She shivers, wrapping her palms around her toes. "Why?"

"They knew each other."

"Well, yeah. Through you."

I shake my head. "His friend Olly told me they *knew* each other, like talked on the phone. Texted. All the time for a few months. Like they liked each other or something."

Kayla's bottom lip drops open. "No way."

"I found her sweatshirt in his bedroom."

Kayla clutches her stomach. "She cheated on Ryan? With Joseph?"

"No, at least I don't think so. Olly said it never got physical. They stopped talking once Joseph found out she had a boyfriend."

"So that's why he started hanging around practice. To stalk her."

"I don't think it was like that."

"No offense, Amy, but it's not like you have the most unbiased perspective on all this." She slaps a hand against the dock. "This means he had a motive."

"All it means is that she lied to me. You too."

Kayla's face softens, a flash of pity in her eyes. "He did, too. He lied, too."

I swallow the lump in my throat. "I know."

Kayla turns her focus back to the tree across the lake, the one that looks like it's on fire in a sea of green. "When we were little, I caught her in a lie."

"What kind?"

"All the time, actually. Small things. She'd lie about what she had for dinner or what kinds of clothes her mom would buy her. Once she told me she was allergic to dairy."

I let out a laugh. "She only drank whole milk in her coffee."

"I caught her eating a quesadilla. She'd make a joke out of it, say I was so gullible when I had no reason not to believe her."

"Absurd. Why do you think she did it? Lied?"

Kayla shrugs. "I never thought to ask. I wish I did."

"Do you think she lied to Ryan, too? Peter?"

"She must have."

We're both quiet, listening to the birds caw, the wind rustling in the trees.

"The underclassmen are supposed to arrive on Friday," she says. "My sisters texted me this morning."

"Wild."

"Board sent out an email saying justice will be served."

I blow a raspberry out my mouth.

"I wouldn't blame you if you transferred for the rest of the year."

"What?"

"It might be easier that way. Just leave it all behind."

I know what she means, that getting away from this place—from the memory of Sarah and Ryan, from Joseph—might give me peace, set me free. But the idea of leaving is absurd, impossible. Not when I still have so many questions, not when the events of the night don't quite line up. My shoulders sag and I drop my hand into the lake, fingers flinching against the cold.

"You know, I've spent so much time thinking about Sarah that I've barely begun to grieve Ryan," Kayla says. "But it's like, he was my friend, too. A dipshit sometimes. Arrogant and a little immature. Competitive as hell, especially with Peter. You'd think they were both trying to win some sort of life prize. But he was one of us. He had a future just like Sarah."

I look out over the pond and can't help but feel a sliver of guilt wedge itself into my heart.

"That's what Peter keeps harping on. 'Everyone only cares about the *girl*. Missing girl. Dead girl. What about Ryan?'" Her imitation is spot-on, down to the hardened consonants, the pointed words.

"He's not wrong."

Kayla pushes herself to stand and turns back toward campus. "Coming?" she asks, but I shake my head.

"I need another minute."

Kayla begins to walk, her footsteps crunchy against a few fallen leaves, but then she pauses and turns around.

"One thing I can't stop thinking about is how he was able to get back into your room."

"What?" I rest my chin on my shoulder, looking back at her.

"I mean, if you say you saw him leave through your window, he'd need a key card to get back in, right? Even if he used the tunnels. They weren't monitoring the doors, but we still swiped to get inside."

"Yep," I say. "Another hole in the case."

"He didn't take yours?"

"Nope." I pat my pocket. "It's been with me all week."

"You know," she says slowly. "Coach keeps an extra one in her locker room. Or she *did*. I looked for it the other day when I left mine in my room. But I couldn't find it."

She lets the words hang between us, the silence indicating

what she means. That *Joseph* could have easily yanked the key card and put it back without anybody knowing.

I let out a gust of air. "Kayla . . ."

"I know," she says. "Just . . . something to think about."

"Right."

"I'm sorry, Amy."

"For what?"

Kayla's footsteps pick up again, hard against the wood dock. "For what's about to happen."

A bout of nausea hits me as I listen to her walk away and realize what she means. Everything is about to get so much worse.

THE DAY
OF THE VIGIL

Liz

"The point of the vigil is to show who Ryan and Sarah were outside of all the news stories." Peter walks fast ahead of me as we're making our way through the auditorium. His laptop is wedged up under his armpit and he's walking with his chin tilted up, like he's on a mission. "And for our community to mourn together as a collective, so we can one day move on."

"How would you describe the mood on campus?" I ask, sticking out my phone to record his answer.

Peter blows out a puff of air. "Well, things have been better since Joseph was caught. I think people feel safer now."

"Mm-hmm." I scribble the word *safer* in my notebook. "But I'm worried too much of the focus is going to switch over to Joseph Stone."

"Exactly." Peter throws up his hands. "Whenever there are big crime stories, they pay so much attention to the killer. Like, think about how much we know about Ted Bundy. Should we really know the Catskills Killer went to Cornell or that he was a competitive skier? I know *that* about him, but I don't know a single one of his victim's names." He shakes his head as if he's disgusted with himself.

I didn't know those details. They may have been buried deep in Yalitza Luna's book, but the intricacies of the Catskills Killer's life never stuck with me. The biographies of his victims did. I can still remember all of their names: Emmy Pinkerton, Roberta Gallo, Ulla Frederick, and Brigette Lim. But I don't say that to Peter. Instead, I recall Yalitza's advice: *Stay quiet. Let the sources speak for themselves.*

"Classic media. My dad is basically the arbiter of it these days at NYNN. The only thing he wants to publish are stories that affect his bottom line."

"Writing about victims doesn't generate revenue?"

"Who knows?" Peter picks up his pace, walking briskly across the quad, and I rush to keep up, careful not to drop my recorder. "All I can focus on is what I can do right now."

"And what's that?"

"Explain what Ryan was like. Make him seem like a real person worth remembering." Peter's eyes drift toward the direction of the boathouse at the edge of campus. "Coach made us do push-ups in the boat whenever someone messed up and Ryan would always be the first guy going, the last one to stop. He just had to be the best at everything, you know? When I ribbed him for it, he would tell me not to take things so seriously, that I should lighten up and have more fun."

"Did you take his advice?"

"Sometimes. But most of the time I think I lived vicariously through him, got off on his stories about stealing his dad's Maserati to take joyrides up the Merritt Parkway. Things like that." He turns to me, eyes wide. "Don't print that—the Maserati thing. His dad would kill me."

I mime zipping my lips and throwing away the key, even though I know I should remind him that he never said the three magic words: *off the record.*

A crack of thunder erupts overhead and I jump. The sky threatens rain, enormous storm clouds forming above us.

"We should get inside." Peter takes a few big strides toward the auditorium. I follow him inside the lobby, trailing behind him as he heads to the backstage maze, housing dressing rooms and rehearsal space.

"I think I have a clear picture of what Sarah and Ryan were like as individuals, but I'm wondering if you can speak to what they were like as a couple?" I ask.

Peter pauses and looks at me with his brow furrowed. Heat rises to my cheeks. Perhaps I've made a misstep, asked something too personal, and I fumble to regroup.

"I mean, they were your two best friends, right? You probably knew them better than anyone. Together and apart. It's not like I spent much time with them so I was just wondering . . ."

Peter's gaze softens. "Right, right," he says. "It was nice when they got together. Made it easy to hang out. No one was unwelcome."

"Totally," I say, as if I can understand those dynamics completely, but I've never had a partner, nor two best friends who got together. I can't even begin to imagine what it's like to navigate a relationship like that.

My only experience dealing with a gushy couple was when Mom had a brief fling with my favorite librarian, the one who made sure they always had *The New York Times* for me to read. Mom lied about it for weeks, even after I saw them kissing in her car, even after I confronted her, demanding she tell me the truth for once.

She stood there in our living room, shocked that I would *accuse* her of something so ridiculous, until finally Grandma came out from her bedroom and told Mom to knock it off and be honest for once.

But all that did was remind me that they had both kept the truth from me. Again.

At least when Ryan and Sarah got together, Peter knew from the beginning. Never had to worry about his friends lying to him.

I follow him through the wings and onto the stage, which looks out on the seats in the audience, all velvet-covered. The house lights are low and you can see all the way to the back, where some folks have begun to decorate the walls with photos of Sarah and Ryan.

Peter seems to recognize someone and raises his arm in greeting.

"Do you want to talk to Ryan's parents? I can make an introduction."

My stomach flips, nerves fluttering. "That would be great."

Peter walks me down the stairs and up the rows until we come face-to-face with an older couple who both look like they haven't slept in weeks. The woman is tall and broad-shouldered, wearing a short-sleeved black dress that falls to her knees, her hair up in a French twist. Her husband is in a charcoal sport coat and khakis, sunglasses perched on his head and a fat, shiny watch on his wrist.

"Mr. and Mrs. Pelham, this is Liz Charles, editor of the school paper."

I extend my hand, and Mr. Pelham shakes it tenderly.

"She's working on a story about the vigil. Hoping to really

showcase who Ryan and Sarah were at Meadowbrook. I was just telling her about how Ryan was such an inspiration to me on the crew team."

Mrs. Pelham nods curtly. "He was an excellent athlete."

"Where are you from, Miss Charles?" Mr. Pelham clasps his hands in front of his middle.

"Milwaukee," I say. "Wisconsin."

"I didn't realize Meadowbrook recruited from the Midwest."

"There are students from all over here." My words are stilted. "We have one of the biggest international populations of all the boarding schools in Connecticut."

"Right." Mr. Pelham frowns. He turns to his wife. "Do we know anyone in Wisconsin?" He says the state like he's trying out the word for the first time, like he's never put those letters together out loud.

She shakes her head. "We do not."

"It's a lovely place."

Neither one of them respond and I glance at Peter, looking for an in. Or maybe an out. But he stares at his shoes as if he's realizing in real time how much the Pelhams did *not* care to meet me.

"Um," I try again. "I'd love to speak with you to learn more about Ryan. We really want to show the world he was more than just a headline."

Mrs. Pelham looks at her husband. "We're going." Her back is to me fast, before I can even respond.

Ryan's father faces Peter, his gaze nowhere near me. "It's an impossible time for us. You must understand."

Peter holds up one hand. "Of course, sir. I'm so sorry I even asked."

Mr. Pelham rests a hand on Peter's shoulder. "You should know better." He glances my way but quickly averts his eyes as he mumbles, "A student reporter. From Wisconsin."

"Of course." Peter bows his head, and Mr. Pelham stomps off, following his wife.

"Wow," I say. "I know his son just died but . . . wow."

"I should have known." Disappointment lingers in Peter's voice. "That was my bad. He doesn't trust the media. Not even a school paper. Not since the NYNN ran that hit piece on his fund."

"What was it?"

Peter waves his hand. "Something about how his workplace was toxic or whatever. Bosses berating analysts and all that."

"Ah." I don't know what else to say or how to get us back on track.

"He tried to sue the whole network, but he and my dad worked something out. Guess my friendship with Ryan came in handy."

"Do you want to go into the family business?" I ask. Most of the kids at Meadowbrook wear their ambitions on their sleeve, myself included. Like, everyone knows Iris wants to be a pediatric oncologist since she was so awed by the doctors who helped save her sister from leukemia. And Kayla wants to be a lawyer like her mom, the Connecticut attorney general. But I've never heard Peter talk about his career aspirations.

"Not as a journalist," he says. "You people make pennies. No offense."

"None taken."

"My plan's to go to business school so I can learn to run the network, like my dad."

"Uh-huh," I say.

"I'm going to be interning at headquarters on the sales side next summer. But, you know, for the right person, I can always call in a favor." He smiles at me.

I roll my eyes at Peter, not taking the bait. "Very funny."

He smiles wide and then heads off to the podium, pulling out the leatherbound folder holding his notes, a signal that our conversation is over.

There's an hour before the vigil is supposed to start, and I'm not sure shadowing Peter while he reads over his speech for the fifteenth time is the best use of my time. What I really *should* be doing is finding ways to get quotes from Egan. I hate to admit it, but I'm terrified of coming face-to-face with her, and I haven't seen her since our altercation earlier in the week. My guess is she's been busy, discussing every single safety concern with parents and board members, trying to figure out how this year can go on as planned.

Since then, I've let Mrs. Herschel be my go-between, but in order to make this story well-rounded, I'll need a quote from her. Hopefully something about how this memorial can help students move on and get closure. But I wouldn't be a good journalist if I let her go without asking about Joseph and Coach Jensen's connection to the school.

I try to focus on the task at hand as I run into Doc Kolner, rounding the hall. "Have you seen Egan?" I ask.

She points down a hallway but doesn't glance up from her packet of papers. "I think she went that way."

I duck my head and weave past the sound booth, until I enter the dimly lit hall. It's empty, but I can hear folks behind doors to dressing rooms usually occupied by theater kids preparing for the spring musical or members of the orchestra who are rumored to use the spaces for hookups.

I tiptoe down the hall, keeping an ear out for Egan's low voice, her sharp, clipped tone. But I don't hear her yet; maybe Doc Kolner was mistaken. Glass shatters inside one of the rooms and I stop, pressing my ear to the door.

"Shit." It's an older man, maybe someone's father, and I wince as he begins to cry. I back away, as if the moment is too personal to overhear. A few steps farther, I finally hear Egan's voice.

"It's a miracle you made the arrest so fast. I almost can't believe it," she says, her words muffled through the door. "Can't tell you how grateful we are that we can get this school year back on track."

But then another voice joins hers. It's male, deep and gruff.

"It wasn't easy."

Egan lets out an agreeing sound, but then her tone changes when she speaks again. "What are you thinking internally now that he's being held without bail?" It's the voice she uses when she's disciplining someone, asking us to shush during a morning meeting. It's one that means business, that has no time for nonsense or jokes. It's one that says, *I have the power.* "You know we need this to be open-and-shut."

I stop moving and press my back to the wall, trying to suppress everything inside me that's telling me to bust open that door and force them to say this to my face. I slide out my phone from my pocket and press record.

"What do you mean, 'What are you thinking?'"

"I mean, I know the evidence is there, or at least some of it, but how soon can this go away?"

"He's pleading not guilty," the officer says. "So, it'll likely go to trial."

Egan sighs. "That means we'll be dealing with the fallout all year. Maybe longer." A pause. "Is there anything you can do to make him plead guilty?"

"He's not budging. I can only muscle the lawyer so much before it becomes . . . you know."

Egan seems to consider this. "Right," she says. "And the evidence is solid, though, yes? The weapon?"

The officer sighs. "Well, the weapon is legit. Traces of blood match the crime scene. But . . ."

"But what?"

I hold my breath, leaning forward, begging him to continue.

"What?" Egan asks again, her voice urgent.

"It was in his car. No question about that. But his prints were nowhere to be found. Not in Sarah's room, not on the knife, even though he admitted it was *his* knife."

"Couldn't he have wiped it down? That happens, you know."

"Oh, does it?" he says, sarcasm in his voice. "There was blood on it, another set of prints. Not Joseph's, not Sarah's, not Ryan's."

"Nothing on Joseph's phone to implicate him?"

"Nope."

"And you never found hers?"

"Nuh-uh."

Egan doesn't say anything, but I can imagine what she's thinking, what the officer isn't saying outright: if someone else's prints are on the knife, then Joseph could be innocent. Someone *else* may have killed Sarah and Ryan and planted the weapon in Joseph's car.

The door opens and I gasp, pressing myself against the wall. The detective walks out and turns the other way, not looking in my direction, and I have barely enough time to sneak down the hall, out of sight in case Egan emerges. Under the cover of darkness, I sink down onto my heels, squatting with my head in my hands. I have to call Amy.

Amy

The outer edges of campus are quiet and empty since most everyone else is at dinner, ahead of the vigil. I skipped, favoring the solitude over sitting at a table, wondering what everyone is saying behind my back. I have sixty minutes all to myself before everyone heads to the auditorium, and every second is another moment of respite until I have to watch Peter take over the microphone to talk about them both.

I let my mind wander, my feet guide me down the path by muscle memory, turning at the brick gate, then toward the pond.

From this distance, I can see Getty House, and I look up and count the windows, three up four over. That's our room. Right there.

For a moment, I stop and think about what would have happened if I had been there when Sarah and Ryan were attacked. I like to think I would have saved them, that my instincts would have taken over and I could have changed history. But I know that's not true. I've never been reactive or brave. Back when the paparazzi would camp outside our home, I'd duck and hide until they left. It never occurred to me to walk up to them and knock their cameras to the ground, to kick and scream and cry until they left. Maybe I realized that would only antagonize them more.

Besides, there's no use in what-ifs. Not now.

My phone rings, a battle cry inside my pocket, but when I look down at the screen, I see it's Liz. Decline.

We've barely spoken since the incident in the social space, and she's the last person I want to hear from right now. When I saw her this morning in our dorm, she was prepping to hang out with Peter before the vigil. She's probably calling to get a comment about my lack of involvement. *No thank you.*

I shove my phone back in my pocket, but it rings again. Liz *again*. Decline *again*.

I shake my head, trying to rid myself of her, and keep walking, getting closer and closer to the athletic complex, a steel door leading to the locker rooms.

No one's outside now and the only sounds come from the breeze whispering through the trees, the creaking of the metal hinges of the supply shed housing all the extra balls and bats and oars. My phone buzzes again and I groan, seeing Liz's name for a third time.

"If you're calling to get me to say something about the vigil, you're a bigger asshole than I thought."

"What? No? Amy, listen, I just heard Egan say that Joseph's fingerprints weren't on the knife."

My heart leaps into my throat. "What?"

"I overheard her talking to one of the detectives."

"So, he could be innocent."

"I have no idea, but I thought you should know."

My mind races, hope pinging in my chest. I spin around, taking in the vast expanse of campus and my gaze lands on the athletic building, only a few yards away. Right through those doors are our locker rooms and all of the coaches' offices.

"Amy?" Liz's voice is frantic. "You there?"

I grunt a response, but my gaze stays fixed on the building ahead. Kayla said she looked for Coach's key card but couldn't find it, but maybe she missed it, maybe it's there. There *must* be a way to get that card and prove that it wasn't used to swipe into our dorm that night.

"I gotta go." I say.

"Wait—what are you doing?"

I hang up, knowing exactly where to go and what I need to look for.

It only takes me a few seconds to get to the side entrance of the athletic building. When I throw open the door, I'm met with the dank smell of sweat. Down the path to the soccer lockers, damp uniforms hang on hooks, remnants of this morning's practice, all of our names and numbers staring back at me.

I step up to Sarah's locker, right next to mine, and run my hand over the metal, cold and unyielding, and my fingers stop at the lock, which had been cut open by the police, a jagged sharp edge where the bolt used to be. I yank it open though it's empty. Only a week ago, she had tossed cleats, extra shin guards, and a few pairs of knee-high socks inside, knowing that someone on the team might need them, that, as captain, she should always be prepared.

Tears prick my eyes and my chest heaves as I shut her locker and turn around, heading to Coach's office off the side.

I run my hand over the wall next to the door, searching for the light switch. My fingers graze the plastic and I flip it up, revealing the small space, barely big enough to qualify as more than a closet. A desk is shoved against one wall, with one chair wedged in behind it and two on the other side, usually reserved for players who have the pleasure of being complimented by Coach or those who are reprimanded, questioned about their dedication, their perseverance. Behind the desk is a corkboard cluttered with Meadowbrook Soccer mementos—lanyards from last year's championships, photos of past teams huddled together around the goalie, heads ducked in focused prayers.

Sarah's face smiles back at me from one of the photos. Her arms are thrown up over her head, her pointer and middle fingers extended in V shapes to signify our victory against Prescot Prep. In the image, Coach is by her side, clapping and proud in her tracksuit.

I tear my eyes away from the photo and let out an exhale. *The key card. Look for the key card.* Usually, it sits inside a plastic sleeve, hanging from a Meadowbrook Academy lanyard on the hook behind the door. But the only thing hanging from the peg is a school baseball hat and an extra whistle. My stomach flips. Maybe it's still here, hiding.

I close Coach's door behind me and scan the room, my heart beating fast, desperate for the answer to reveal itself. The wall opposite Coach's desk is lined with bookshelves full of sports books and binders, disorganized with no blank space left. No lanyard. I turn back to her desk, pausing at the tall metal filing cabinet.

Each drawer's contents are designated by a small laminated label: STUDENT STATS. COMPETITION NOTES. RECRUITMENT. COACHING DOCS. I yank on the handle to the first one, but it stays shut, held in place by a lock. The second one is the same, but when I tug on the drawer labeled RECRUITMENT, it opens swiftly, sliding all the way out with a bang.

Inside is a row of folders, tabs pointed up, indicating different regions in the country, different universities where Coach has sent players in the past. I thumb through brochures for small colleges in the Northeast and big state schools in the Midwest, and find all of the papers are packed tightly together, barely leaving space to open a folder in its entirety.

Except toward the back.

Near the rear of the drawer, there's a dark sliver of space between folders, indicating a blockage. Something stuck in there, preventing the pieces of paper from sitting flush. It could be nothing, another errant whistle or a ballpoint pen. But maybe, just maybe, it's Coach's key card, made bulky by the lanyard.

A breeze picks up, drifting through the window, and I shiver. But then a crack of thunder rips through the sky, causing me to jump in the air. It's only seconds before the rain comes, slapping at the window in a violent, furious sound. I try to steady my breathing, to ignore the crush of water hitting the roof as I extend my arm and reach my hand to the back of the drawer, my fingers descending in between the folders.

I close my eyes and feel around for a plastic, rounded edge held up by a cotton string. But that's not what I feel. That's not what's there.

I wrap my fingers around something slim and solid, a rectangle block that feels so much like the device in my pocket, and my eyes snap open as I pull the object up, folding it into my hand. I stare at it in my palm, my mind blank until I finally register what I'm looking at: a phone.

I tap the home button to find it dead. The screen doesn't blink.

It could be Coach's, a spare. Or one she found in the locker room or on the soccer field, just waiting to be returned to its owner.

But those are wishful thoughts, impossible truths.

The phone is naked, no case, and still I know what I'll find when I turn it over. A Meadowbrook Soccer sticker and a Cape Cod decal. A tiny chip in the top left corner from when it fell off the second-floor landing in Getty House last week.

I drop the phone on top of the open cabinet like it's on fire. Like I shouldn't touch it.

Because what I'm looking at, what I found tucked inside Coach's files, hidden like contraband, is Sarah's missing phone.

Liz

I pace back and forth in the small space between the backstage and the dressing rooms of the auditorium and stare at my phone, which I've been white-knuckling since Amy hung up on me. I don't know if I'm waiting for her to call me back or for the courage to call her lawyer, but all I can do is let my feet take me back and forth across the carpeted walkway as the rest of the vigil planners move in a synchronized choreography to finish putting things in place.

If Egan and the police are working together to pin the murders on Joseph when they know he might not be guilty, this is a huge story—hell, it's illegal. I could call Mrs. Herschel, but based on her actions this week, there's no way she would turn on Egan. She'd probably run back to her and tell her everything I heard, find a way to hand me over to the detectives, too.

"Hey, you okay?" Peter stops midstride, a manila folder under his arm, and rests one hand on my shoulder. "You're practically shaking."

His eyes are narrowed in concern and his head is turned sideways, one lock of his curly hair bouncing up and away from his head. My stomach buzzes and I can't tell if it's a warning or a sign to trust him. I claim the latter.

"Actually, can we talk for a second?"

Peter nods and motions for me to follow him down a set of stairs to a landing beneath the stage, often used as a trapdoor during plays. It's darker down here with low clearance overhead. But it's quiet and private, and I'm grateful there aren't rushing teachers or crying parents around to hear this. Peter leans in, his face lit only by a few small cracks of light coming through the ceiling.

"What is it?" His eyes are wide with concern and he licks his lips like he's nervous, not annoyed to be taken away from his duties.

I don't know where to start, how to explain what I overheard. But Peter takes a step toward me and reaches for my hand.

"It's okay," he says. "You can tell me."

I clear my throat, testing my voice, and then the words spill out of me. "I overheard Egan and some cop talking about Joseph," I say, the words running together. "They have someone else's prints on the weapon, not his." I lean in so close I can see the soft stubble on Peter's chin, the tiny hairs between his eyebrows, the smudge on his glasses. "I think someone else killed Sarah and Ryan and they're trying to frame Joseph."

Peter's mouth drops open and I can see his back molars, clean and white.

"No," he says, a whisper. "That's . . . horrible."

"I know." I nod, suddenly relieved that I confided in Peter. "I made a recording." I hold out my phone, the screen turned up to Peter, showing him the voice memo.

"Can I hear it?"

My thumb hovers over the display, the truth right there in front of us. Without hesitating, I press down and hit play.

Amy

By the time I get back to my room in Holbrook, I'm out of breath and soaked from the rain. My hair drips onto the wood floor and I press my back to the door, my shirt sticking to my skin. I spin around and turn the lock behind me, as if someone might come in at any second.

Sarah's phone is like a grenade in my hand and I set it down on my desk as gently as I can. My face stares back at me in the screen, a mirror mimicking my own horror. The entire run back, I was desperate to charge it and turn it on, but now that I'm alone inside, I'm not sure I want to find out its contents.

Or why it was in Coach's possession.

Coach.

My hands form fists and I raise them up, hugging them against my head, trying to understand this. There's only one reason Coach could have Sarah's phone, so obviously hers.

She wanted to help Joseph cover up the murders.

A sob escapes my chest and I know what I need to do.

With shaking hands, I grab a charger and shove it into Sarah's phone. All that's left to do is wait. I could call the police now, turn it in, and let them figure out what's on here, if it's significant. But the last time I tried to do what I thought was right, I only made things worse.

It only takes a few minutes before there's enough battery to load the home screen. I enter her password with muscle memory, grateful that we always gave each other our codes, never considering we had anything to hide. But maybe now we do.

I stare at her home screen, a photo of the beach taken from the deck of her family's Cape Cod house. My throat itches and I wipe a hand along my face.

Right as I'm about to open Melody's app, a knock at the door jolts me upright.

"Amy?" Coach's voice rings out, but everything in my body freezes. I hold my breath, desperate to be still. She shouldn't be here, not after Joseph's arrest. Egan asked her to stay away, a formality until they fire her for good.

"Amy, I know you're in there. I saw you enter through the front door." Her voice is gentle but stern. Something scratches against the door and then a beeping sound rings out, unlocking the door. She must have a key card after all. "Amy, I'm coming in."

I stare at Sarah's phone, her whole world right in my hands. The lock unlatches and I yank Sarah's phone from the wire and stuff it into my pocket just before the door swings open, revealing Coach standing there, rain-splattered in a tracksuit, her face downcast.

"There you are," she says, her voice still. "I've been looking for you."

A gasp hitches in my throat and I know what I have to do.

Run.

Liz

Peter's staring at my phone, white noise from the end of the recording hanging in the air. The rest of the school is starting to arrive, based on the rising volume of voices in the auditorium.

"Holy shit," he says. "I can't believe you got all that."

We're both standing there, staring down at my palm, but then Peter reaches forward and plucks the phone out of my grasp.

"Hey," I say, and reach for it, but Peter turns around, shielding it from me with his body. "Give it back," I say, nerves tingling in my chest. I wiggle my fingers, my arm extended. But Peter's got it, blocking me with his shoulder, and he's staring at it like it's a weapon, like it's dynamite.

"Peter, come on."

In an instant, he throws it against the far wall, the sound of glass breaking, metal crunching, as pieces hit the floor.

"Peter!" My voice is a shriek and I drop to my knees, trying in vain to reassemble the device. I catch my finger on a piece of broken glass and wince as it draws blood, dripping onto the cement floor. I look up at Peter, who's standing over me, a look of shock on his face. "What the hell?"

It takes a second for him to regain his composure, as he smooths down his hair, adjusts his glasses on the bridge of his nose. Then he kneels so we're at eye level. "I know you think you're a vigilante crime reporter, but you're out of your league here." Peter's voice is more urgent than it was a moment ago. A little higher.

I stand up, trying to steady myself and sort through all the questions in my head. But Peter mimics my motions, and before I can ask any of them, he darts across the room to the door from where we came, the one that leads back up to the auditorium, where the rest of the school is now waiting for the vigil to start.

"Peter," I say, my voice wavering, as I try to follow him out of the basement. "What's going on?"

It's useless, though, because before I can get to him, he's passed through the entryway, slamming the door behind him. I reach for the handle to pull, but just as I make contact, I hear a soft *click*, the sound of a door locking and Peter's footsteps running farther and farther away, leaving me here, trapped and terrified, wondering what Peter is hiding.

Amy

"Amy, wait!" Coach's voice is nearly drowned out by the wind, but I don't turn around. I keep running toward the auditorium, where the rest of my class is gathering, preparing to pay respects to Ryan and Sarah. There's safety in numbers, safety in other people being around to stop me from being so scared.

I can hear Coach panting behind me, and I push forward, trying not to think about what she might do when she catches me and realizes I might hold more evidence to put Joseph away.

Even if his fingerprints weren't on the knife, like Liz overheard, and even if he says he didn't do it, the fact that Coach has Sarah's phone means one thing: she's been lying to us all week.

I take a hard left and pull up to the side door of the auditorium.

"Amy!" Coach calls behind me. "Stop! I know you were in my office."

I block out her voice and wrap my hand around Sarah's phone inside my pocket. It has the answers. I know it does. But I can't look at it now. I have to get away.

I throw open the door and stop for a moment. There are three different hallways, three different ways to run. Coach is close behind and I don't have much time. I blink, choosing the path closest to my right and take off, not knowing where it will lead.

The hall curves right and I follow the walls as the lights get dimmer and dimmer. Up ahead, there's a ramp leading down toward the basement of the auditorium. I hear a door hinge opening—Coach entering the building—and pick up my pace. She won't be able to catch me, won't know which way I ran, but still, I need to put as much space between us as I can.

I keep running, fire burning in my lungs. I'm now in a dimly lit hallway, only illuminated by small white lights stamped into the floor, guiding down a ramp that leads to a steel door.

There's only one way to go and I push through it, stepping inside, praying there's a way out on the other side, that I didn't just seal my fate. But as soon as the door closes behind me, I stop short.

Liz is standing in front of me, her mouth agape and her eyes wide. "Amy?" she asks. "How the hell did you find me?"

Liz

For a moment, I'm too stunned to move. My focus shifts from Amy to the broken shards of my phone, my lifeline to the world, scattered across the floor.

I start. "What the fuck is going on?"

Amy's chest heaves and her breathing is shallow as she climbs to her feet and tries to steady herself, moving beside me. She extends an arm and opens her fist, revealing a phone in her hand.

"Sarah's phone," she says, catching her breath. "I found it in Coach Jensen's office."

I shake my head. "What are you talking about?"

"She was covering for Joseph," Amy says. "I'm sure of it." She glances behind her at the closed door. "She was chasing me here."

I press my knuckles to my temple and shake my head. "How did she get it?"

Amy shakes her head. "I don't know." She starts pacing back and forth in the small space. "What if he gave it to her to keep safe? That must be it. He wanted her to cover for him." Her heel crunches against the broken bits of my phone strewn across the floor and she looks down, registering the remnants. "What the . . ."

"My phone," I explain. "Peter smashed it when he heard the

recording I made of the police admitting to Egan they didn't have Joseph's prints on the knife."

"What?" Amy's voice is small.

"Yep. I guess he got freaked out that the school year wouldn't continue or something."

"That doesn't even make sense. Does it? I feel like I'm losing my mind."

I glance at Sarah's phone, my heart leaping into my throat. "Have you looked at it yet?"

Amy shakes her head. "Coach caught me in the dorms right when it was charged."

"No time like the present."

Amy stares at the black screen in front of her but doesn't move. Suddenly she looks up, her eyes red. "I'm scared."

I nod, swallowing the lump in my throat. "I am too."

"What if I learn things about her I don't want to know? About Joseph?"

"You probably will."

"That is not helpful."

"It's the truth, Amy."

She nods and presses the home button, illuminating the screen. "It has five percent," she says.

"Well, we better work fast."

Amy

I keep my eyes on the screen as I tap to Melody's app to see all of our hidden messages. Familiar names jump out at me. *Kayla, Ryan, Amy.* The class group thread. *Julian.* Nothing from Joseph, though I try not to focus on what he might have deleted when he stole her phone and gave it to Coach.

I look closer and try to parse out the order the texts came in on the night she and Ryan were killed. I was texting with Sarah as late as midnight, when I left the party and went to Joseph. There's only one person she texted after that: Peter.

My heart rate picks up. *Peter.*

I swallow the lump in my throat and try to slow my breathing. It's not abnormal that they might text, even late at night after a party, even when they both went home with other people. I tap his name with my thumb and am greeted by a wall of text from Peter.

My eyes move faster than my brain can comprehend, trying to make sense of what I'm looking at.

"What is it?" Liz asks in front of me. I can sense her intrigue, her desperation, but I ignore her and focus on the words in front of me.

The most recent message was sent at 12:04 a.m. the night of

the murders. Thirty minutes after I left to meet Joseph. An hour before we got home.

I need to see you. I'm coming over NOW. I don't care if he's there. We need to talk.

My heart starts to race as I scroll up to what seems like the very beginning of this conversation, which started just after the party ended.

Peter: Are you okay? That was so fucked up with Amy.

Sarah: It's fine.

Peter: You're not still mad at me, are you?

Sarah: I told you tonight. I need some space. I don't like when you try to grab me like that.

Peter: Grab you? What are you talking about?

Peter: Seriously? What did I do? I can't apologize if I don't know.

Sarah: I'm too tired for this.

Peter: Let's talk about this in person. Can I come over?? Kick him out.

Peter: Come on. He's just going to hurt you.

Peter must have sent these from Kayla's bed, after she went to sleep, too drunk to register his movements. I read the texts over and over again, my mind swimming with possibilities. Sarah's words—*grab me like that*—sticking in my brain. I close my eyes and put myself back in the boathouse before our fight. There was a moment, wasn't there? When Peter's palm grazed Sarah's hip. When he held her in place like she was his. I wrote it off as intimacy between old friends. But what if . . . what if it wasn't?

"Amy?" Liz asks, and finally, I shove the phone into her face, the texts there for her to see.

Liz's eyes scan the screen and she gasps when she reaches the end. "Peter went to your room. Peter was there."

Liz

I press my lips together as I try to figure my way out of this mess. But it's impossible—Peter was the last person to see Sarah and Ryan alive that night and he didn't tell anyone about it.

"If Peter went to Sarah's room, then how the fuck did Joseph wind up with her phone?" I ask.

A loud bang erupts in the tight quarters and I spin around to see the door swinging open, Peter standing in the frame, looking just as he did an hour ago, except now he's got on a tie and a blazer, his hair combed and neat.

"Shit," he says, closing the door behind him. "I should have known."

Amy yelps and reaches for my hand, squeezing it tightly. We're both quiet, fear building in my middle as I search Peter's face.

His gaze moves to my hand, which is wrapped around Sarah's phone, the battery holding on at just a percent or two. But he doesn't know we've seen the texts. He doesn't know what we've found.

I try to make my voice sound as calm as possible. "Should have known what?"

"That someone had picked up her phone," he says, almost sad. "I just didn't think it would be one of you."

"What are you talking about?" I grasp at anything. "This isn't . . ."

He shakes his head. "Sarah and I had shared locations for years. I set an alert for it to notify me when it was turned on so I could find it, find out who hurt her. I just didn't think it would be *you*."

"What? Peter, are you—"

But I can't get the rest of my sentence out because Amy rushes from behind me and lunges for Peter, aiming for his middle. Peter grunts but deflects and then the horrifying sound of a body smashing against cement rings throughout the room as he shoves Amy to the ground.

Everything slows in my brain as I try to figure out what's happening. Peter's on all fours, Amy trapped below him, and she lets out a scream. The terror on her face is real, unavoidable, and my stomach fills with dread.

"Amy!" I reach for her hand and yank as hard as I can, pulling her out from under him. I step between the two of them and push Amy to the other side of the room. It takes him a second to get his bearings.

Amy shakes, but stays steady on her feet, her eyes trained on Peter even as he steps closer to us, moving forward inch by inch.

"This is all a misunderstanding," he says.

"How could this possibly be a misunderstanding?" Amy asks, reaching again for my hand. Her ponytail has fallen out of place, her cheeks red, stained with tears. "I know you went to her room the night they were killed. You were the last person Sarah spoke to. You were *there*."

"Stop trying to cover for Joseph."

Amy shakes her head. "I'm not covering for him. I wouldn't. Not anymore." She widens her stance, leans forward on her feet. "I found the phone in Coach's office. We read the messages."

Sweat begins to bead at his hairline and up close I can see his lips are chapped, his eyes roaming and afraid. He's as terrified as we are, afraid of being outed for who he really is. What he's done. If I can wrest the power back, he'll crumble under the weight of the reality of his actions.

It's like what Yalitza Luna wrote in her book after confronting the Catskills Killer in an interview done while he was in custody:

Many murderers cannot face the horrors of their actions. They build up stories about how they were wronged or how their victims deserved to die. They become the good guys in order to live with their past. But once they come to understand the truth, they are only faced with one monster: themselves.

I let go of Amy's hand and move closer to Peter. I listen for the sounds of voices up above, of our classmates gathering for the vigil, the one that Peter painstakingly planned in order to make himself look good and righteous, like a mourner.

I push down any fears, the ones that tell me no one will find us down here, that Peter will win, that he will kill us all in order to free himself.

But I am not alone, and I'm not afraid of Peter. The only thing that scares me is not knowing the truth.

"You did this, Peter." My words are slow. Deliberate. "You killed Sarah and Ryan. Your prints are on the knife."

Peter shakes his head. "The cops didn't say that. You heard them. They don't know who touched it."

I take another step toward him, fueled by rage and courage, a furious sensation boiling in my stomach. "You were with Kayla that night, in her room," I say, speaking slowly at first. The pieces are coming together in my head. All I have to do is get them out. Peter's hands form fists, white knuckles by his sides.

"But something happened between you and Sarah. You asked her if she was mad at you, and she wouldn't say. She didn't want to see you. She didn't even like you. But you went anyway. You didn't need a key to get in because Sarah and Amy were so careless. So trusting. Isn't that right?"

"Stop," Peter says. "Stop it right now." His voice warbles, betraying his consistent confidence, his usual poise under pressure.

Amy thrusts a finger at him. "You heard them hooking up and you grabbed Joseph's knife from the coffee table. You barged in on them and you . . ." Her voice cracks and erupts into a sob.

"Stop it," Peter says, his voice rising. "Stop. Stop."

I shake my head. He doesn't deserve to ignore the reality of what he did, the pain he caused. "You took Sarah's phone so no one would find what you wrote, even though the messages were in Melody's app. You left them for dead then snuck out the tunnels, just like Kayla said. Dropped the phone somewhere along the way and went back to your room like nothing ever happened." I shake my head, almost not believing what we're saying. "You planted the knife in Joseph's car. You made everyone think he did it. You . . ."

"You murdered them." Amy's matter-of-fact, dejected, her voice flat, the truth holding weight we both can't quite comprehend. "You killed your two best friends in the world because . . ." Her eyes go wide and when she speaks again, she's pleading. "Because why? Peter, why?"

Peter turns away from us and for a second, I think he's going to make a break for it, run for the door, leave us behind. But he doesn't. He keeps his gaze on us, his eyes moving slowly between Amy's face and mine.

"You don't know anything," he says finally. "Neither of you."

"Then tell us," I say. "Tell us what happened. Explain the messages. Explain why you smashed my phone. Tell us *why*."

"It wasn't supposed to happen this way." His voice is quiet and even, terrifying in the cold darkness of the room. "I thought Ryan had gone home by then, that I could finally talk to her *alone* without him being there. He was always there."

My heart leaps into my throat and I reach into my pocket, desperate for my phone, to record what he's saying, what's about to happen. But my fingers don't find anything, and I remember it's on the ground in a million pieces. I look down at Sarah's phone, but with only a percentage of battery left, I have nothing, no recorder, no backup. Just the three of us.

I glance at Amy, who's keeping her face still, her fists clenched.

"You hated that, too," Peter says to her. "She kept ditching you for him. Think of how I felt. I was there for her when she caught her mom cheating with the tennis pro in middle school."

"What?" Amy's voice breaks. "I never . . ."

"When she found out about Julian."

"She told you." Amy covers her mouth with one hand.

Peter presses his thumb into his chest and leans forward, nearly lunging at us. "I knew more about her than anyone ever would." His brow wrinkles and the corners of his mouth turn downward. "She was my best friend, my . . ."

I shake my head. "Wasn't Ryan your best friend?"

"Ryan was a fool. Desperate to compete with me over everything—school, crew, Sarah." Peter shakes his head. "The sick thing was that we made each other better. Both got our PRs on the water trying to kick each other's asses. Hell, he made me good at history because I kept trying to beat his score." Peter scoffs. "But he never understood the fact I was simply . . . better. He couldn't even cheat well. You know I caught him red-handed with that test and he didn't even try to hide it? And I thought Egan had the balls to investigate and take him to the disciplinary committee."

"You're the one who tipped her off?" But Peter doesn't hear me. He just keeps talking.

"He spoke about that test the same way he spoke about Sarah, about *everything*—as if he was entitled to her, as if he *deserved* her! He had no idea how lucky he was to be with Sarah, talked about other girls all the time, as if Sarah was a starter girlfriend, a stepping stone to something greater." Peter starts pacing, barely registering our presence anymore. His tongue darts out from his mouth, coating his upper lip fast, like a snake.

"And Sarah . . . she was so oblivious. She'd rather text *Joseph* than me. I caught her doing that. Told her she was being ridiculous for entertaining the idea of being with him." He looks to Amy. "You know what she said? She said it was nice to have someone to talk to who actually listened to her. As if no one—not me, not Ryan, not *you*—actually heard her."

Amy starts to stay something, but I clamp my hand over her mouth, stifling any noise, anything that might cause Peter to stop talking, to stop admitting what he's done. We need to hear all of it.

"At that party," Peter starts, "I tried to tell her all of this, but then you two fought and she stormed off." He shakes his head.

"Later, I caught them, right there on her bed, hooking up. As if she hadn't even read my texts. As if he wasn't driving a wedge between you and her. The knife was sitting there. I didn't know it was Joseph's, not then. Not until later when I saw his initials carved into the handle. It was just staring at me. I only waved it around to scare them, but Ryan came at me." He pauses, looking at me. "I had to use it. I had to defend myself."

Amy shakes her head. "And then, what? You killed him by accident and decided you had to kill Sarah, too?"

Peter's skin pales. "I didn't mean to hurt her. It happened so fast."

Tears prick Amy's eyes, but she keeps going. "Once you realized what happened you knew you needed to blame someone, right?" But then she pauses. "The knife was there when I got back. It was sitting right on the coffee table."

Peter turns his face up, his chin pointing at us. I watch his Adam's apple bob up and down like a pinball. "I came back," he says quietly. "I dropped it on the table when I left and came back to get rid . . . I heard you and Joseph and . . ."

Amy shakes her head. "You blamed him because Sarah liked him more than you, too."

Peter shakes his head. "She didn't even want him," he says. "But you know what? He *did* go after you to get back at Sarah. I'm sure of it. He would have done anything to get her attention. You and Kayla were the same, always prancing around, trying to win her over."

I inhale sharply, shocked by his words, but Amy acts faster. In one motion, she steps forward and pulls an arm back, making a fist. Her hand connects directly with Peter's jaw and a cracking sound erupts in the room as Peter falls to the ground, a strangled sound coming from his throat.

"Holy shit," I whisper.

Amy looks at me, her eyes wide like she can't believe what she's just done.

Peter starts to stand, wobbly on his legs, and turns back to us, clutching his face. Blood trickles out the side of his mouth.

"Now you see how crazy she is," he says to me, nearly breathless. "We can turn this around, you know." He nods in Amy's direction. "We can say she was part of it. You and me, we can prove it. I'll get you any job you want at New York News Network. I promise. Your whole life . . . everything you've ever wanted."

A rage fires up in my belly, consuming and ferocious, but I tamp it down, sense an opening.

"Oh yeah?" I ask.

"Liz, what the fuck?" Amy whispers behind me.

"Let me hear him out," I say. Amy shudders, but she doesn't see what I see. A small latch right beside him. One that's unmarked and nearly invisible, blending in with the walls. One that looks like the other handles hidden beneath campus that lead to the vast network of tunnels underneath the school.

I grab Amy's hand even as she tries to wriggle away from me, and walk in a circle, knowing Peter will mirror my moves. He does and pretty soon we're in opposite positions, the latch right behind us.

"What's the offer, Peter?" I say, trying to keep my voice as serious as possible.

"Monsters," Amy mumbles under her breath, but with her

hand still in mine, I position both of our palms on the latch behind us, out of Peter's eyesight. Amy's lips part and I know she feels it, understands the plan.

"Well," Peter starts. "We'll get you a guaranteed internship, on track to becoming a full-time reporter. Any beat you want, and—"

But we don't hear the rest. Not a word. Because in an instant, Amy and I pull the latch and a door springs open. I pull her by the hand and together we run as fast as we can, knowing we have no other choice.

Amy

I take off after Liz, throwing the door closed behind me, but it's pointless in keeping Peter at bay. I hear him panting not too far behind us.

It's even darker in the tunnels than it was under the stage, but as soon as I get through the door, I spot a metal pipe wedged up against the wall in the corner and an open electrical unit in the ceiling above where it's supposed to be installed.

"Liz," I call. "Help me."

She spins around, fear in her eyes, but when she spots the pipe, she doubles back. I shove my shoulder up against the door as Peter tries to come through. "Prop it up at an angle."

"There's no knob," Liz says, frantic. "It won't stay."

"We need to hold him off for a little. Until we can get out of here."

Liz grunts as she tries to position the pipe so it keeps the door closed, but my heart beats fast knowing every second we waste is another that Peter's able to come up with a plan.

"You know this is a lost cause!" Peter calls, but I shake my head, looking at Liz.

"He's dead wrong."

Liz nods and heaves the pipe up so it catches against the tiny gap in the door, bolting him in, at least for now.

I yelp with surprise and pick up my pace. "Come on."

Peter bangs on the door behind us, but it doesn't open. We take off running down the dark, dim hall until we come to a four-way split. I pause, looking down each length. But Liz doesn't hesitate.

"This way." She nods to the left. "This goes up into the auditorium. Backstage."

"You're sure?" I ask, but there's no time to be certain. Behind us, the clanging sound of metal rings out through the tunnels, and I hear labored breathing, Peter coming up behind us.

"Let's go." Liz takes my hand and I follow her down the hall.

"No one will believe either of you," Peter calls. "You have no proof I was there."

"Fuck him," Liz says, her eyes narrowed as we run side by side. She's panting hard, like she hasn't run in years, and I can sense her slowing. But I can't let her. Not now. Not when she's helped me get this far.

We get to an elbow in the tunnels, where the only way to go is right. My heart lurches when I see what's at the end of the hall: another doorway outlined in a bright light shining from the other side.

"Almost," I say, coaxing Liz, who's fallen behind. But when I turn around, I see that Peter has nearly caught up and he's gaining speed. Another few steps and he'll be in line with us.

I face forward, suddenly aware of all the ways he might kill us. A slammed head into the cement wall. An accidental trip into the concrete floor. A concealed weapon he's now comfortable wielding when he thinks his life, his future is in danger.

But not now. Not tonight. Not when Liz and I are so close to exposing the truth.

The door is only a few feet away, and I glance behind me to

see Peter catching up, a horrible gleam in his eye. He extends his hand toward me.

"Give me Sarah's phone, Amy. I'm only going to ask you once." He's panting now, out of breath.

"Absolutely not." The words slip from my tongue, but I don't act fast enough to avoid Peter's body slamming mine to the ground, his hands reaching for the phone buried deep in my pocket. "Stop!" I scream, throwing my hands up in front of me. I can't see Liz, can't hear if she's reached the door. All I know is that Peter's pinning my arms down with one hand, shoving a knee so deep into my stomach it causes me to lose breath.

I force myself to look at his face, but his eyes are dark and furious. My stomach lurches as I realize where I've seen this look before—that night at the party. From my perch in the corner, I watched as he approached Sarah, laughing as their foreheads bent close to one another. It didn't seem strange at the time, what happened next. But now, now I understand it all—the way he reached for her, placed his hand on her waist. His fingers extended up, covering her flank, as he yanked her close. Sarah had pushed him away, her mouth a circle of surprise. Peter had tried to hold her in place, to keep her still, to himself. But she dodged his grasp, moving away, to Kayla and Ryan. Perhaps to safety.

I had looked at Peter for only a moment, seen the rage on his face and discarded it as a symptom of friendship, of adolescence, of nothing.

That was when I approached with the popcorn, unaware of what had transpired or what was lurking in Peter's mind. If only I had realized what his actions had meant sooner, that all of them boiled down to one single word: *mine*.

I blink, seeing Liz's face hovering behind Peter's, fear in her eyes. "Go," I whisper, but she doesn't. Liz moves fast, grasping at Peter's collar, trying desperately to pull him off. It's no use. Liz has no strength, not when she spends all her time behind a computer. I try to fight Peter, to push him off, but he doesn't budge, not until he finally grasps Sarah's phone and pulls it from my pants, rolling off me with a sweet moment of relief.

I try to reach for it, but Liz pulls me back. "Let it go," she hisses.

"No fucking way. He can't get off."

"He won't." She grips my hand with hers and pulls me toward the door, a few inches from us.

I have no choice. I have to believe her. My chest fills with a surge of hope, as Peter clambers to stand and turns to face us.

With one hand on the door, I spin around and stare at him, this monster, bloodied from my fist, with wild eyes and glasses askew. He's panting, desperate.

I spit in his direction at the same time Liz throws open the door, blinding us both with lights so bright I have to shield my eyes. When they finally adjust, I realize what I'm seeing: the entire senior class staring back at us from the velvet seats in the auditorium. The door didn't lead us toward the wings or the dressing rooms. No. It led us right onto the stage. Liz must have known all along.

I look to my left and see a podium, Kayla standing behind it, gripping the sides. She's wearing a maroon Meadowbrook sweater, her hair tied in a simple side braid. She looks perfect, except for her eyes, which are wide in shock.

But then there's a hard shove from behind, Peter's breath on my neck, and in an instant, I realize, *he doesn't know where we are.*

"You're going to regret this," he says, his voice carrying. "You think you won't seem like his accomplice, Amy? That Liz didn't help you pull it off for a story? It's almost too easy."

He gives me one final shove, and I let my body go limp as I fly through space. The room turns upside down and my ears fill with gasps. People stand in their seats, cover their mouths with their hands, wonder why Peter Radcliffe is beating up on Amy Alterman on stage during the vigil.

I close my eyes and pray for the first time since my bat mitzvah. I pray for everyone to find out about Peter, what he did and how. I pray for Joseph to be released, for his survival. I pray for Liz, grateful she was here this whole time, that she didn't leave me to fight Peter on my own. And then just as I see the stage floor beneath me, the dark wood coming at me hard and fast, I pray for Sarah and Ryan, picturing their faces as I knew them: smiling and flushed, fresh off a run or a meal at the diner. I pray for their forgiveness, that they are remembered for more than the way they died, for who they hurt or how. I pray for their safety in another realm, for lives extended, for the unknown to be kind and joyous and filled with warmth.

I pray.

Liz

"Amy!" Her name erupts from my lips, so loud it echoes in the rafters. I rush to her, lying on the stage, unmoving. I press my ear to her mouth and realize she's breathing. She's okay.

I spin around and see Egan is rushing the stage from the wings, her fists clenched by her sides. "All of you, off the stage. Now."

Peter's staring at her, unblinking, frozen in time. I look him over, rumpled and bleeding, his hands by his side. But he has it. Right there, in plain sight.

"That's Sarah Oliver's phone," I say, making my voice as loud as I can. "Amy found it. Peter killed them." The words are spilling out of me, bleeding into one another, but I know I don't have much time before I can get it all out. "He's been obsessed with Sarah for years. Tried to frame Joseph by putting the knife in his car. There are messages on there between them. He . . . he . . . did it all."

"She's lying." Peter's voice is loud and persuasive. "She's trying to cover for Amy. She helped Joseph. The phone was in Coach's office. She's . . ."

The audience is quiet and I look to Egan, trying to figure out what to say or do. Amy groans beside me, starting to stir.

She blinks and makes eye contact with me, fear and pain all mixed up together. "Is it over?" she whispers. But it's not. Not yet.

I turn to Peter. "Admit it."

Peter shakes his head, his face turning red. "This is ridiculous."

Down in the audience, Ryan's parents spring to their feet. Sarah's mother sits with her hands wrapped around the handle of her pocketbook, her mouth forming the shape of an oval.

"Prove it." I turn to my right and see Kayla emerge from behind the podium, her hand outstretched toward Peter. "Give me her phone."

"What? Come on, Kayla."

Kayla's palm faces upward, but from here I can see her fingers are shaking, nerves running through her. "Let me see her phone."

There's a loud rustling in the crowd and when I look down, I see Sarah's and Ryan's parents moving toward the stairs of the stage.

Peter clocks them, too, his face growing redder. "You know me." He says it again, but this time his voice breaks.

Kayla wastes no time. Within two steps she snatches Sarah's phone from his hand. It only takes a moment before her face falls. Before she reads the messages, too.

"Kayla," Mrs. Oliver says, her voice barely a whisper.

Kayla nods and hands them the phone. "It's all here."

Mrs. Oliver lets out a guttural noise, one that causes a shiver to shoot down my spine.

Beside me, Amy pushes herself to sit, pressing her palm to her temple. "It's over," she says, no longer a question. "It's over."

EIGHT MONTHS LATER

Liz

I unzip my graduation gown and let the front fall open, polyester billowing at my sides. The rest of the class is gathered in little groups on the quad, posing for photos with parents and friends, the backdrop of Meadowbrook Academy behind them in snapshots they'll frame or tuck inside scrapbooks to show their children decades from now.

Was this the year of the murders? they might ask, and everyone in our class will have the same answer: *yes.*

Amy and I plop down on the steps to the library, away from everyone else, a calm settling between us.

"We made it," she says, her voice flat but at ease.

"Somehow, some way."

She knocks her shoulder with mine and I'm reminded again how strange this new feeling is, the one that reminds me I have an ally, a friend. A *real* one. All it took was a double homicide, being locked inside a trapdoor basement, and a total shit show of a memorial assembly to link us together forever.

But after everything that happened this year, I'm not sure I could have made it without her. She'd never say it, but I know she feels the same.

"When are you shipping out again?" Amy asks, even though I told her this morning.

"Two," I say. "If all goes according to plan, we'll be back in Milwaukee tomorrow, the old hatchback smelling of McNuggets and farts." I scan the campus for my mother, but I know better. As soon as the ceremony ended, she and Grandma went back to the bed and breakfast, right next to Rex Taylor's. I didn't even try to make them stay, wanted to say goodbye to this place on my own.

"You sure you don't want to do your summer internship from Palo Alto? We have like forty extra bedrooms."

"Nah," I say. "You don't want me hanging around." Though by now I know that's not true. But we'd talked about this, how it might be good for her to spend some one-on-one time with her dad, just the two of them. He's taking the summer off to relax at home, do some hiking in the Redwoods with Amy.

"Eh, you'll be too busy with Yalitza to hang out anyway." Amy smiles and I can feel her pride as genuine.

"You may be right." After Peter was arrested, Yalitza told me she was leaving NYNN to write a book about Ryan and Sarah, about all of us, and hired me to be her research assistant. I hesitated, unclear if working on something like that was appropriate, given my involvement. But Yalitza assured me that we could include a disclaimer, explained that not all journalism was unbiased, that it was okay to infuse my own experience into this one. We decided to work in the gray area, to allow this story to live in the nuance.

Besides, at Yalitza's urging, I ended up writing a first-person piece about what happened in the tunnels and how we came out alive, what I had learned about student journalism along the way. Once I sent it to her, she gave me the best advice I'd ever received: *Don't publish this in the school paper. Aim higher.*

When it came out in *Vanity Fair*, she sent me a small bouquet of flowers and offered to write my recommendation for Northwestern's journalism school *and* the Page One scholarship.

Acceptances to both came just before the new year.

But it all felt wrong, like I had hurt others to get there, like I had capitalized on pain and death and hardship, used it all for my own gain.

I pull out my Moleskine and jot down these thoughts so I'll be ready to ask Yalitza when we start work on Monday. Maybe she'll have the answers.

"Hello, girls." I look up to see Mrs. Herschel standing in front of us, wearing a blue poplin shirtdress and a scarf tied around her neck. Her hands are clasped in front of her and she's got a glassy look in her eyes.

"Don't tell me you're sad to see us go."

She wipes a tear from one eye and waves a hand. After the assembly in September, she was the first adult I saw, waiting in the wings, and she didn't leave my side all day, not when the police questioned us, not when we watched them take away Peter in handcuffs, and not when we were able to get my recording of Egan talking to the police off my cloud and hand it over to the board.

"Ready, Liz?" She points off toward a woman wearing jeans and a navy blazer, a notebook and pen in hand. "Time for *you* to be on the other side of things now."

I groan. "I shouldn't have agreed to this. It's so unprofessional. Amy, why don't you do it?"

Amy shakes her head. "I've had about enough press to last me a lifetime. Plus, this'll be good for your cred. She's a media reporter. You're talking about ethics in student journalism."

"Fine."

I stand to leave and Amy does, too, and for a moment, we face one another, our eyes meeting at the same height. This unlikely friendship, the one that sustained me, that's bound by exposed secrets and utter honesty. I know Amy's not big on affection. Not a hugger or a hand-holder or even a shoulder-bumper. Her eyes say everything and a current passes between us, knowing and certain.

"See ya," she says.

"Of course." Though we both don't know when that may be.

We nod at one another and I follow Mrs. Herschel toward the woman from *The Washington Post*, knowing that Amy's still behind me, cheering me on as she promised she would.

Amy

Liz walks over to that reporter, her head held high and her cap in her hand, and I swipe a hand across my face, catching a stray tear. I've been doing that a lot over the last eight months, the crying. But I don't try to stop it anymore. It's easier to let the pain out. It recedes eventually. That's what my therapist has been saying, at least.

Over on the other side of the quad, I see Kayla, Hillary, and the rest of the soccer girls posing with Coach Jensen. They let her come back in October, after Joseph was cleared, after she explained that Joseph *did* find Sarah's phone when he left my dorm, dropped on the grass outside the dorm. Coach kept it hidden because she didn't want the cops to pin the murder on him. But the new head teacher, some import from a Quaker school in Rhode Island, issued a public apology and offered Coach the opportunity to stay, at least for this year, to see us through.

She catches my eye and waves, beckoning me over. I hesitate, but then I see Kayla look my way, her eyes lighting up.

We've softened on one another, bound together by Sarah and Ryan and even Peter. I don't think we'll ever be as close as either of us was with Sarah, but the frustration I felt with her is gone, and all I can summon now is empathy. She had no idea who Peter was. None of us did. A horrific realization.

I feel a pull toward the soccer girls, the people who I spent so much of my high school experience with, even though I dropped off the team in the fall. Playing without Sarah was too much, too heartbreaking. Besides, I was never even that good.

But I stand anyway, letting my robes fall around my ankles, tickling my bare skin. Dad's off in Fielding House, catching up with Lisa Brock, who was *not* pleased with me after the stunt Liz and I pulled. But after I told her I might be interested in learning more about the legal system, she said I could shadow her all summer and even into the fall if I wanted. I think I'll take her up on it since I'm taking a gap year in order to feel a bit more grounded before going to college.

I've talked to the Olivers and the Pelhams about setting up a scholarship in Sarah's and Ryan's names here at Meadowbrook. They welcomed the help.

I take a step toward the team, feeling a wave of nostalgia sweep over me. But before I make it to them, someone tugs on my hand and I spin around to face Joseph.

"Hey," he says. He's wearing khakis and a wrinkled white button-down, his hair parted to the side and his cheeks pink from the heat. He smells of butter and basil, fresh summer herbs that have just begun to sprout.

I'm shy suddenly, unsure how to act toward him after so many months apart. We tried for a few weeks after Peter's arrest, spoke on the phone and met up at Rex's in town. But I found myself pulling away from him, unable to trust him after all those months he spent lying to me about knowing Sarah. He understood when I broke things off and admitted that it might be best for us both to have new centers of gravity that did not include each other.

It was easy to avoid one another, to forget the way his smile spread across his face or the way his fingers flexed by his side when he was nervous. Now that he's here in front of me, it's like the air is leaking from my lungs.

"Congrats, grad," he says, a smile fighting its way onto his face.

"You too," I manage. "Coach said you made it out with honors."

He nods and I can tell he's proud, as he should be. It wasn't easy after missing so much school in September, after having so many eyes on him, so many rumors swirling. "I'm going to culinary school over in Hyde Park," he says, looking off toward his mom, who's got her eye trained on us.

"That's amazing." I mean it, too. "Are you here for the summer?"

Joseph shakes his head. "Going to Oregon to visit my aunt for a while. Work at a restaurant in Bend. I need some time away from here, you know?"

I let out a laugh. "Yeah. I definitely do."

His smile widens. "Where are you headed?"

"Home." I shrug. "Going to take some time to figure out what I want to do next."

He seems to consider this. "You know, the West Coast isn't that big."

My heart leaps into my throat, but I know there's no way I can continue this, that I can say *yes, let's keep going, let's try again.* Especially after knowing that he lied about Sarah, about whatever was going on between them. So I shake my head. "Any other time and . . ." I start, but I can't find the words.

Joseph nods. "I figured, but I had to take a shot, right?"

"Amy!" I spin around and see Kayla beckoning me over. "Team photo!" I hold up my hand in recognition and turn back around to face Joseph.

There's so much to say to this boy, this person who lied to me, whose life is so profoundly changed by the people at this school, the ones who almost drowned in their quests to save themselves.

He smiles at me, his movements grounded and calm, and I see the same boy who made me feel safe in his car, who kept me warm and made me homemade jams, loaves of banana bread.

How lucky I was to be close to him. How lucky I was to know Sarah and be loved by her—be loved by Joseph, too.

Saying goodbye to him means saying goodbye to her, goodbye to this place that made me, then broke me. It healed me, too, in a way. Taught me that I could survive. That I could trust again. That I'd find a friend in someone like Liz.

"I'll see you later, Amy," Joseph says, walking away, though we both know that's a lie.

And still, before I join the soccer team, before I leave this place for good and I embark on finding purpose in this new, strange world, I say it back, knowing the words are heavy and false, one last lie we'll tell each other.

"See you later, Joseph."

Acknowledgments

Thank you to Alyssa Reuben, my brilliant and kind agent, who has guided me through this industry with care and a bird's-eye view of what really matters.

I am so lucky to work with Rūta Rimas and Simone Roberts-Payne, two editors who are the best brainstormers, collaborators, and comrades an author can ask for. Their generosity, humor, and intelligence drew out the nuances and depth of this story when I couldn't quite see them myself. When I say dream team, I mean it.

Casey McIntyre, Razorbill's beloved publisher, passed away on November 12, 2023. Casey was instrumental in starting and championing my career and did the same for so many authors for so many years. Casey's big, bright smile, her wonderful laugh, and her enthusiasm for children's literature continues to inspire me in my work. Her warmth and creativity will live on in the books she helped bring into this world and the authors she nurtured.

Elyse Marshall has been my publicist since day one and has always made me feel like *anything* is possible. I love collaborating with you. Thank you to Jaleesa Davis for all of the extra help.

Thank you to Jen Klonsky and Jen Loja. I am always indebted to you for the ways in which you support my work and make me feel at home at Penguin.

The team at Penguin Young Readers and Putnam is unmatched. Thank you to the people who make, promote, market, and sell books for a living. Your work is invaluable and I am so appreciative: Rebecca Aidlin, James Akinaka, Alex Campbell, Christina Colangelo, Kate Frentzel, Alex Garber, Bri Lockhart, Abigail Powers, Shannon Spann, Felicity Vallence, Natalie Vielkind, and Kelly Young.

Kristin Boyle designed this beautiful cover with art from Bron Payne. Thank you for the attention and thoughtfulness that went into creating this showstopper.

Olivia Burgher and Sanjana Seelam, thank you for ensuring my work travels far and wide, often beyond my wildest imaginations. My adoration runs deep.

James Munro and Kim Ryan have helped my books reach audiences all over the world. If I could say thank you in all of those different languages, I would.

Thank you to Liv Guion, Liza Mullett, Stella Irwin, and Laura Lujan, aka the all-star team of WME assistants. I can't wait to say I knew you when.

My dear and trusted friend Josh Goldman gave me the idea for *The Meadowbrook Murders* in a throwaway text one afternoon, and I am very grateful to him for inspiring Liz and Amy's journey.

I am in awe of the booksellers, librarians, teachers, bookfluencers, and readers I have interacted with over the years. Your excitement for new and riveting books is contagious, and your support has been incredibly meaningful. Thank you, thank you, thank you.

Growing up, I heard so many stories about my mother's time as a student at a New England boarding school, though those years did not include the kinds of difficulties Amy and Liz endure (thank goodness!). I am so appreciative that she shared these special memories of her own coming of age with me and that she brought me along to her high school reunion in the spring of 2024. Go, Penguins!

Life is sweeter as an aunt, and I am absolutely tickled that I get to escape into worlds of silliness and make-believe with my favorite kiddos, Luke and Charlotte. To their parents, Halley and Ben, I love you very much.

My mom and dad have made my writing career possible with their encouraging words and endless support. Growing up with you two as my backstop has been nothing short of marvelous.

Thank you to Ziti, our sweet little noodle, and, of course, to Maxwell for listening to me plot out loud and offering to hug, help, or hear; and for all the unnoticed things you do to make our little life complete.